Cursing the Darkness

Rex W. Last

Cursing the Darkness

Vanguard Press

A CIP catalogue record for this title is
available from the British Library.

ISBN 978 1 80016 958 6

Vanguard Press is an imprint of
Pegasus Elliot Mackenzie Publishers Ltd.
www.pegasuspublishers.com

First Published in 2023

Vanguard Press
Sheraton House Castle Park
Cambridge England

Printed & Bound in Great Britain

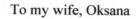
To my wife, Oksana

Acknowledgements

A big thanks to my wife, Oksana, who, as ever, pored over drafts of the book and made many professional and insightful comments on my short-comings. What's left is mine and I very much hope you like it.

'It is better to light a single candle than to curse the darkness' (Eleanor Roosevelt)

Author's Note

To labour an obvious point, this is a work of fiction and the Nuremberg and characters of the book exist in my imagination only, historical figures aside. Anyone familiar with that lovely city will recognise well-known sights and shake their heads sadly at the topographical liberties I have taken. What is real, though, is the dreadful dilemma which faced my characters and countless others like them in the 1930s. However, it turns out that hope may be possible even in the darkest of times.

For an account of how this book came about, a gallery of images of Nuremberg and details of my other recent books and YouTube presentations, please go to www.locheesoft.com.

Prologue

These events took place in 1935 in the Bavarian city of Nuremberg, a powerhouse of National Socialism, where the annual National Congress of the Nazi Party was held every autumn. For one small group of Germans, two incidents were particularly momentous.

It was a snowy night in January when a bizarre patient bleeding from two bullet wounds hammered on Dr Johann Voss's front door in search of urgent medical attention. Some months later, a dark rainswept evening, skies heavy with the threat of snow, proved life-altering for the same small group, as that was the night Adolf Hitler came to supper.

Chapter One

Dr Johann Voss locked the driver's door of his Adler saloon and set out to walk across the cobbled market square and up the steep hill towards Nuremberg's eleventh-century castle walls. The unusual circular watchtowers, capped with conical slated roofs, gleamed in the dying rays of the sun. It was an exceptionally mild evening and the pavements were crowded with people taking a late stroll. By the roadside, dirty piles of winter snow were slowly melting.

Many of the men wore traditional Loden green jackets and the women showed off decorative Dirndl dresses with their gaily-coloured aprons. But amongst them were a scattering of ugly Brownshirt uniforms and increasing numbers of young lads proudly sporting the smart outfits of the Hitler Youth, with their prominently buttoned shirts, dark neckerchiefs fastened by a woggle, short Lederhosen and jaunty caps. Some bore swastika armbands as they strode beside their parents with a proud adult military swagger rather than the casual, playful meanderings of a child.

Across the city, the tinkling warning bells of the trams formed a constant background to the bustle of the streets.

Many cars and lorries were out and about, some belching clouds of black smoke. These days ever more military vehicles would thunder past, loaded with troops singing bawdy songs and shouting at the passers-by.

The steep red roofs of the half-timbered buildings with their neat rows of square mansard windows emanated a tranquil, almost dream-like quality but they too were scarred by the long red streaks of brash Nazi banners with black swastikas on a white circular ground. Yet another festive parade in honour of the New Germany was in prospect, and Johann shook his head sadly at the way in which German civil society was becoming increasingly regimented and militarised.

His wife, Elise, who worked alongside him as his practice nurse, encouraged him to take these regular evening strolls in his beloved medieval old quarter to clear his head from the stresses and strains of daily work as a general practitioner. He was finding it increasingly dispiriting to practise medicine in Nazi Germany, as the brutal doctrines of fascism insinuated themselves more and more into all aspects of daily life. He regularly encountered patients who presented with the sadly familiar symptoms of depressive illness induced by the inhumanity of the society in which they were constrained to live. For their ills there was no medicine, he mused, and little chance for me or them to challenge the crazed direction German society was taking.

He paused before a shop window. The store sold china and gifts and, here too, Nazi trinkets were on offer. Johann suddenly noticed his reflection in the display window, a tallish figure with a thinning mop of dark hair, a warm, friendly face and an untidy, rumpled grey suit. Unconsciously, he pushed back the spectacles on his nose and gave himself a mock Nazi salute. He instantly regretted his foolish action and peered nervously about him to see if anyone had noticed. No, not a soul. Thank God for that.

Johann continued on his way uphill and, as he passed the Sebalduskirche, he heard the rich vibrant sounds of the organist rehearsing. He was drawn inside and for a while let himself become lost in the majesty of a Bach fugue played on the church's elderly chamber organ. As the music resolved itself in a final, strident chord and the reverberations slowly faded, he reluctantly emerged from the cool, echoing shade and out into the busy street.

He continued up the steep pathway which led past the house where, in the early sixteenth century, Albrecht Dürer had once lived and worked. Germany had produced so many great cultural icons—painters, musicians, philosophers and writers—yet their positive legacy had been powerless to stem the evil Nazi tide. Some creative artists had fled the country, a few had shamefully locked step with the régime and others still had withdrawn altogether from cultural life.

Again and again, his mind grappled with the intractable question: why was he so utterly powerless in the face of the madness which had gripped his fatherland? Why did he have to be borne along by the relentless tide of mass hysteria for this evil parody of an idealist doctrine? He had once been a keen supporter of the Social Democrat Party but he had withdrawn from involvement when it became too dangerous to challenge the political orthodoxy openly, and now any expression of dissent was cruelly and ruthlessly suppressed.

Growing ever more despondent, he turned left in front of the castle wall where the flower beds were beginning to display their spring blooms. He sat down wearily on a wooden bench to one side of the path and scanned the lights of the city spread out before him. If you made yourself ignore the Nazi banners slapping arrogantly in the light breeze, Johann thought, it would be just another normal day in a beautiful medieval city coming to a quiet and tranquil end. But it wasn't. Germany, he was convinced, was hurtling headlong into an insane tyranny which would inevitably end in wild military adventures, threatening, for the second time this century, to engulf the whole of Europe and the world beyond.

He couldn't comprehend the senseless horror of it all, not least the treatment being meted out to the Jewish community in Germany who had lived amongst their fellow citizens for centuries through good times and bad. Yet now, they were being pilloried as 'Untermenschen', sub-humans, members of an alleged global conspiracy which after the Great War culminated in the 'Dolchstoss', the supposed stab in the back by Communism and international Jewry and the humiliation of Versailles, both of which were now cornerstones of the Nazi foundation myth.

For Johann, the so-called Jewish question was not just a social and political affront to human dignity, it was intensely personal. He had married a half-Jewish girl, Ilse, whom he loved deeply, and whose parents had perished in a racist attack shortly after the Great War. To protect her from the growing tide of anti-Jewish sentiment, he had succeeded in arranging for the identity papers of a terminally ill young woman patient, who had no known relatives and who, despite his best efforts, had died in his care, to be exchanged for those of Ilse, who now became Elise.

Organising that switch of identity was a mere pinprick of a challenge against the rising tide of Nazism, made possible by his knowledge of the bureaucracy and the paperwork required for birth and death certificates. He yearned to be able to mark up a more substantial achievement, anything which would make a real impact on the wider community. Without, of course, unduly compromising his personal safety or that of Elise.

At least his wife's sister, Ursula, was translating her aversion towards Nazism into genuine positive action and risking everything in the process, he thought enviously. She and her husband, Wolfgang Schmidt, lived with their children in Waldheim, a large rambling country house Wolfgang had inherited from an uncle, and they gave shelter and support to Jews and non-Jews alike who were fleeing from the brutality of the state. Johann knew that husband and wife also belonged to an underground movement which assisted those in peril of their lives to make good their escape from Germany, and he enviously applauded their commitment and the huge risks they were taking in the name of humanity.

From his jacket pocket, he took out a small leather-bound notebook which contained a personal diary of his daily activities and private reflections on his life. He opened it and pushed back the glasses on his nose to examine the most recently written page.

It was a kind of internal monologue which his wife strongly encouraged him to write, not just as a therapeutic exercise but as an actual record, a kind of time capsule which might, one day, be passed on to his children, or read by people from a later generation as a warning against fascism and a heartfelt appeal for them to promote democracy and freedom wherever they could. Johann had always nourished a secret desire to become a writer, and this account of the descent of Germany, as he called it, served as an outlet for his private literary ambitions, as well as helping him to maintain his sanity in an increasingly mad world.

But, he wondered, what can I actually do? Challenge the state and you will be struck down, physically assaulted, imprisoned, dragged away to one of the newly-constructed concentration camps along with left-wingers, intellectuals and artists who did not fit the accepted mould, or with homosexuals, gypsies, the handicapped and others regarded as unworthy of living in a Nazi paradise.

He was so caught up in his despondent reverie that he failed to notice a pair of Brownshirts staggering drunkenly towards him. As they drew near, one of them stopped in his tracks, swaying slightly. He raised a truculent arm skywards and snapped in a slurred voice, 'Heil Hitler!'

As Johann failed to respond, the other Brownshirt stepped aggressively forward, prodded him roughly in the ribs and repeated the salutation.

Suddenly becoming aware of what was going on, Johann stood up hastily from his seat and responded with a ragged Hitler salute and a muttered word or two of apology. The Brownshirt sneered, 'A touch more enthusiasm, friend, otherwise, things could go badly for you.'

'Yes, yes, I am sorry,' said Johann limply, but, mercifully, the inebriated duo had already lost interest in him. They marched unsteadily onwards, on the lookout for more potential victims and the nearest tavern.

Angry and humiliated, he slumped back on the bench. He hated himself for his submissive response, but if he had refused to react to their salute, what purpose would it serve? He could have been roughed up or even badly beaten and his solitary protest would be utterly futile. He, the doctor, would be the one in need of emergency medical care.

Drained and deflated, he rose with an effort and made his way wearily down the steep cobbled incline to his car and the short journey home.

Chapter Two

Light snow began to fall as Johann parked the Adler in his driveway, locked it and walked up to the house. He fumbled in his trouser pocket for the house keys and was just about to turn the lock, when the heavy wooden front door swung open and a slender dark-haired woman stood before him, haloed in the porch light wearing a big smile, a thin nightgown and very little else.

'Good evening, sir,' said the woman. 'Can I help you?'

'Yes, madam,' replied Johann, pushing the spectacles back on his nose, 'indeed you can. Do you have a bed for the night for a poor lonely doctor?'

'I think I might be able to arrange something. My charges are quite reasonable.'

Johann looked her straight in the eye for a moment, then the pair burst into laughter and he embraced her warmly. He wagged a mock stern finger at her as he gently eased her into the hallway and closed the door behind them.

'So now you're demanding payment for your services. Our Führer would not approve of a good German hausfrau selling her body to the highest bidder, now would he?'

'Only if it was for the greater glory of the Reich,' she giggled.

'So,' he said, standing back with his hands on her shoulders, 'tell me, nurse, is there some solemn medical duty that I have to perform?'

Elise blew into his ear. 'Come, doctor. You are needed upstairs urgently. There's a patient waiting to be examined internally.'

Johann stood there for a second or two, still holding her at arm's length. 'Then we mustn't keep her waiting, must we?'

They rushed up the stairs to the bedroom and urgently tore off their clothes. As he stood there naked in front of her, she looked admiringly down at the angle of his erection and snapped, 'Heil Hitler!' The two of them collapsed in helpless giggles onto the bed.

A little while later, they lay side by side in the large wooden-framed fourposter. She looked at him in that intense, quizzical manner she always adopted when she was concerned about him.

'What's wrong, Liebling?' she demanded softly.

'I acted like a coward again this evening,' he replied. 'Why do we have to be such faint-hearted creatures?'

She did not reply, just looked steadily into his eyes, waiting for him to say more.

'I was sitting on a bench looking out over the city and generally feeling sorry for myself, when two damned drunken Brownshirts came marching along, demanding I bawl out "Heil Hitler" or get myself a sound beating. What could I do? What can anyone do now these thugs have such a stranglehold on power?'

She ran her hand gently through his hair. 'Don't despair so, Johann. You are forgetting what you keep telling me. Let them have their petty victories, let them believe they have the upper hand. But, for all their power, they cannot get inside our heads and hearts to change how we think and believe.'

'I know, I know. But fine thoughts versus an all-powerful state—that's not much of a contest. And, anyway, they've already wormed their way inside the heads and hearts of millions of our fellow citizens.'

She sat up and looked sternly at him.

'Together, you and I have made a stand, remember. You gave me a new identity; otherwise, I'd be in danger of being transported off to one of their concentration camps and you too would be in serious trouble for having married into a Jewish family.'

He smiled faintly.

'And,' she continued, 'you don't just do nothing. You note down all your thoughts and concerns in your diary— and, if it's little else, it is a record of what one honourable man holds dear in the face of impossible odds.'

'Writing is hardly the highest degree of bravery,' he countered. 'Unless, I suppose, my words of wisdom were to fall into the hands of the Gestapo. At least, my scribbles are a kind of release for me, letting me search for a faint ray of hope that, one day, the Nazi creed will be eradicated and a new and better Germany will emerge from the ashes. One good deed is fine and laudable, provided you get away with it.'

He paused and looked long and hard at her.

'But when you've done that good deed,' he continued sadly, 'it's gone and passed like it never happened. Good deeds don't thrive in isolation. One good deed demands another, and another, and so it goes on. 'What's the old phrase? "One swallow doesn't make a summer."'

'It'd take an awfully large flock of swallows to make the meanest difference to our Nazi paradise,' she conceded. 'But, surely, it's better to roll with the punches when we must and seek out opportunities to challenge the régime as and when we can?'

'You're right, I suppose. But the trouble is, those opportunities must be precious few and far between. I can't see one coming our way any time soon, can you?'

Again she gave a quizzical look. 'You never know,' she replied. 'You just never know.'

Johann lay there, staring at the ceiling. A minute or two later, physically and mentally exhausted, he fell asleep, still wearing a troubled expression on his face.

Chapter Three

His repose did not last for long. The nightmare which regularly came to haunt him was, once again, tormenting him, as it had ever since his last involvement in the brutal world of national politics. In it, he found himself attending his final Social Democrat rally in a local Bierkeller, listening to increasingly desperate calls from speaker after speaker for the moderate left-wing in Germany to rise up and challenge the pitiless domination of the Nazi Party and its political thuggery.

Ernst Gräber, a respected local leader and member of the Reichstag, was just completing his impassioned speech, when the doors at both sides of the stage were smashed open and a gang of stick-wielding Brownshirts yelling, 'Heil Hitler!' charged in among the platform party, seizing them one by one and dragging them away. Almost immediately, the thugs were back again, leaping off the stage to pursue their violent attack into the body of the hall.

Panic erupted. The audience stampeded for the exits, scrambling over benches, chairs and fellow Party members in their frantic attempts to elude the feral onslaught. As they reached the entrance, many bloodied and injured, they were forced to state their name and address to the Brownshirts manning the door. One particularly villainous-looking individual, having noted Johann's particulars, snapped, 'Now we know where you socialist scum live, we'll be round to pay you a little visit one night soon.'

Then the scene would shift to the darkness of their bedroom at home. In the depths of the night, a sudden imperious hammering at the front door would shatter the silence. Shaking with fear in his dream, Johann stumbled down the stairs to the front corridor, fumbled with the locks and bolt and flung open the door. There, before him stood the villainous-looking Brownshirt, laughing maniacally, rattling a collecting tin and demanding, 'Donate generously to the Winterhilfswerk!' The Winter Aid Fund was a Nazi programme which claimed to raise money for the underprivileged in the cold winter months and the can rattlers could be pretty ruthless in their demands for 'voluntary' donations.

At that moment, Johann would wake in a cold sweat, trembling with fear. Elise would stir in the bed beside him and whisper softly to him to relax and go back to sleep.

'It's all right, Liebling. It's just that stupid dream again.'

For a long while, he would listen anxiously to the small noises of the night before he finally managed to settle back to sleep.

But, this time, nightmare fused with reality. Now it was actually happening. When Johann sat up in bed to shake off the dream, the violent hammering persisted.

His wife, drowsy with sleep, muttered, 'What is it? Who can that be at the door?'

'I don't know, but don't worry, it's probably just some patient emergency. I'll deal with it.' He tried to calm her concerns but his words did not carry much conviction.

Trembling despite himself, he swung his legs out of the bed, flung on his dressing gown, shuffled into his slippers and hastened apprehensively down the stairs. Was this the night when he would be confronted with a political reckoning? Could someone have managed to read the subversive thoughts in his diary? Had those two drunken Brownshirts at the castle succeeded in tracking him down?

The knocking became ever louder and he was aware of a high-pitched voice outside half shouting, half screaming incomprehensible words. Taking a deep breath, he switched on the outside porch light, unlocked the door and nervously edged it open.

Before him, in the now steadily falling snow stood, thank the Lord, not the mad Brownshirt of his nightmare, but the bloodied figure of a skinny young woman, bright ginger hair in a pigtail, face in deep shadow, clutching her left arm as it oozed blood on to the doorstep. Blood was also seeping from her right thigh, black like tar in the pale porch light. As he instinctively reached out to assist her, she stumbled and fell into his arms, muttering, 'He shot me, the bastard. Twice. H- help me, please.' At which, she lost consciousness and collapsed in a heap, and a light dusting of snow fell from her clothing.

Johann hefted the woman's limp body into the entrance hall and gently lowered her to the floor. He took a quick nervous glance to left and right along the silent, empty street, closed the door and secured it firmly. Turning off the porch light, he gathered her up under her arms and manhandled her into his consulting room. As he did so, Elise called out to him from the top of the stairs.

'Are you all right, Liebling? Who was it at the door? Do you need me to come down and help?'

'Yes, please. It's a young woman with a couple of nasty-looking bullet wounds.'

'Bullet?' There was a tremor of fear in her voice as she swiftly fastened her dressing gown and hurried down the stairs.

Johann lifted the young woman on to the treatment table and turned his attention to her injuries, ripping back the thin material of her blouse sleeve. The bullet had passed through the muscle of her upper arm, leaving simple entry and exit wounds which he proceeded to clean and prepare for stitching. Elise sought out the surgical thread and needle as he closely examined the wound.

Mercifully, no major blood vessel had been caught by the path of the bullet. The patient remained unconscious as he carefully sutured the injury.

'Right, Elise, now let's take a look at the young lady's thigh.'

Although he was preoccupied with the urgent medical attention the young woman clearly needed, Johann was all the while half aware that there was something rather odd about her, that all was not as it seemed. But he forced his concerns to one side and continued with the task of locating and treating the wound.

It was only when his focus shifted to her bloodied upper thigh, that he realised with a sudden jolt what had given him such cause for puzzlement. He had become increasingly convinced that there was something very strange about this patient and, when he lifted up her skirt to inspect the injury, he was amazed to see not only that 'she' wore no undergarment, but that her genitalia were far from being feminine.

In fact, they were very clearly male. Not of massive proportions but, unmistakably, a penis and a brace of testicles. So the 'she' was evidently a 'he'. But why was he disguised as a woman? And how was this connected with the bullet wounds he had suffered?

Elise gave a shocked little cry. 'In all my time as a nurse, I've seen some unexpected sights, but this one beats the lot,' she said, laughing despite herself. 'I'd better clean the makeup off his face, I suppose.'

'Yes indeed. But we must remember that we are medical practitioners and our task is to try and make our patients better regardless of their condition,' Johann replied, himself struggling vainly to keep a straight face. 'Still, our young gentleman here is going to have quite a bit of explaining to do.'

Because the exit wound in the thigh was jagged around the edges, it took Johann and Elise a good twenty minutes to complete their work, after which, he gently smoothed down the patient's skirt, washed his hands thoroughly and sat down in the leather chair next to the treatment table to wait for him to regain consciousness and offer an explanation of what exactly was going on. Meanwhile, Elise was mopping up the bloodstains on the hall floor and in the consulting room.

'Thank you, Liebling. You go on up to bed and I'll stay here with our Herr or Fräulein whatever, in case there are any complications. Good night, Elise.'

She kissed him, gave their unusual patient a final questioning glance and tripped lightly up the stairs to bed.

Johann yawned and rubbed his eyes. After a few minutes, his head nodded onto his chest and, despite himself, he fell into a light sleep, to be rudely awakened an hour or so later by a loud shriek and a hand jabbing him none too gently in the ribs to attract his attention.

The patient was sitting upright on the edge of the table, clearly in shock from the bullet wounds and also badly frightened by his predicament. In a light, tremulous voice that could have been either male or female, he said, 'You must be the doctor. Sorry to have disturbed you in the middle of the night, but as you can see, I was shot by this half-crazed Nazi and your surgery was the first and nearest place I could think of.' He paused, clearly embarrassed.

'I presume, as a doctor, you know about... ' He looked pleadingly at Johann, who was endeavouring to keep a neutral expression on his face.

'I mean, I can explain why I'm dressed as a woman with no knickers... My name is Rudolf, by the way, Rudolf Fischer... but everyone calls me Rudi... I really must thank you for patching me up... I'm afraid I haven't got much money... '

'I'm Johann, Doctor Johann Voss. Pleased to meet you.' Their formal handshake felt a little bizarre, given the less-than-conventional circumstances of their meeting.

Despite his injuries, the young man quivered with nervous energy and stared earnestly at Johann. 'I hope I'm making some sense, I must owe you... ' He suddenly paled and keeled over sideways on the table. Johann moved forward swiftly to ease him back onto the pillow.

'You really must take things gently,' said Johann. 'You've been hurt pretty badly and you've lost a fair amount of blood, much of it on my front doorstep. But, first of all, I must give you something for the pain. We'll worry about the money later.'

He reached over to the side table, handed his patient two tablets and passed him a glass of water to help him swallow them.

'Now, you really must take things easy and only tell me what you've been up to when you feel strong enough.'

Rudi smiled apologetically, reached up and removed his ginger pigtailed wig to reveal a short crop of untidy fair hair. His eyes scanned fearfully around the room and, finally, rested on Johann again. He paused for a second or two, then nervously cleared his throat.

'No, I must explain to you right now... I really need to tell you the full story... ' His voice took on a wary note as he scanned the walls of the consulting room. 'Can I assume that the absence of a portrait of the Führer might indicate... ' His voice trailed away, worried as to how he should express himself without getting into political hot water.

Nowadays, even the most private of conversations could lead to disastrous and potentially fatal consequences, and here he was about to open his heart to a total stranger. Still, the man was a doctor and could be counted upon, at the very least, to keep a confidence. Or could he?

Johann smiled. 'Are you trying to ask me if I am a Nazi Party member or, at the least, an ardent follower of our great leader?'

Rudi looked him in the eye, his expression nervous and questioning.

'Let me put it this way,' continued Johann. 'I used to be a supporter of the Social Democrat Party until our local association was shut down a while back after a brutal attack by Brownshirts. Some of the injuries suffered that night were far worse than those you have just received, so I am hardly a devoted fan of the Third Reich.'

'Gott sei dank,' said Rudi with a relieved sigh. He attempted to sit up again but Johann restrained him.

'You really have to lie down quietly and give your body time to recover.' A pause. Johann smiled. 'But, despite that, I must admit that I am pretty curious about how you managed to get yourself into this bizarre situation.

'Do tell me why you dressed up as a woman, apparently without bothering to put on any underwear, and turn up at my front door in the middle of the night, shouting and screaming with blood pouring out from two rather unpleasant bullet wounds? Neither of which, I should add, are particularly life-threatening, but you'll be pretty stiff for a while and you really will have to take things very easily.'

Johann paused, spread out his hands as if to say, now it's your turn. Tell me what this is all about.

Rudi sighed, nodded resolutely as if he had made a big decision and said, 'Right. I am going to trust you. I'm no friend of the Nazis myself, far from it, as you'll see when I explain why I've been wandering about in this unusual disguise.' He gestured at his feminine wig and dress.

Johann nodded and settled back in his chair to listen.

Chapter Four

'I have a sister, Anneliese. She's my dear little sis, a couple of years younger than me and, as children, we were very close indeed. That is until we left school and went our separate ways. She's very bright and managed to get a place at university, despite the government's restrictions on the advancement of women. You know, the "Kinder, Küche, Kirche" slogans—make the womenfolk look after the kids, cook the dinner and go to church and let the men get on with the really important stuff. She managed to rise above all that propaganda claptrap and complete her education as a lawyer.

'But I was a late developer and the black sheep of the family, couldn't make my mind up what to do and was generally not regarded as a dutiful and productive citizen. After a few months of trying a number of jobs and failing miserably at them all, I finally landed a temporary position as a stagehand and dogsbody at the Sommerkabarett in the city centre.

'One morning, I happened to be strolling past the Cabaret building near the main station and saw a sign in the booking office window advertising a vacant post for a scene shifter. I took a deep breath, marched in and told them I was just the man they were looking for. And, for some unaccountable reason, they believed me.'

Rudi paused, reached for the glass on the side table and took a sip of water.

'I loved every minute of it, especially ogling the girls in the dance troupe as they performed for the paying customers, but most of all, I admired the comedians and their sharp satirical barbs at politicians of every shade and their take on life in general. To me, the Cabaret had become the last refuge of political satire, a place where you could—within limits—speak your mind without being beaten to a pulp or thrown into jail. Or both.

'It also held out to me the chance to become the actor I'd always secretly wanted to be. And, now, here I was on the lowest rung of that ladder, aching for an opportunity to do more.' Johann gave him an encouraging nod. Despite his injuries, there was a vibrant vitality and naïve earnestness about Rudi and Johann could hardly wait to discover what had driven him into his present bizarre predicament.

'Well, one night, the Cabaret was full to bursting as usual, with a large gang of uniformed men from the local barracks seated at the best tables, and also the regular crowd of Brownshirts accompanied by a dozen or more of the local ladies who—how shall I put it?—might otherwise have been out catching their death of cold walking the streets in the snow.

'Everything was going well until our chief resident comedian, Rolf, staggered out to perform his last routine of the evening. There was clearly something amiss with him, and when he crashed into the scenery as he made his way on to the stage, it was pretty clear that he had been hitting the bottle even more enthusiastically than usual.

'As a rule, he could manage to struggle through his performance, drunk or sober, but on this particular night, he was so plastered that halfway through his first sentence, he produced an enormous belch, thrust out a stiff Nazi salute and collapsed in an untidy heap on the floor. The audience gave a ragged cheer, clearly not too sure whether this was all part of the act, but I knew he really had passed out and was unlikely to rejoin the human race for quite some time.

'So, I made up my mind. With my heart pounding like a hammer, I took my courage in both hands, strode out from the wings and into the glare of the spotlight. I raised both hands up to the audience and waited until the laughter and catcalls had subsided a little.

'"Meine Herrschaften, I have to inform you that my friend here has had a vision of the Führer and has fainted away in a state of sheer ecstasy." That set off a cacophony of whistles and guffaws from the audience. I bent down and sniffed at the unconscious Rolf, who had begun to snore loudly, much to the amusement of everyone present.

'Miming a doctor with his stethoscope examining a patient, I poked and prodded the recumbent form and shook my head with exaggerated distress. I gestured to two stagehands to fetch Rolf and drag him off the stage. Out of the corner of my eye, I could see the stage manager having a fit in the wings but I ignored him.

'"His condition may possibly also owe something to the local schnapps." Loud laughter. "So, I fear that he must be allowed to continue to dream that he has been transported into Herr Hitler's castle in the air, and… that I, that is, my humble self must take poor Rolf's place."

'I glanced over into the wings. The stage manager was gesturing frantically at me but I turned resolutely away from him and faced the audience. I said in what I hoped was a clear, confident voice, "I hope that's all right with you—so may I be your charming and entertaining host for the next little while?"

'The audience, most of whom were not far short of being in the same condition as Rolf, roared and stamped their approval and I launched into a routine which I had been privately practising in the hope that I'd be allowed one evening to perform for real. The stage manager simply gave a gesture of despair, put his head in his hands and let me get on with it.'

Another sip of water. And a pause for dramatic effect, Johann thought to himself. He really does enjoy his role as an actor, on and off the stage. Rudi carefully put the glass down and prepared to continue his tale.

'To my great surprise, I was a hit. The audience adored my attempts at humour and, in the wings, the stage manager heaved a great sigh of relief and actually joined in the applause. As for me, I loved losing myself in a stage performance and almost literally becoming someone else for a few brief moments.

'When it was all over, I wallowed in the applause and cheers from the audience. As the curtain fell, the one thing I wanted to do was to get out on stage and do it all over again. And, after a bit of an argument with the stage manager, that's precisely what he agreed to. Rolf was fired and I became one of the resident comedians.'

He paused, wincing at the pain as he tried to shift his wounded arm into a more comfortable position.

Johann asked him, 'Are you sure you are strong enough to continue?'

'Of course, just let me get the rest of my story off my chest. Then you'll see how I came to be battering your door down in the middle of the night, dressed as a girl and riddled with bullet holes.

'I was almost too successful, as my particular routine involved a whole load of political satire and, as you can imagine, in times like these, even in the Cabaret, you have to tread carefully. I also mixed my comedy routine with a quick change act, dressing up as everyone from Hitler to the girls off the local street. And, night after night, I brought the house down.

'One evening, my sister, Anneliese, joined the audience to watch me. She was on vacation from the university and curious to see what her alleged failure of a brother was up to. I was determined to put on my best performance and I suppose I may have been trying just a little too hard.

39

'I started off with a fairly harmless Hitler joke. It went something like this: Hitler calls his closest advisors to a meeting at which he declares, "I hereby order the execution of ten thousand Jews and one parrot." For a second or two, there's a stunned silence.

'Then a senior army officer demands, "What do you want to kill a parrot for?" Hitler smiles and replies, "There. I told you. We are a nation of bird lovers, and no one cares about the Jews." That went down pretty well, as I remember, so I carried on with my usual stuff, which included a couple of quick costume changes.

'I'd just told my joke about the British officer on the eve of the battle of Waterloo who asks his batman to get him his red coat so the blood won't show, and his batman says that means he will have to put on his khaki shorts. Then, after a pause for laughter, I added, "I used to wonder why Brownshirts wear that particular colour—and now I know!"

'Loud applause and a gale of laughter swept around the audience, except for one particularly thuggish Brownshirt, who took great exception to my words of wit and wisdom—but, to be honest, the man was far too pissed to take anything in the right spirit.

'He crashed and staggered his way towards me, much to the merriment of the rest of the audience. Our two bouncers shoved and elbowed their way towards the intruder, who was struggling on his hands and knees up the steps to one side of the stage, hurling abuse at me and threatening me with death, fire and brimstone and Lord knows what else, and not necessarily in that order. In a lull in the uproar, I proclaimed at the top of my voice, "Look, he thinks I'm Hitler. He's actually crawling up to me!"

'More hoots of derision rose from the audience. Howling with beery rage, the drunken Brownshirt lunged at me, fell headlong on the stage and was finally manhandled off into the wings by the bouncers. His imprecations could be heard getting fainter as he was half carried, half dragged along the corridors behind the scenes and unceremoniously thrown out of the rear of the building.

'What I did not know was that my sister, frightened by the uproar in the auditorium, had fled the building and was nervously waiting for me at the stage door. I worked through the rest of my act and made my departure, leaving the next turn, a troupe of jugglers, to try and hold the audience's attention. As I was making my way towards my dressing room, the janitor told me that my sister was hanging about anxiously outside and in a bit of a state, and would I please go and meet her as soon as possible. I sprinted down the corridor and out into the rain-swept cobbled street.

'Of my sister, there seemed to be no sign at all. I looked around and, at first, I couldn't see anything in the darkness, but after a second or two, I could just make out the Brownshirt dragging her down the alleyway by her coat collar. Sis was putting up a good fight but she was no match for that big brute, drunk or sober.

'The bastard was actually trying to rip her underwear off with one hand as he hauled her through the mud and filth of the gutter. As you can see, I'm not exactly a heavyweight but I charged straight at him and leapt on his back. We crashed into a heap on the ground and I set about battering the Brownshirt with every ounce of my rather small being.

'I was so inflamed with rage that it took my sister a heroic effort to drag me off the man. By this time, he was so blotto that he was barely offering any resistance and Anneliese was beginning to fear for his safety. We left him there lying in a puddle of vomit, muttering incoherently to himself, and sis and I hastily made our way back to our parents' home where she was staying. She was half hysterical with relief, calling me her hero and all sorts of nonsense, so I told her to recommend me for the Iron Cross First Class. I suspect I may have to wait quite a while for that little award to turn up.'

Rudi paused. Reaching over to the side table, Johann passed him the glass of water.

'Are you sure you're up to continuing? Or are you too tired?'

Rudi smiled. 'No, no. Nearly finished. Must get it all over and done with in one go.'

He passed the empty glass back and continued his account. 'I was determined not to let matters rest there. My sister had been thoroughly traumatised by what could have escalated into the nastiest kind of sexual assault. I was horrified that one of the local Nazis had so completely lost all sense of decency and respect for others he felt he could act like he was master of the universe. He believed he could treat the rest of the population, women in particular, as his personal playthings.

'So, I faced two problems: first, to find the piece of shit who had assaulted Anneliese and then to work out how to make him pay for what he'd done. There's no way I could beat the brute in a fair fight unless he was paralytically drunk, so I had to dream up some alternative scheme.

'After some head-scratching, it occurred to me that the best way of punishing Herr Brownshirt and show him up as the complete asshole was, to publicly humiliate him in front of his mates and turn him into a laughing stock.

'Humour is my sharpest and strongest weapon. This creature regarded himself as some kind of sex god who could ravish any woman he took a fancy to, but it didn't take me very long to dream up a means of cutting him and his masculinity right down to size.'

Another pause. Rudi breathlessly waved off Johann's concerned enquiry before he had a chance to speak.

'Don't worry about me. I really must tell you the final bit of my story. Then I can rest for as long as you like.

'Two days later, it was my night off, so I went out in search of my prey. Less than an hour later, I'd managed to track him down to a sleazy bar up a side street near the river. It was a well-known haunt of the more obnoxious specimens of the Brownshirt fraternity and, when I put my head round the door, there he was in a corner with half a dozen of his mates.

'They were well into their third or fourth beer of the evening, laughing and joking and generally having a good time. But I was pretty pleased to note that he sported a black eye and a selection of cuts and scratches to his face.

'I went across to the bar and asked the well-endowed young lady serving the beers where the manager was. She looked me over sceptically and demanded to know why. I told her I was an old school friend of his and needed to talk a private matter over with him.

'She gave me a long suspicious stare then, making up her mind, she pointed at a curtain to one side behind the bar and said, 'He's working on the annual accounts, so don't blame me if he bites your head off.'

'I did actually happen to know the owner slightly, as he had been at school with me in the class above. Fortunately, he recognised me and told me he'd seen my act a couple of weeks earlier and loved it. And, better still, he shared my opinion of the whole bunch of Brownshirt thugs.

'His problem was that they had become one of his main sources of income but when I told him what this particular specimen had tried to do to my sister, he willingly consented to go along with my plan to cut the brute down to size in front of his pals. I'd brought a bag with me containing one of my changes of costume, which I had been practising for use during my act, and quickly slipped into the dress and wig you found me wearing when I banged on your door.

'When I put my mind to it, I can be pretty convincing as Little Marlene—that's the name of the young girl I've been practising for my act—and so I sidled up to the group who were telling bawdy jokes to one another and inveigled my way into the conversation.

'A couple of wisecracks later, I was actually sitting on the knee of my sister's attacker and he had his grubby hand firmly placed halfway up my skirt. Now, was the time to pounce, so I commanded the assembled mob to silence and informed them in the gravest tones that their esteemed colleague was concealing a deadly secret which could destroy him if the Nazi hierarchy found out the real truth about him.

'They all looked bemused, some of them laughed, others stared into their beers in a puzzled way, but they were all bursting to know what I was about to reveal. My sister's attacker looked suitably dumbstruck.

'"And, meine Herrschaften," I continued, "what do you reckon this secret might be?" Pause for dramatic effect, then I announced, "He goes around attacking innocent women." I paused once more. "But you knew that already, eh?" My eyes swept around the mystified assembly. Nods of agreement and a tipsy giggle or two came by way of reply.

'"The real secret is that he chases after women in order to prove he isn't a closet homosexual! And now he has come after me because he fancies me. He knows what I really am… and now I am going to prove it."

'I hoisted my skirt up to my waist, demonstrating to them that I was indeed of the male gender. There was a moment's shocked silence and then, the lot of them, with one notable exception, burst into hoots of raucous laughter which drew the attention of the whole bar. As you know, the Nazis don't exactly approve of homosexuals and tend to pack them off to the nearest concentration camp.

'The notable exception to the merriment had turned puce with rage. I got the general impression that my next move ought to be to beat a rapid retreat, so I shoved him off his chair and made a dash for the door, accompanied by ragged cheers from his fellow Brownshirts. I was halfway down the street, when he staggered out of the bar behind me, waving his sidearm in his hand and bellowing a string of obscenities in my direction. Then he fired three times.

'The first shot hit a dustbin with a deafening clang, but with the next, I felt a burning sensation in my left arm, quickly followed by a painful jolt to my leg. I looked at the Brownshirt in horror, as his friends who had rushed out after him were drunkenly trying to wrestle the gun out of his hand and drag him back into the bar.

'When I pulled myself together, I decided I was in some danger and also in serious need of medical attention, so I bound up the injuries as best I could. Then I recalled that your consulting room was just a couple of stops away on the tram, so I managed to struggle my way here. A colleague of mine at the Cabaret once recommended you to me. And here I am and that's my tale, for what it's worth.'

Johann could hardly suppress his delight at what Rudi had done to his sister's assailant and laughed out loud at his exploits.

'You are damned resourceful, my young friend,' he smiled. 'And I am truly envious of the fact that you actually struck back at the bastard in the way you did. I wish I had the courage and the opportunity to do anything remotely like that. I am full of admiration for you.'

They looked quickly around as a soft feminine voice added, 'Me too. Brilliant, Rudi, quite brilliant.'

Elise stood in the doorway, smiling broadly.

'How long have you been there?' demanded Johann. 'Quite some time. I heard voices and, surely, you didn't expect me to stay in bed like the dutiful wife when this young man had such a splendid tale to tell, did you?'

Chapter Five

As the morning sun caught his face through a thin gap in the curtains, Johann sat up suddenly, instantly awake and for a few confused seconds trying to fathom out where he was. Sitting in the uncomfortable chair he used in his consulting room and aching all over, that's where. On the examination table next to him, Rudi was still fast asleep, snoring gently.

A little later, the door opened and Elise appeared, yawning. The tart aroma of coffee drifted in from the kitchen.

'Happy Sunday,' she whispered.

'You too,' he replied. This was the one day of the week when they had no regular consulting hours, and most times, it was an opportunity for them to be together and alone, away from the cares of their medical practice. But not this weekend, it seemed. They took another look at their patient, who seemed unlikely to rejoin the land of the living for some time yet.

'Has he been awake since telling his story?' she asked. 'Not at all,' Johann replied, leading her out of the room and closing the door gently behind him. 'After what he's been through, he'll need all the sleep he can get.

It was around eleven o'clock when a gentle knock on the sitting room door informed them that their patient was, at last, up and about.

'Do come in,' called Elise.

The door swung open to reveal a sleepy-eyed Rudi, still dressed as a young girl but without the wig. He advanced uncertainly into the room and collapsed into a chair.

'Ouch,' he said. 'I think someone shot me. Twice.'

All three laughed, breaking the tension of the previous night's crisis and its aftermath.

'Coffee?' asked Elise. Rudi nodded earnestly.

Elise went off to the kitchen as Rudi turned to Johann and said, 'Can't thank you enough, you literally saved my life.' An embarrassed pause. 'What do I owe you?'

'Let's say that your little course of treatment is on the house. I feel I owe you far more for that inspiring account of how you struck back at a truly unpleasant Nazi bully. It was just unfortunate that he managed to hit you a couple of times with his gun.'

'Are you really sure about the money?'

Johann waved his question away and smiled. 'Now it's up to you to rest and recover. By the way,' he continued, 'are you going to be able to continue with your comic turns, as all those Brownshirts will, surely, recognise you from that girl costume?'

Rudi laughed. 'There's nothing to worry about there. I'd just been practising that routine, and I'm sure I'll be able to use that outfit on stage which, as I said, I'm going to call "Little Marlene". The way his pals reacted to the drunken bully told me that they were genuinely delighted that someone had, at last, put the man firmly in his place. He'll be out of action for some time, I suspect, licking his wounds—and nursing his battered pride.'

Elise reappeared from the kitchen, carrying a tray of cups which she handed around. Taking the third cup for herself, she sat down next to Johann and asked, 'What shall we do with him, Liebling? Turning up in the middle of the night like that, and disturbing our beauty sleep?'

'I told him I'd charge him treble and ban him from the practice.'

'Good thing too,' she responded cheerfully.

Johann leaned forward, placing his cup on the low table before him. 'Look, Rudi, I know you are still in shock from your injuries and probably want nothing more than to go home and rest. By the way, I'd be happy to take you there in the car. But,' he added, 'there is one matter I'd like to talk over with you before you go if you don't mind.'

'Talk away, I'm listening.'

Johann looked at Elise, who nodded at him in encouragement.

'We both applaud what you did by way of retribution for the attack on your sister. We particularly admire the fact that you didn't meet violence with violence, but simply cut the man down to size and made him look extremely foolish. It certainly ought to discourage him from behaving as mindlessly as that ever again.

'I personally have long wanted to be able to achieve something positive like you did, but up to now, I've done nothing much more startling or remarkable than put my thoughts and experiences down in a daily diary. Pretty poor stuff for a rebellion against an almighty state, you'll agree.

'Without going into details, one of Elise's family has been far more active than we have in assisting people of all kinds whom the Nazis seek to harm, for whatever reason, and we are more than keen to do something positive and practical too.'

He paused, took a sip of coffee and looked at Rudi, who nodded thoughtfully.

'Carry on, Johann.'

'I was more than delighted to be able to assist you last night. What I did by treating you was no more than a very minor gesture against the Nazi state, I know, but you and your splendid story have increased my appetite to do a great deal more.

'What I have been considering is bringing together a group of four or five people, including Elise here, who would be prepared to take similar positive action as and when the opportunity arises. It could take the form of helping a political opponent of the régime to find an escape route out of the country, or meting out retribution for just the kind of mindless brutality your sister experienced.

'You might well argue that one person or just a small group can do relatively little, but I am firmly convinced that doing something, however seemingly petty, against the Nazis and all they stand for is vital if we are to maintain our humanity and our cherished civilised values. Do nothing and we are no better than they are.

'So,' he continued, taking a deep breath, 'we wonder if you would be willing to join the group if I can call it that, which I am in the process of trying to put together. So far, I haven't actually spoken to anyone else, but there are at least a couple of my patients who I know share our views and might well leap at the opportunity.'

Rudi looked thoughtfully at both of them. After a pause, he nodded.

'Yes, of course, I'd love to join you—especially because of what I did last night and your response to it. But can I suggest we keep it just between the three of us for now, that is until we come across an opportunity to act and to demonstrate that we really are able to do something which has a genuine impact? Only then, should we think about extending the group, as you call it, to four or five people. We really ought to establish a track record before seeking to involve others.

'Besides, the real problem nowadays is being able to trust anyone because the state has eyes and ears everywhere. Any potential new member would have to be an individual who has already seriously crossed swords with the Party and, for that reason, is strongly motivated to take positive action against the régime.'

Johann and Elise smiled and nodded enthusiastically at his response.

'Agreed,' they said in unison, and they all shook hands to seal their pact.

'Now,' said Rudi, 'before we transform ourselves into knights in shining armour, let's consider a couple of practicalities. I know where you are, of course, but do let me have your telephone number so I can contact you. As a poor struggling comic actor, I don't have access to a phone, and the best way to get in touch with me is via the janitor at the stage door. He'll know where I am and when my acts on stage finish for the evening.'

He turned to face Johann.

'And I'd be very grateful to accept your kind offer of a lift back to my apartment. I do hope it won't be long before some real opportunity comes along. I've begun to get quite an appetite for these little adventures. I do hope that something turns up quite soon.

'There's just one other problem, though,' he continued and they looked nervously at him. 'Could you possibly lend me some clothes as I don't want to parade the streets as Little Marlene at this time of day. Especially with no knickers on.'

The three of them burst into laughter.

Chapter Six

Number 49 was constructed on an even grander scale than the other stone-built detached houses in the Parkstrasse, a broad tree-lined avenue which sloped gently down in a long sweeping curve towards the River Pegnitz. Built on rising ground, the house boasted a deep-pitched roof hugging a row of eight mansard windows. On the double-fronted ground floor, large picture windows overlooked generous lawns and mature shrubberies dusted with a light covering of snow. The gated front entrance gave access to a circular gravelled drive leading up to the porticoed main entrance, and to the right, a large outbuilding housed a two-car garage on the ground floor and accommodation for up to four servants on the upper storey. The entire property was surrounded by a low stone wall.

The Birnbaum family had lived there ever since the house had been built just after the end of the Great War. During the years of military conflict, Eli Birnbaum had increased his wealth, as his clothing factories supplied some of the German uniforms and specialist equipment demanded by an ever-swelling army and navy, and as the war went on, an increasingly crucial air force.

He had purchased the house outright as a family home for himself and his new wife, who in due course bore him two daughters. Other well-to-do families moved into the neighbouring houses as they were completed, most of them businessmen like Eli who had emerged from the hostilities more prosperous than before, and soon, the avenue puttered and coughed to the sound of automobiles—the latest and most expensive models, of course—which chauffeured husbands to work, children to school and wives to the upmarket shopping areas of the city with their cafés and bars and shady walks.

When hyperinflation and the Great Crash of '29 came and, with it, yet more depression and unemployment, some of the houses fell empty and, for a while, even became derelict, with weeds and brambles invading the manicured lawns and immaculate gravelled drives. Number 49 accommodated one of the more fortunate families. Eli had converted much of his savings into paintings and antiques, and his factories still produced a limited but growing number of uniforms after a brief period of closure and mothballing.

Eli was now beginning to expand his business abroad, but he had never taken his good fortune for granted. He sponsored and supported many charitable undertakings and was always generous in assisting friends and family members who had fallen on hard times. He was much loved by his workers who respected him as a compassionate and sympathetic employer, and all who knew him admired him for his generosity of spirit and unassuming ways.

As part of his involvement in charitable causes, he organised an annual exhibition of his private collection of pictures and sculptures in the long gallery which ran the length of the rear of the house, and those lucky enough to obtain a ticket for the viewing plus a lavish buffet and dance were persuaded to part with considerable sums of money in support of local orphanages for abandoned children.

Now, the country was undergoing yet another great upheaval, and the domination of the Nazi Party was viewed with very mixed feelings by the residents of the Parkstrasse. Some families, seeing business opportunities in the rise of a disciplined, militaristic government, enthusiastically embraced the new régime. Others were far more cautious, and as a survivor of two decades of alternating business success and near disaster, Eli was deeply suspicious of the ability of the Nazi Party to control the huge aspirations which it had set for itself and to ride the tiger it had let loose amongst the German people.

Privately, he was seriously alarmed at the growing tide of anti-Semitism and its potential consequences for his family, his business and the wider Jewish community. Eli's cousin, Ham, had been a member of the German international rowing team, and Eli was saddened and concerned when Ham was banned, along with all other Jews, from organised sport when the Nazis came to power, long before the 1936 Olympic Games in Berlin. But even more unnerving, was the way in which the Nazis had cleverly averted a potential international boycott, convincing countries like America that Germany was a tolerant and fair-minded land which welcomed all people regardless of their race or colour to their peaceful international festival of sport.

For the meantime, though, Eli continued to pursue his manufacturing achievements, and he and his wife slipped gracefully into their middle years along with their well-off friends and relations. Their elder daughter, Ruth, continued to pursue her studies at the local secondary school, where her violin playing drew universal praise, and her sister, Naomi, had started Kindergarten, where she was loved and cherished by staff and pupils alike. However, even for the children, the atmosphere in school and playgroup alike had recently grown increasingly unfriendly towards Jewish pupils.

It had seemed that the Birnbaums might survive the 1930s as they had the turbulent decades which had preceded them. But the danger signs could no longer be disregarded, and that is why Eli Birnbaum had privately been making urgent preparations to effect his family's evacuation from Germany if the situation became untenable.

One Spring evening as dusk began to fall, a net curtain twitched in the ground-floor window of a much smaller dwelling on the opposite side of the avenue. It was a former gatehouse sitting on its own tiny patch of ground and it was very much out of place amongst the wealth and opulence of the rest of the avenue. Its sole occupant was one Winifred Bucher, an embittered spinster whose fiancé had been torn in two by a burst of machine gun fire in the dying days of the Great War.

Since then, consumed with envy at the comfortable lives of others, she had eked out an embittered and solitary existence with her dachshund,, Spitz as her only companion. Like many Germans disaffected by defeat in war and the vicissitudes of life in the Weimar Republic, she had been seduced by the blandishments of the Nazi Party, not least because her brother, Leopold, had been swept on the back of his active Party membership from total obscurity as a factory accounts clerk to the post of Deputy Bürgermeister, much to the disgust of colleagues who were appalled that they had been overlooked in favour of such a boot-licking upstart.

It was her brother who, three years previously, had bought the gatehouse for her and he continued to support her financially when the need arose; two good deeds which served only to fuel her antagonism against all those more fortunate than herself.

But the greater part of her venom was reserved for the people who resided in the opulent houses of the Parkstrasse which surrounded her humble home, and most particularly, for the occupants of number 49. Not only were they enterprising and successful and at the heart of local society life, they were also Jews, and the Jewish people, she was convinced, were one of the direct causes of her life of unremitting misery and frustration.

Moreover, her brother, Leopold, had toiled away as a lowly employee of the Birnbaum family's local clothing factory before his meteoric rise through the Party ranks.

So, it was hardly surprising that she was obsessed with the comings and goings of the family opposite, and that evening, she was shocked and concerned by an unusual amount of activity throughout the house. All the lights were burning and she could just make out the shadowy forms of people moving urgently from room to room, carrying what appeared to be piles of clothing and other possessions down to a central collection point in the main living area, a huge and well-appointed space large enough to accommodate a tennis court.

She wondered what on earth could have caused such a commotion in the family. And, then, a sudden thought struck her.

Was it possible that these rich Jews were actually preparing to make a run for it, to flee the country from the retribution which was long overdue to them and which they must not be allowed to escape? Unaware of the fact that the bustle in the big house was caused by nothing more sinister than special preparations for their younger daughter's fifth birthday on the following day, Winifred became convinced the Birnbaums were on the brink of clandestine flight from the country and that they should be stopped at all costs. But how?

In that instant, she called to mind a conversation with her brother a year or so previously. He had dropped in to take her to tea in the fashionable hotel opposite the main railway station. Out of kindness to his sister, he would occasionally give her such little treats, which she meanly interpreted as part of his attempt to rub her nose in his wealth and underline her inferior status.

In fact, he had always been greatly fond of Winifred and deeply sympathised with her over the sad loss of her fiancé and the financial hardship she had faced as a consequence. Leopold, it appeared, was almost two different people: soft-hearted and kindly to friends and family, but in public life, an utterly ruthless autocrat, a man without pity or the tiniest shred of compassion.

Amongst the potted palms and the clatter of expensive china, Leopold had told Winifred the story of himself and his wife, Marie, when they were an engaged couple in the 1920s with little prospect of acquiring more than a pokey rented tenement flat in a drab quarter of the city. Marie had always loved bright shiny things, the outward display of wealth and status which resolutely eluded their grasp.

Their one small luxury in a life of drudgery and impoverishment was to take the tram on a Sunday afternoon to the city outskirts and just stroll around. Most often, they would end up walking with crowds of other couples and their families through the woods that bordered the city to the southwest. On this particular Sunday, however, they jumped on a single tramcar unit which took them up to the prosperous suburb of Altdorf, where they alighted at the top end of the Parkstrasse and set off to stroll aimlessly down the tree-shaded avenue. As ever, their conversation turned to money and the prospects of a life of near penury.

Leopold had been an early active supporter of the Nazi cause, joining in the mid-1920s, long before the so-called 'March Violets', opportunist new members who later scrambled onto the Party bandwagon in 1933 when the Nazis came to power. Trapped in a repetitive office job which provided little satisfaction and no chance of advancement, he had smouldered with resentment at the cigar-smoking bosses with their fur-lined overcoats and chauffeured limousines, and he became a willing convert to the Nazi Party with its grandiose promises of prosperity for the downtrodden and advancement for the faithful.

Marie adored nice clothes and furniture and spent much of her free time ogling the shop windows of the upmarket retailers in the city, like her husband, bewailing the cruel fate that had condemned them to a life of drudgery with little hope for the future. As their discussion became ever more embittered, a large black Mercedes Benz saloon whispered past them. Suddenly, Leopold stopped in mid-sentence and stabbed an angry finger at the luxury vehicle.

'Donnerwetter, that's my boss's car,' he exclaimed. 'And that's him in the back, too.'

A hundred yards ahead of the pair, the car turned slowly into an entranceway and stopped. They watched enviously as the chauffeur stepped out and opened the double metal gates. Getting back into the vehicle, he eased it up the driveway.

'Let's go take a peek at where he lives,' said Marie, and the two of them hurried down the avenue until they arrived opposite number 49. The size and splendour of the building, together with its extensive grounds, held Marie spellbound and Leopold himself felt the sharp sting of pure envy.

'Some day, I want to live in a house just like that,' said Marie covetously. Then, she paused, and continued with all the venom she could muster, 'No—I want to live in that house.'

Her husband raised his chubby hands in a despairing gesture. 'There's no chance of that ever happening, my dear, more's the pity.'

Winifred Bucher smiled wryly as she recalled Leopold's account of that Sunday afternoon conversation and called to mind her own chippy response. 'Well, brother, one day, that dream may actually come true. Stranger things have happened.'

When, at last, Leopold was beginning to prosper as a rising star in the local Party and he was able to purchase the gatehouse opposite number 49 for his sister, he insisted that it was pure coincidence. It was simply an excellent deal from a bankrupt shop owner and set in one of the better locations in the city.

He had, he swore, completely forgotten about his wife's longing to own a place like number 49 and even that she had lusted after that particular house, but Winifred was convinced that he was at least partly motivated by a desire to demonstrate his newly-won status and power and emphasise her cruel dependency on him. However, she had eagerly accepted the chance to move from her drab flat in the city centre, and, now, it took her less than a moment's thought before she stepped over to her telephone, another gift from her brother. As she lifted the receiver, the dachshund yapped at the machine.

'Quiet, now, Spitz. I'm just ringing my brother, Leopold. Go and sit on your bed.'

The dog looked enquiringly at her, then trotted off and deposited itself on a cushion by the empty fireplace.

When Leopold picked up the receiver, she greeted him and spoke conspiratorially.

'Brother, do you remember that house opposite me and what you told me Marie had said about it? The house she had always wanted? Of course, you know the family are Jews, the Birnbaums, the people you used to work for in that crummy factory of his. I think they are all about to make an attempt to leave the country, as there are lights on all over the house and the place is a hive of frantic activity. So, it could well be in your interest to contact local SS Headquarters and pass the information on. They may act upon it, and then, you never know, you might just be able to turn your wife's dream into reality... '

She let the tempting thought hang in the air, and for a few seconds, she could hear nothing but the faint hiss and crackle of the phone line. Then, her brother coughed in that irritatingly self-important manner he had adopted since his rise to local fame and fortune.

'Ah, yes, I do remember now. I did tell you that Marie had once hankered after it, but that was a long time ago. Nevertheless, thank you, my dear sister,' said Leopold, his voice only slightly blurred by the first of several evening brandies, 'I'll consider taking the matter up and I am most grateful to you for your information.'

Pompous ass, thought Winifred, putting down the phone and moving back to the window to observe her neighbours across the way, who she so keenly hoped would not be neighbours for very much longer.

All too soon, that hope would be tragically realised.

Chapter Seven

Just before six the next morning, the quiet of the Parkstrasse was shattered by the din of motor horns and shrieking brakes as the SS arrived to teach yet another Jewish brood a lesson they would never forget. At the last minute, this particular household—father, mother and two daughters—had been crammed into the schedule for the next regular transhipment to a concentration camp in the south of the country and SS Leutnant Erpenbeck was not best pleased. He had been dragged out of his comfortable bed and the arms of his current mistress at some ungodly hour of the morning in order to deal with this extra consignment and the least little irritation was going to tip his pent-up anger into naked aggression.

Pointing at the sign on the gatepost, he snapped, 'That's the house, number 49. Let's get this over and done with, men.'

As usual, it was the duty of the Obergefreiter, the lance corporal in charge of the squad, to march up to the ornate double front doors, knock imperiously and demand that the head of the family appear. There was a long silence and the Obergefreiter was about to renew his door battering when he heard the sound of bolts being drawn and a key turning. The door swung half open to reveal Eli Birnbaum in his dressing gown. He peered through sleepy eyes at his unwelcome visitor.

With a steady voice, he demanded, 'What is going on here? Why are you hammering at my door at this hour of the morning?'

But his eyes, moving rapidly from the Obergefreiter to the car and lorry parked at the end of the drive and back again, betrayed his fear. For a moment, the Obergefreiter was daunted by the man's outward display of calm dignity, but he swiftly recovered. Pulling himself up to his full height, he shouted,

'You have been indicted as an enemy of the Reich and you and your family will get dressed immediately and within fifteen minutes... we will be removing you from your home to a transit location for further transportation, er, and resettlement.'

His usual smooth delivery faltered as a sweet little girl, eyes wide with curiosity, appeared round the door. A mass of dark curls framed a smooth-featured face with full red lips. In her right hand, she held an ancient stuffed doll, its head lolling comically to one side.

'What is happening, daddy? Who are these people? Are they here for my birthday?'

She spoke in a thin young voice coloured by the hollow-ounding vowels of the profoundly deaf. Her father looked down at her, smiled faintly and spoke slowly to her so she could lip-read.

'Nothing to worry about, Naomi. Just go back inside and daddy will sort it out.'

The Obergefreiter thought to himself, what's happening to the lot of you is that you are about to get carted off to a concentration camp where you'll all rot to death. But why did that damned sweet little girl have to mention it was her birthday? Secretly, the Obergefreiter hated this aspect of his work, but why should he challenge what the Führer and Reich demanded of him, not least, because he had a decent corporal's wage in his pocket and a wife and family to support? After all, he was only obeying legitimate orders. So, he assumed his best military bark.

'Hurry along now. Time presses. We can't hang around here all day. There are other addresses for us to visit before the morning is done. You have fifteen minutes to pack necessities into a suitcase.'

He turned sharply round and marched back down the drive, before Eli Birnbaum could respond. Just let us get on with it, his demeanour said, and the quicker it's over and finished with the better.

When the Birnbaums finally emerged, there was the usual deal of fuss and bother. The mother was close to hysteria, shaking with fear and trying in vain to maintain a measure of self-control. Still clinging to her rag doll with one hand and her mother with the other, the younger girl, suddenly sensing that something terrible was threatening their secure and happy life, began to howl and scream inconsolably.

By contrast, the father preserved his dignified posture and sought in vain to calm his wife and younger offspring. The elder daughter, Ruth, a tall wisp of a girl with long black hair, stepped quietly along behind her mother, a small suitcase in her right hand. She mirrored the calm external poise of her father, although inside, she too was in turmoil, as she knew full well what had happened to some of the other Jewish children from her class at school.

As they stumbled down the drive carrying hastily filled suitcases, the Obergefreiter snapped an order and two of his team ran smartly forward to urge the family to hurry along, as the Leutnant's patience was clearly wearing thin. Before they reached the end of the drive, mother and father found themselves being unceremoniously dragged out on to the pavement. And when the younger girl's lamentations reached screaming pitch, one of the soldiers lost his temper and snatched her rag doll away from her.

'Stop that bloody row, you little Jewish bitch,' he yelled.

'Leave her alone, you brute!' snapped the older girl. 'Get your filthy hands off my sister.'

The soldier just laughed and swirled the doll around his head. Leutnant Erpenbeck stood impatiently looking on, slapping his leather gloves against his side and letting his subordinates manage the situation, one he had witnessed dozens of times before. He sought to give the impression that he was above such undignified displays and that the Jews ought to damned well shut up and accept the fate they so richly deserved.

Then, as his eye roved over the elder daughter, his grim mood lifted a little and a lustful sneer flickered across his features. Not bad for a little Jewish virgin, he thought. Not bad at all. Perhaps today won't be as tiresome as I thought. I must have a little word with my Obergefreiter as she could well provide me with some well-deserved entertainment after a long and tedious day.

Naomi was now shrieking with fear and despair. Exasperated, the soldier flung the doll across the road to land on one of the tramlines that ran down the central reservation. Hysterically, the little girl began struggling violently to free herself and Erpenbeck was tempted to reprimand the soldier for over-reacting. But why make a fuss, he thought, they… we are just Jews they are dealing with. Third-class citizens on the road to nothing more sinister than a happy relocation camp, or so the national propaganda machine tells us.

At that instant, a tram came clattering down the gentle decline leading to the main shopping district and the square opposite the station and, as it drew nearer, the girl's lamentations mingled with the rattle and squeal of the wheels on the track. The tram came ever closer and, in that moment, the little girl suddenly wrenched herself free from her mother and dashed across the road to recover her precious doll. She had just reached her prize, as the tram, its alarm bell ringing furiously, drew level with her, emergency brakes screeching stridently. There was a faint thud, and a blur of movement as Naomi's body was swept under the wheels of the tram.

'Naomi!' howled her mother, who would have dashed across to try and save her, but she was roughly held back by one of the soldiers. Grief-stricken, she collapsed by the roadside as if her very life had been torn from her. But it wasn't her anguish which was so profoundly moving, it was Eli's grimly quiet words and the soldier's response which were truly heart-breaking.

He said, calmly and almost gently, 'She was deaf. That's why she didn't hear the tram. She was deaf, damn you.'

The soldier swung round and snarled, 'Just another bloody Jew crushed, just like the lot of you should be. Not worth the buckets of stupid tears you're crying over her. Get into the damned truck and bloody well be smart about it.'

The Obergefreiter signalled to one of his unit to stand guard at the front door of the house and wait for the specialist removal vans to come and confiscate any goods of value. The house would be cleared and ownership of the building transferred into the possession of a deserving Party member, presumably someone of considerable rank and in good favour. After all, it was a pretty substantial dwelling.

The mother was still sobbing in despair and the elder daughter covered her face with both hands. Eli Birnbaum turned back to take a long sad look at his house as if to bid it and their life there farewell, and helped his anguished wife and surviving daughter up into the truck. Leutnant Erpenbeck shoved his gloves into his coat pocket and whispered private instructions to the Obergefreiter.

The truck set off in a cloud of exhaust smoke and the Leutnant hopped into his Mercedes, slammed the door and drove swiftly after them. Family number one dealt with for today. Another five to pick up before bloody lunchtime, he muttered to himself. No peace for the wicked. Especially me, he smirked, his mind playing back the image of the tall slim elder daughter and her soft budding breasts. Especially me.

As the sound of engines faded down the road, the tram remained stationary on the line. The Obergefreiter walked smartly across to where the driver was stretched out on the ground, peering under the body of the vehicle. He prodded the man with his foot and demanded, 'What can you see down there? Is the damned child alive?'

The driver slowly raised himself up, brushed his uniform trousers and, near to tears, replied with a sad shake of the head, 'What's left of the poor lass is jammed in the undercarriage. She's just a mangled mess, that poor little girl. Dead in an instant.'

The Obergefreiter shoved him brusquely to one side and bent down to inspect the undercarriage himself. Satisfied that Naomi was indeed deceased, he rose to his feet, brushed the dirt off his trouser legs and snapped at the driver, who was standing disconsolately next to him, 'Get back in the tram, man, and drive us off. We are going back to the main depot. Now!'

The Obergefreiter clambered up after the driver and sat down behind him. Meanwhile, the passengers, staring blankly ahead, sat motionless like dolls in their seats. After all, it was nothing to do with them. Whatever had happened was clearly sanctioned by the state, and you just had to accept it. But what had occurred to the little girl was tragic and traumatic all the same. If only Uncle Adolf knew about some of the atrocities taking place in his name, they were sure he would not allow it. It was actually the people around him who were really at fault, not our dear Führer.

The tram bell tinkled importantly as it accelerated away down the line towards the town centre. As it did so, a curtain tweaked in the small former gatehouse opposite Number 49. Inside, just visible in the shadows, Winifred Bucher, her expression contorted by shock, muttered wretchedly to herself, 'God in Heaven, I didn't mean that to happen. They shouldn't have killed her. That poor dear child. It's all their fault.'

She found herself shaking from head to foot and told herself to get back under control and calm down. After a few moments, she resolved to take her beloved dachshund out for a breath of fresh air. That would clear her head and give her time to remember that she had only been doing her duty as a citizen, and if something had gone disastrously wrong as a result, she was not to blame. That was entirely up to the SS officer and the men under his command.

'Come on, Spitz. Let's go for a walk.'

The dog unravelled its body and stumpy legs from its cushion by the fireplace and wagged an enthusiastic tail. After putting on her threadbare black coat, which she had worn in public ever since she had received the news of the death of her fiancé all those years before, she reached down and attached a lead to the dog's collar.

Outside, the road was clear again and the tram was only just visible in the distance. It was as if nothing had ever happened. Winifred and the dog crossed over to the central reservation, where she bent down again and released the lead.

'Be careful, Spitz. Keep well away from the road, now.'

The dog yapped and waddled off to sniff the lampposts and tree trunks for any invasion of its territory. Winifred slowly walked over to the tram stop and sat down on the bench.

She looked across at number 49 and, as she did so, a black high-sided van swept into the driveway, past the still open gates and up to the front entrance. Four men leapt out and marched into the house along with the soldier who had been left to guard the property. She wondered what they were up to. Perhaps they were securing the building to prevent attacks by burglars or, even worse, looters.

A motor car went past then another tram clattered up from the city and stopped in front of her bench. The driver glanced enquiringly towards her, but she shook her head. The bell pinged and the two-car set trundled off up the incline towards the city limits.

After a little while, she became aware of Spitz panting at her feet and looking up at her in eager anticipation.

'What is it, boy?' she asked, still focussed on the happenings at number 49.

Spitz yapped to draw her attention away from the van and the workers who, to her puzzlement, were loading it up with articles of furniture and paintings from inside the building. Perhaps the Birnbaums had already arranged for the house to be cleared before the arresting party made its appearance, she persuaded herself.

Then she looked down at her dog—and let out a blood-curdling shriek.

Spitz looked at her inquiringly. She screamed again and again. Gasping for breath, she shouted, 'Dear God, Spitz. What have you got there?'

Spitz wagged his tail as if he was being complimented on his find. In a hollow by the tram track, he had stumbled across a bundle of dark hair attached to a ball, which he had dragged over to his mistress for her inspection and approval.

What Spitz had chanced upon was Naomi's severed head, brutally disfigured by the impact from the tram, but still just recognisable. The girl's dark dead eyes stared straight at Winifred as if begging her to explain what had happened.

'Leave it alone! Leave that damned thing alone!' she shrieked at the dog, who jumped back, shocked at his mistress's vehement disapproval. Normally, she would have patted him on the head when he retrieved lost balls or other similar items, but, now, she just roughly reattached his lead with quaking hands, forced herself to her feet and strode hysterically off towards her gatehouse, gulping air into her lungs and dragging the unfortunate animal behind her.

An hour later, a truck from the transport department appeared, charged with finding and removing any possible traces of the accident. One of the workers came across Naomi's bloodied head and laughingly held it up like a trophy to his mates before throwing it into a waste bin. Across the road, in the gatehouse window, the curtain twitched again and Winifred Bucher turned away, her face grey with horror.

Extract from the Nürnberger Zeitung,

Last night, Deputy Bürgermeister Bucher visited the dwelling of his unmarried sister, forty-seven-year-old Winifred Bucher, to find her body hanging from a beam in the kitchen. Her faithful dog, Spitz, had been killed by a single blow from a knife. Herr Bucher stated that his dear and much beloved Winifred, a war widow, had recently been suffering from depression and that her sad demise was a result of her personal sufferings. Foul play is not suspected. The funeral will be private with family flowers only.

Chapter Eight

Thomas Braun was the embodiment of the Nazi Aryan ideal. He was tall, blond, blue-eyed and boasted the physique of a bodybuilder, a man who took regular exercise and had been a successful amateur boxer in his younger days. Now in his forties, he could still go three rounds with the best of the young bloods in the boxing gym. But Thomas was no mindless bruiser, he was a sensitive and intelligent man who loved art, music and books and who would rather spend a spare half hour in a library or museum than on a windy, muddy playing field or in a boxing gym reeking with male sweat.

His parents had been too poor to fund him beyond basic schooling, but he succeeded in working his own way through an apprenticeship as an electrical mechanic. His rapid advance up the promotional ladder culminated in his appointment in 1932 as the Chief Engineer for Transport in the Nuremberg tramways central workshops, the youngest employee ever to be elevated to such an important position in the city.

He was the archetype of the good family man. He had married relatively late, at the age of thirty-five, and his wife, Gertrud, was a slender, auburn-haired woman with sparkling blue eyes who lit up any room she cared to walk into. And she could cook too. Their two children, one boy, one girl, were both attending Kindergarten and were bright and eager, anxious to enjoy life and reach out to new experiences.

All of this conspired to make him the ultimate local poster boy of the Party, the epitome of the successful working class lad who had fought his way up to the top by dint of hard toil and strength of character, and he was on the receiving end of a rash of overblown plaudits from the local propaganda press. He was a Party member, but only because he had little choice but to join if he wanted to progress in his career. He kept well out of the political limelight, preferring to let others take centre stage. He was, in fact, almost too good to be true.

There was just one blemish to taint this perfect image, one tiny secret he could never divulge for the sake of his own safety and that of his family. Put simply, Thomas Braun loathed everything the Nazis stood for and, in particular, the institutionalised thuggery and blind racism which defiled the Party at every level. He particularly despised the arrogant notion of Aryan supremacy and the adulation of physical fitness and physique at the expense of the intellect and the imagination.

More than most people, his dilemma was acute. He loved his job and excelled at it. Away from the workshop, he had been happily married and had bought a neat detached house for his wife and family. He was the envy of many of his peers, but he felt like a fish out of water in the brash militaristic intolerance of the New Germany, and in private, he seethed with repressed anger at the lunatic direction Germany was hell-bent on pursuing.

He was enjoying a rare day away from the pressures of work with his children as they played in the sunlit garden of their suburban home when the telephone jangled stridently from within the house.

A few moments later, an irritated Gertrud called out to him that his deputy was on the line, apologising for the disturbance, but he stressed that it was a matter of great urgency. As Thomas lifted himself out of the garden chair, he wondered what the problem could possibly be. Heinrich Wagner, his Deputy Chief Engineer, was competent enough to manage just about any problem the local transport system could throw at him, from breakdowns and collisions to a serious fire in the main workshop, so it was with a sense of foreboding that he marched quickly over to the kitchen door.

As he passed his wife, she said to him, in a voice tart with annoyance, 'He sounds as if he's in a real panic. I've never heard Heinrich sounding so anxious.'

Thomas gave a concerned nod, wondering what on earth the crisis could be. Well, he said to himself, there is only one way to find out. He strode into the hall, picked up the receiver and said,

'Yes, Wagner, what is it? You know I hate to be disturbed at home unless aliens have landed or the entire city network has been blown up by the Communists.'

'I'm afraid it's worse than that, Herr Braun.' There was no hint of amusement in his voice, which caused Thomas to adopt a more conciliatory tone. Somewhat embarrassed, Thomas cleared his throat and paused for a second.

'You mean, it's political? SS, for instance?'

'Yes, Herr Braun. SS it is. And straight from the top. There's a tram just arrived at the main workshop which needs to be quarantined and cleaned out by you and me in person, and no one else is allowed to go near it. The incident which occurred is.to be described officially as a collision between the tram and a dog.'

'Dog?' questioned Thomas incredulously. 'Has someone run over the Führer's personal shepherd hound?'

'No, Herr Braun. Just an alleged animal belonging to a local Party chief.' A pause at the other end of the line. 'But the driver, who's pretty well shaken up, informed me that it was actually a little Jewish girl he had run over and killed by accident. Worse still, the SS were present at the time and involved in it up to their necks.'

'So, we're dealing with another SS cover-up, are we? It certainly won't be the last time. I'm on my way. Give me twenty minutes, Wagner.'

'Thank you, Herr Braun. Again, sorry to bother you, but when the SS gives an order, you don't challenge it, unless you want to be on the next trainload to the concentration camps.'

Thomas slammed down the receiver, angry at the disruption to a day with his children. He looked round sharply to find his wife actually holding his coat and hat ready for him. That's odd, he thought. For some time she had been acting somewhat coldly towards him and he was at a loss to understand what was going on. Perhaps she resented the demands of his job, or maybe they were just going through the kind of phase which can happen to any married couple. It was curious that she was now diligently playing the role of the dutiful wife, but he might as well go along with it. So, he forced a smile and said, 'Thank you, my dear. I'll be back as soon as I can.'

As he turned into his personal parking space, Thomas could hear the familiar din and bustle of the workshops. He clambered out of the driving seat to see his deputy hurrying towards him, dressed in a dark grey boiler suit over his business clothes and carrying a spare outfit for his boss. He also handed him a set of protective shoe covers.

'Thank you, Wagner. Let's get this over and done with.'

As he struggled into his boiler suit, Wagner told him that the tram was located in a far corner of the workshop and that the two duty security guards were in attendance.

'Where is the driver?'

'I sent him home, sir. The poor fellow was in tears, and I can't honestly blame him. Causing the death of a young girl with your tram isn't something you expect to happen every day. Especially when it was an entirely avoidable tragedy and not his fault at all.'

'Pity, I would like to have had a personal word with him. Ring his home if he has a telephone or get a message to him to the effect that I fully understand his distress and that he should not expect to have to return to work until next Monday.'

'Consider it done.'

They marched off briskly in the direction of the offending tram.

As they approached, one of the security guards stiffened and gave a smart Hitler salute. Thomas pretended he hadn't seen the man, swept past him and marched straight up to the two-coach unit, one of the more elderly trams which had been plying the routes of Nuremberg for decades but were still well-maintained and roadworthy.

'Get me the steam cleaner,' he said roughly. 'Then I'll climb down into the pit and find out what all the fuss is about.'

He eased his way gingerly down the oil-slicked concrete steps to the inspection pit. Picking up a lamp on the end of a long mains cable, he switched it on and held it up to the undercarriage. For a moment or two, he couldn't see anything out of the ordinary, but as he scanned the beam further along, he suddenly stopped. The red tangle of flesh and the obscene whiteness of splintered bone caught up with a girl's dress turned his stomach and, despite himself, he bent over and retched.

'You all right, Herr Braun?' Silence.

'Herr Braun?'

Wagner scrambled down the steps and placed a hand on his boss's back. 'What's wrong, sir?'

Thomas stood up stiffly and, in reply, pointed the lamp at the offending spot.

'Donnerwetter.' Wagner himself was struggling to retain his own breakfast.

'Get me that damned steam gun and a bin, and I'll clean up my vomit and that—dreadful mess.'

Wagner hurried off to do his bidding, and quickly returned with the requested equipment.

'Off you go now. I'll deal with this.'

'Don't we have to try and collect the remains of the deceased?'

Thomas shook his head angrily. 'A little Jewish girl? That lot just regard her as no more than carrion, to be taken away in a rubbish bin.'

He stopped abruptly, aware of the imprudence of his comment. Wagner nodded.

'It's all right, Herr Braun. I couldn't agree more. But we would be wise to keep our views to ourselves.'

As Thomas undertook the grisly task of steam cleaning the undercarriage of the vehicle, he wondered how far the excesses of the SS and their brutal soldiery would go before they were held to account, but that was never likely to happen, he thought bitterly.

The fierce jet of steam dislodged the fragments of bloodied flesh and bones, unrecognisable as parts of a human body, which fell to the ground with a sickening thud. Gagging again, Thomas shovelled the remains into the bin for disposal. He swept the steam jet along towards the rear of the wagon and, after several minutes of utterly distasteful work, he suddenly stopped. High up and jammed behind the rear leaf spring suspension, he could just make out a small deformed bundle, which looked very much like a second body.

He took a deep breath to compose himself, fetched a short ladder and, perched on the uppermost rung, reached gingerly up with a long-handled rake to try and dislodge whatever it was that had become thoroughly stuck in the mechanism. With a couple of firm tugs and the bundle suddenly came free and fell lightly to the ground.

Thomas put the ladder to one side and bent over to pick up the small cloth object. He could not hold back a choking sob when he realised what it was. The remains of a rag doll, one arm wrenched off, head lolling limply to one side, its remaining eye staring unblinkingly up at him, it was evidently a much-loved possession mangled in the violence of the collision. For a moment, he was too distressed to react. Then he reached into his coat, pulled out a large neck scarf, wrapped it round the doll and stuffed it into his pocket. As he did so, a sharp military voice snapped,

'Anyone down there?'

Thomas looked up guiltily, but he was fairly certain that whoever the voice belonged to had not seen him pick up the doll.

'Direktor Braun here. I am just finishing up. Wait a second and I'll be with you.'

He continued working with the steam gun until all evidence of the doll and its owner had been washed away then, bent half double, he walked the length of the wagon, checking that everything was now in order. As he reached the top of the steps, he saw Wagner standing nervously next to an arrogant-looking SS officer.

'Herr Direktor,' he said formally, 'this is Leutnant Erpenbeck, come to ensure that his orders have been properly carried out.'

Thomas looked distastefully at the man. 'I have personally cleaned out all the remains and have placed them in a rubbish bin for disposal.'

Erpenbeck sniffed. 'We are grateful for your discretion and rapid response, Herr Direktor. Do ensure,' he added with a sinister warning note in his voice, 'that no one else has knowledge of this unfortunate incident. It was a dog that ran into the path of the tram, you understand, and you were called upon to check the undercarriage as the animal belonged to a high-ranking official and there was a chance that the creature was still alive. Is that clear?'

The Director and his deputy nodded. Erpenbeck slapped his gloves against his black coat, swung around on his heel and marched out to his waiting Mercedes. As the vehicle swung out of the courtyard, Wagner muttered under his breath, 'Arschloch.'

Thomas responded with a snort as he handed his work gear back to his deputy. 'Ill-advised, Wagner, but absolutely correct. The man is a total asshole.' Sickened by the whole episode, he continued, 'I'm off back home. Do you need me further?'

'No, sir. Not at all.'

'Don't forget to contact the driver. You have done well today, especially given the circumstances.'

The two men shook hands in silent acknowledgement of their common disgust at the entire episode.

As he drove back through the city, the tears coursed down Thomas's face. He imagined one of his own children being cut down by the mindless savagery of a Nazi thug, and he banged his fist against the steering wheel in anger and frustration. He was beginning to wonder how much more of this Nazi paradise he could tolerate.

Chapter Nine

That evening, Johann waited for the rain to clear before he drove into the city for his regular walk. Elise had to urge him to go despite his objection that he really ought to deal with a backlog of paperwork. But she knew that now, more than ever, he needed time to himself and space to think. Every day was becoming a more painful challenge for both of them, filled with conflicting demands and moral dilemmas. He had tried to scribble a few sentences in his diary but the words refused to come easily, so he reluctantly took her advice and drove towards his usual parking space by the market square.

Instead of going up towards the castle, Johann decided to cross the bridge over the Pegnitz and head in the direction of the Lorenzkirche. He looked beyond the market square with its handful of empty stalls towards the Frauenkirche, the Church of Our Lady, just one of many celebrated buildings in a city crammed with architectural treasures.

A tourist couple were pointing at the clock face high up in the church façade, where the celebrated Männleinlaufen, the 'little people walking', took place every day at noon. A mechanical automaton of painted models of the electoral princes would move shakily past the Emperor Karl IV and make their obeisances to him. It was one of the great tourist attractions of the city, but it too was framed by garish Nazi banners which overlaid the timeless Gothic architecture with a sinister fascist patina.

Johann moved on over the river bridge towards the main shopping streets and the twin spires of the Lorenzkirche. There were few people out and about as the rain had been heavy and more was threatened by the dark clouds hanging low overhead. Lost in thought and more determined than ever to find some means of hitting back at the vile and inhuman Nazi dictatorship all around him, he strode pensively onwards. As he passed the end of an alley, he paused. He thought he could hear a faint whimpering sound like an animal in pain. He looked nervously about him and picked his way cautiously towards the sound. Halfway along the dark, narrow passage, he could just make out what appeared to be a pile of rags huddled in a doorway.

He edged cautiously forwards, reached out and gently touched a torn and bloodstained coat.

'Nein!' Hoarse with pain and dread, the pile of rags shrank fearfully away from him. The voice was that of a young girl, clearly terrified out of her wits. As his eyes became accustomed to the gloom, he could see that she was aged about fourteen, her face and clothing smeared with blood, her arms and legs bound tightly together with strips of material.

'Please don't be afraid,' Johann whispered, 'I am a doctor. I can help you.'

In reply, the girl tensed, jerked her slender legs up in a foetal position to reveal that they too were badly cut and bloodstained. He squatted down beside her.

'Tell me your name, would you please?'

A pause, and a sob, then, 'Ruth. I'm Ruth Birnbaum.'

'Well, Ruth Birnbaum, I'm Doctor Johann Voss, and I am going to cut those cords for you,' he said softly. The girl was clearly traumatised and he decided that the best approach was to talk gently to her, to comfort her and try to determine the extent of her injuries.

'Nein,' said the girl hysterically, 'don't do that, he'll be back for me. Please don't let him get at me again.'

Johann told her to relax and reached into his pocket to withdraw a penknife. He unfolded the blade and released her arms, then her legs. The girl whimpered again, clung fiercely to him. 'Don't let him get me, please, no, please, please.'

'It's all right,' he replied soothingly. 'I am here to help you. No one is going to hurt you, not any more. Now, Ruth, try and be calm for me and breathe steadily in and out. I'll soon have you away from this place.'

'Sorry,' she whispered, 'I am just so frightened. That man was so awful towards me and did such dreadful things to me.'

She shuddered with cold and fear, but her eyes were bright and intelligent. After her initial hysterical response, he could see that she was beginning to confront a horrendous situation with a measure of restraint and dignity unusual in one so young.

Johann said, 'Look, Ruth, I'm going to take you back to my surgery and clean up your injuries for you. My wife works with me as my nurse and she will help to take care of you. But, do tell me, who is this man you are so afraid of?'

A longish pause, then her words rushed out, 'He says his name is Erpenbeck and he is an SS officer and, if I let on to anyone, he'll come and find me and shoot me dead. This morning, it was one of his soldiers who was responsible for my sister, Naomi, being killed by a tram in front of the whole family. Then they carted us off in the back of a lorry and rounded up more people. Once we were loaded into railway wagons in the station goods yard along with the other families, a soldier sought me out and took me away in a fancy car.'

She shuddered and burst into tears, sobbing breathlessly. 'I ended up in Leutnant Erpenbeck's apartment, where he struck me several times, threw me on the bed, ripped at my clothes and then he… ' She choked on her words and fell silent.

'Never mind Erpenbeck. He's not here now, and I won't let him harm you any more. You can tell me all about your parents when we get back to my office.'

In reply, she began to half cry, half whimper again, but she managed to continue, 'When he'd finished with me, he kept on hitting me, then bundled me into his car and threw me out here on the street.' A pause.

'My parents... you have to free them,' she urged. 'You have got to free them. Otherwise, they will end up in one of those horrid camps and die.'

'Ruth,' Johann spoke gently, realising the full horror of what Erpenbeck had done to her as it dawned on him why she and her family had been arrested. Ruth, of course, a lovely Jewish name. He looked compassionately at her.

'We'll talk about your parents later. For now, we must concentrate on helping you. You've clearly had a terrible shock and suffered a very nasty experience. I want you to try and relax and do as I say, and I'll soon have you out of this place and safe in our house.'

He gently released her, then, holding her at arm's length, asked, 'Can you walk?'

'I... I think so. Yes. But it hurts, between my legs. It hurts so.' She struggled painfully to her feet, half stumbling sidewards, but, in a moment, she had forced herself upright, her back leaning against a doorway. As she steadied herself, she gave Johann a half smile and said, 'I... I think I can manage to walk now.'

'Come on then, my car is just by the market square. It won't take us long to get back.'

Twenty minutes later, he pulled up outside the house and switched off the car lights.

'Wait here and I'll help you out.'

He got out of the car, closed the door and walked round to the passenger side. As he did so, a light came on in the front doorway of the house, sending a bright splash of yellow along the path to the front gate.

As he opened the car door, the girl whispered fearfully, 'Who is that in the house?'

He smiled. 'Don't be alarmed, it's my wife, Elise. She always worries so when I go out late for a walk to clear my head. And, as I told you, she's my practice nurse too. So, she will be assisting me in dealing with your injuries and helping to make you better.'

Ruth slowly lifted herself out of the car and walked unsteadily towards the house door. She looked calmly at him and in a quiet, grown-up voice said,

'Thank you, Dr Voss. But I don't think I will be really better for a long time.'

The front door opened and Elise stood there in the porch light.

'Johann,' she called out softly. 'Who have you got with you?'

'I found this young lady injured and distressed in the gutter and I simply couldn't leave her there. She's had a pretty dreadful experience and will need all the loving care and attention we can give her. She's called Ruth, Ruth Birnbaum, and she and her family were arrested by the SS. One of them was responsible for her little sister, Naomi, being killed in front of them all. To make matters worse, she was later forcibly taken to the apartment of one Leutnant Erpenbeck, the SS officer in charge, and assaulted in the nastiest possible way. And then he just dumped her in the gutter.'

'Come along in,' said Elise softly. 'We'll soon have you cleaned up.' To Johann, she added, 'That man must be pretty sure of himself to tell her his name. The SS is getting more arrogant with every day that passes.'

Elise gently took Ruth by the hand, smiling warmly as she led her into the consulting room and helped her up on to the table.

'Now, Ruth,' said Johann softly, 'I'm pretty sure that the kind of attack you have suffered so cruelly at the hands of that SS officer is a particularly private and personal matter, so would you prefer my wife to treat you?'

Ruth nodded gratefully, and Johann placed his hand on Elise's shoulder. 'I'll be in the kitchen, Liebling,' he said and left the room.

As Elise carried out her examination and cleaned up the deep cuts on her thighs, she talked quietly to Ruth, telling her the blood from inside her was natural to a girl who had not been with a man before and that the pain he had caused by the brutality of his assault would go away in time. However, the external wounds she had suffered were quite extensive and her husband would have to deal with them.

She called out for Johann to come and complete the rest of her examination and decide what treatment was required. He had brought a steaming cup of coffee back with him and Ruth took a sip of it. The ghost of a smile flickered across her battered features.

'You are both so kind,' she said in a half-whisper. 'Not least because I'm... '

Elise nodded. 'Jewish?'

'Yes.'

'We treat everyone here without fear or favour,' said Johann. 'A patient is a patient, and race doesn't matter to us.'

When he and Elise had finished dealing with her cuts and lacerations, Ruth thanked them both, then looked pleadingly at them.

'What is it?' enquired Johann.

After a pause, Ruth said in a very quiet voice, 'I hate to ask you for anything more, but... '

Her voiced trailed away and Johann prompted her. 'You mean—your parents?'

She nodded furiously.

'Mum and dad will be frantic about losing Naomi and worried sick about me too, as I was snatched out of their arms shortly after we were all loaded into that railway wagon in the goods yard.'

Johann and Elise exchanged glances, and Elise nodded to him in encouragement.

Johann considered his answer carefully, then said slowly, 'Look—I can't promise you anything, but I have a friend who, I know, will be able to help me at least to find out what's happening to your parents. But I'll have to go out now to talk it over with him and it may well be some hours before I get back.'

'I'm not letting you go out by yourself,' said Elise firmly. 'I'm coming with you. But what are we going to do about Ruth here?'

Ruth responded with a determined smile. 'As long as I can lock myself in, I'll be fine. After all, it will be you who are taking a risk, and all for two people you have never met. And,' she added more hesitantly, 'Jews at that.'

She reached forward and embraced Elise. 'Thank you—and Dr Voss—again so much. I was left for dead, and you have brought me back to life. Anything more would be a huge bonus. Bless you, both.'

Johann went over to his medical cabinet and selected a couple of small items of equipment which he stuffed into his coat pocket, then said, 'Right, we're ready to go now. I think I have everything we might need.'

Johann told Ruth to lock the front door, ignore any phone calls and let no one in until they returned.

As they left, he put his arm around Elise and said, 'Looks like we are at last going to be able to do something positive against this damned Nazi government. Let's go and call on Rudi and see what we can do to help find Ruth's parents.'

Smiling despite himself, he added in a flippant whisper, 'At least we are helping a real girl this time... '

Chapter Ten

'Wait here in the car. I'll go along to the stage door and see if I can find him.'

Johann pulled his coat around him against the wind and made his way down the alleyway that ran alongside the Sommerkabarett. The glow of a cigarette in the shadow of the stage door betrayed the presence of the doorkeeper. Johann walked up to him and asked about Rudi.

'Just finished his act for the night,' growled the man with a voice roughened by years of smoking. 'Give me a minute or two and I'll dig him out for you.'

The red tip of the cigarette spiralled to the ground. He twisted the stub with his heel and entered the building. A few minutes later, Rudi came bounding out, still fired up by his stage performance.

'Johann.' A quick shake of hands. 'So, what can I do for you?'

'I believe we have chanced across an opportunity to take some positive action, but what I have in mind could be pretty dangerous and it will involve you wearing your SS officer uniform and digging out a Gestapo greatcoat and hat for me.'

'In that case, I'll just pop back to my dressing room and pick them up. Where's the car?'

Johann indicated the main street where the Adler was parked. 'Round to the left near the city wall.'

'Fine. I'll be out in five minutes.'

When Johann had completed his account of Ruth, her rape, her sister's death and the plight of her family, Rudi, appalled by what he heard, responded enthusiastically.

'We really must have a go at finding her parents. The least we can do is to let Ruth know where they are and what is happening to them. And, if we get really lucky, we might just be able to free them.'

Johann was delighted with his response. 'This is exactly the kind of opportunity we were hoping would arise, and Elise and I are keen to do what we can. It would be worth it just to see the expression on Ruth's face if we can give her news of her parents.'

'I suspect that they will be under guard somewhere in the marshalling yards alongside the main railway station, so we'll have to get dressed up in uniform and take a look.'

As he drove, Johann discussed with Rudi how they might deal with trying to find the Birnbaums and then doing their best to release them. He swung into a back street alongside the main station and parked the car. He kissed his wife and said,

'You stay here with the car, Elise, and we'll go and see what we can do, if anything.'

'Fine. Do be careful, both of you. If you recall, there's a road running along the embankment which overlooks the rear of the marshalling yards. I'll move the car over there so you can make a quick getaway if things get ugly.'

'Good idea.' Johann bent over and kissed her. 'See you soon. Fingers crossed.'

Johann and Rudi struggled into their uniforms, left the car and walked back across the central tram terminus and into the station entrance. The building was crammed with people, both soldiers and civilians, searching for their train or waiting to meet friends and family. In the din and bustle of the crowded main concourse, the two of them nearly came to grief when a passing soldier gave them a stiff-armed salute and snapped, 'Heil Hitler'.

It took Rudi a couple of heartbeats to remind himself that he was decked out in the full black uniform of an SS lieutenant, but he recovered quickly enough to return the salute and greeting. He even managed an approving nod in the direction of the soldier, a young private clearly still wet behind the ears. The lad blushed and moved smartly away with a spring in his youthful step.

'That was a bit tricky,' breathed Johann. 'But at least it proves that you make a pretty convincing SS officer.'

Rudi gave him a nervous smile. 'It's a bit different from getting togged up in fancy dress for a vaudeville act, though. If you make a mistake there, they just boo you. You don't get arrested and shot—unless you're really bad, that is.'

Johann pointed over to his right. 'I think we ought to go in that direction.' Keeping a wary eye open for any more soldiers anxious to salute them, they briskly crossed over to a narrow archway and entered a side corridor. 'At least it will be quieter here.'

As they passed a large glass window opening onto the left luggage office, Johann inspected his reflection. He was dressed in a black overcoat with a trilby hat and an official-looking briefcase, looking every inch the sinister Gestapo agent. He pushed his glasses back on his nose and smiled at Rudi.

'We make a lovely couple,' he said. 'Let's hope we will be just as convincing when it comes to dealing with the soldiers guarding those poor people in the goods wagons.'

The corridor took another turn and they found themselves facing a closed door bearing an official notice stating that only authorised personnel were allowed beyond this point, together with a stern warning that infringement of this regulation would attract the appropriate severe punishment.

'And what might that be?' mused the actor. 'Relocation to one of those holiday camps they're busy building in the countryside, perhaps. Or being forcibly held down and compelled to listen to Hitler's speeches repeated over and over again for a fortnight.'

They paused, looked nervously at each other and then Johann took a deep breath and pushed at the door.

'Here we go,' he said. 'No turning back now.'

The door swung open and they found themselves out in the open at the station end of the main goods yards. It was a dim, noisy, echoing space, with row after row of stationary wagons snaking out into a darkness broken by an occasional spotlight. In the middle distance, a locomotive was being coupled to a long line of open trucks, steam gushing from its sides and chimney stack.

A worker appeared from underneath the first truck, signalled to the driver in his cab and the engine snarled and steamed impatiently. Just beyond it, a gantry displaying a half dozen red lights rose out of the gloom. A signal clicked down, one of the lights turned muddy green and the locomotive worked itself into a frenzy as it ground into motion, dragging some thirty or so trucks behind it, clattering and clanking into the night towards the main line for the south.

Suddenly, a spotlight came on just to their left and Johann and Rudi retreated nervously into a recess in the wall.

'What do we do now, Herr Gestapo officer?'

'Take a deep breath and look round. Remember, we really must try and act as if we own the place and have every right to be here. Have you got any idea where they might be holding the Jewish families?'

They peered about them without success. Just then, the spotlight was switched off and they found themselves back in darkness.

'Might as well try over here,' suggested Johann, as they picked their way behind a line of open wagons. They found themselves staring at five or six empty tracks, so they walked on, carefully stepping over the rails and avoiding puddles from the recent rain. Suddenly, Johann stopped.

'There,' he whispered.

In a far corner, a dozen closed wagons were lined up behind a low fence, with a small hut guarding one end. The yellow glow from an oil lamp standing on a wooden table highlighted the face of a young soldier reading a newspaper.

Faint noises could be heard coming from the wagons, weeping, muffled cries and sounds of movement. Johann gestured to Rudi to follow him across towards the hut. When they reached the fence, they saw a large official sign bearing the legend, 'Keep out, Jewish transport'.

'Trust us Germans to be bureaucratic and efficient as ever, especially when we are at our most cruel and brutal. At least it tells us where the families are being detained.'

They slipped through a gap in the fence and Rudi promptly caught his foot on a metal bucket, which clanged like a bell in a church tower.

In the hut, the soldier looked up nervously, set down his paper, rose to his feet and made for the door. He paused indecisively, rushed quickly back to the table to pick up his rifle, ran back to the door and flung it open.

'Halt! We– Wer geht da?' He stood there, vainly trying to untangle the sling of his rifle and appear menacing to whatever threat might be lurking out there in the darkness.

Rudi swiftly regained his composure and marched smartly up to the soldier who, recognising the insignia of

SS rank, brought his right arm up in a stiff salute and said smartly, 'Heil Hitler.'

Rudi casually returned the greeting and snapped, 'Where is the rest of your guard detail?'

'Sir?'

'Surely, you are not out here on your own, soldier?'

'Er, yes sir, the other three guards were sent off to help deal with a disturbance at the main station. I have been left here to keep guard.' There was an awkward silence. 'If you forgive me, sir, the Jews are all locked up for the night and are pretty subdued. They are hardly likely to try and escape.'

'Not very satisfactory, soldier. But not your fault, I suppose.'

Rudi looked enquiringly at Johann, who fumbled officiously in his briefcase and extracted a sheet of paper. He passed it smartly to Rudi, who cast a self-important eye over it and gave a convincing impression of reading out its contents.

'Earlier today, SS Leutnant Erpenbeck ordered the removal for interrogation of one Ruth Birnbaum, female, fourteen-years of age. Following information elicited from this witness, he has determined that the two other members of her family currently in your control be released into our custody for transportation to Gestapo Headquarters to undergo detailed questioning. They are … ' He turned the sheet over. 'Eli Birnbaum, male, fifty-years. Lea Birnbaum, forty-five-years. Duly dated and signed Wilhelm Erpenbeck, Leutnant.'

Rudi carefully kept his sheet of paper well out of the soldier's view. It was an advertising bill for the next month's performances at the Sommerkabarett.

'Sir. My inventory of detainees is in the sentry hut.' Rudi nodded, and the soldier executed a fairly smart about turn and marched off to retrieve the document.

The two exchanged glances and waited until the soldier returned, carrying a clipboard with a list of names and personal details. The soldier scanned down the entries, shook his head, flipped over the first page and examined the second sheet. Halfway down, he paused and nodded.

'Yes sir. Here it is. Married couple Birnbaum. Wagon five. The numbers are stencilled in white paint on the side doors.'

Rudi nodded. 'Thank you, soldier. Now we'll make our way to Wagon five and release the two named individuals into our custody.'

The soldier stared at him. 'Sorry, sir, you cannot do that.'

'Gott im Himmel, man, why not?'

'I do not have the keys to the trucks in my possession.'

'In that case, how on earth did Leutnant Erpenbeck succeed in arranging for Ruth Birnbaum to be taken away for interrogation? And where are the damned keys, anyway?'

Rudi snapped angrily at the soldier, trying to keep the initiative on his side and to prevent him from even thinking of asking awkward questions, not least why the two of them had not dealt with the keys issue before coming to the station.

'Sir,' said the soldier, looking distinctly ill at ease. 'I believe Leutnant Erpenbeck brought the keys with him from where they are held at Gestapo Headquarters for security reasons.'

There was a moment's chilly silence. Rudi and Johann stared at one another as the soldier shifted uncomfortably from one foot to the other.

Johann cleared his throat. 'I do beg your pardon. Of course, I have the keys somewhere here.' He made a pantomime of feeling in his overcoat pocket. 'Yes, here they are. Sorry about that, Leutnant. In the rush to get to the station, I completely forgot that I had signed them out and brought them with me.'

He swung round to the soldier and snapped, 'You and the Leutnant here can be sorting out the paperwork while I go and release those two detainees into my custody.' Before the soldier could think of another objection, Johann set off in search of the wagon where the Birnbaums were held.

'Right, soldier, lead the way,' barked Rudi. 'We haven't all night, you know. The information they hold is crucial to the Reich and must be extracted from them as swiftly as possible.'

The soldier moved towards the hut and Rudi marched smartly after him.

The instant the two crossed the threshold, Johann stopped in his tracks, spun round and sprinted back to the door of the hut, shouting to Rudi, 'Put your hand over his mouth and pin him down.'

As Rudi swiftly obeyed his request, a hypodermic needle appeared in Johann's fingers and he stabbed it into the neck of the soldier, who was too shocked and surprised to defend himself. He quickly depressed the plunger and, as he withdrew the needle, said, 'That young fellow will be out for several hours now, so set him down on the chair. From a distance, it will look as if he is taking a sneaky nap. Now, though, we have to deal with the problem of the key.'

He looked around. 'As this is a railway hut, there ought to be a toolbox of some kind here.' They searched amongst the untidy clutter until they discovered a small work chest on the floor with a battered wooden lid.

'Yes, this must be it.'

He flung open the lid and peered inside. 'Here we go. These bolt cutters should do the trick. Come on, Rudi, we have prisoners to release... '

They rushed over to the line of closed wagons and soon came across the one with the crudely painted sign, 'Wagon five' on the side.

Johann shouted out imperiously, 'Gestapo here. We are seeking Eli and Lea Birnbaum. Call out if you are present. And be sharp about it.'

Silence, then frantic whispers and shuffling of feet. A dignified but frightened male voice said, 'I am Eli Birnbaum. What do you want of us?'

'Silence and obedience for a start,' snapped Johann. He clambered up to the sliding door of the truck and examined the padlock. He whispered urgently to Rudi, 'We should have no problem forcing the door open. Pass me the bolt cutters, quickly.'

It was the work of a few seconds to smash the lock, shift aside the bar and slide the door halfway open.

"Eli and Lea Birnbaum—get down! Now! Bring your possessions and be smart about it.'

Two middle-aged figures, each carrying a brown leather suitcase, came forward and half slipped, half fell down from the truck. Johann grabbed them both and whispered, 'Come with me and don't utter a word.'

They stumbled over the railway tracks and, after a moment, Johann signalled to them to stop.

Quietly he said, 'Please do not be afraid, I may be dressed as a Gestapo officer but that is just a disguise to help me find you and rescue you. My friend, Rudi, is also here to assist. You can thank your daughter, Ruth, who begged us to come looking for you.'

Lea Birnbaum sobbed and Eli said in a voice choked with emotion, 'How can we ever begin to thank you? We were convinced that we were on a one-way trip to the concentration camps… '

Johann said, 'Let's forget about thanks for now. We're by no means out of the woods yet. We still have to get you and Ruth to a safe house in the country which I know of, and then you have to find a means of escaping from Germany. I presume you had been making plans for that.' He gestured to his right. 'Come this way, quickly. I have a car waiting for us.'

Meanwhile, Rudi, still in his role as an SS officer, marched back to the wagon, leapt effortlessly up and spoke to the other occupants. 'By order of the Gestapo, you are hereby released. Move quickly and quietly over in that direction'—he pointed away from the station to a group of buildings in the distance—'and find your own way back home. I suggest you all make urgent arrangements to leave Germany before we are tempted to come after you again.'

Rudi signalled to Johann to escort the Birnbaums across the tracks and up the slope to where Elise had now parked the car, whilst he busied himself with the bolt cutters on the next wagon, telling the people inside to make good their escape and passing the tool to a young prisoner whom he ordered to open up the rest of the wagons and be quick about it.

Rudi raced back after Johann and the Birnbaums, but as he caught up with them, he stopped in his tracks and whispered urgently, 'Oh my God. Look!'

Three military-looking figures had just emerged from the deep shadows of the station building and were strolling unhurriedly in their direction.

'Damn,' said Johann. 'That must be the other members of the guard detail returning from the disturbance in the main station building. What on earth are we going to do?'

'We are in a pretty tight spot. We can't outrun them and take the Birnbaums with us. On top of that, they have rifles and we don't.'

At that instant, one of the three soldiers stopped and pointed and gestured in their direction. Then they broke into a clumsy trot.

'Shit. They've seen us. We're cornered.'

As the soldiers quickened their pace and grew rapidly closer, a sudden piercing scream tore through the night air, which stopped all three of them short. The screech came from the roadway next to the goods yard, and a second or two later, it was repeated.

'Help! Help! they're after me!' yelled a woman's voice.

The soldiers stood looking about them, clearly uncertain as to what they should do.

Another scream rent the night air, even more strident than the first two, and that made up their minds. They turned sharply to their left and sprinted off in the direction of the distressed woman.

'Well done!' said Johann. Rudi looked puzzled.

'That was Elise, coming to the rescue,' Johann said quickly. 'Now, we must get the hell out of here before the soldiers realise they have been duped.'

Gesturing to the Birnbaums, Johann urged them to run towards the embankment leading up to the side road where the car was parked. As they did so, the soldiers could be seen rushing about in the shadows calling out to Elise, who was now acting the role of an innocent passerby and calmly strolling down the road above the marshalling yard. She gestured towards a clump of bushes halfway up the slope to indicate that the screaming had come from that direction.

'Clever girl,' said Johann breathlessly, 'with a bit of luck she will have just about saved our skins.'

The four staggered up the incline away from the rail tracks, Johann and Rudi carrying the cases. Eli Birnbaum supported his wife, who was badly disorientated and seemed scarcely able to comprehend what was happening to them.

As they reached the top of the embankment, the Adler was rolling slowly towards them, with Elise at the wheel. At that point, they could hear angry shouting from the soldiers who had suddenly realised that they had been deceived by Elise's diversionary tactics. Two of them were now charging towards the workers' hut, where their unconscious colleague was still slumped over the table and the third was running full pelt towards the embankment to try and cut them off. Suddenly, he stopped and pointed his rifle at them.

'Halt!' he yelled.

As the four of them scrambled frantically towards the car, a shot rang out and, at the same instant, there was a loud bang from the bodywork of the Adler.

'Drive, drive!' shouted Johann. They scrambled in and the car sped off with a screech of tyres. Two more shots were fired, but, fortunately, they missed. Then they were round the corner and under the bridge carrying the main lines from the north into Nuremberg station. As Elise sped past the city opera building, Johann finally slumped back in his seat, hugely relieved to have escaped a very dangerous situation. He reached down to touch his leg. 'Damn,' he muttered.

'What's wrong, Liebling?'

'Nothing. Just a little scratch and a lot of blood. Must have caught my leg on some loose strands of wire fencing as we climbed up the embankment. We were in something of a hurry and I wasn't taking much notice of where I was going. Now, let's just get back home. Herr and Frau Birnbaum, we are now taking you to our house. The lady driving is Elise, my wife, and the nasty-looking SS officer is my good friend, Rudi, in disguise.'

For a while, they drove in silence as Johann tried to bandage up his injury with a handkerchief. Suddenly, from the back seat, Lea's voice came, hoarse with emotion.

'How is Ruth?'

Elise replied gently, 'She has suffered a very nasty experience at the hands of an SS officer, but she is a very brave young lady. My husband found her and brought her back to our home. Johann's a doctor, by the way, and I act as his nurse. She's waiting for you there now, and I'm sure you'll give her all the love and support she'll need to recover from her ordeal.'

In reply, Lea burst into tears. Losing one daughter was cruel enough, having the other brutally assaulted on the same day was too much for her.

Back at the house, Ruth and her parents were tearfully reunited. Elise insisted on taking Johann into the consulting room where she treated his leg. Fortunately, it was not too deep a cut, but it was long and jagged and required several stitches. Then they returned to the others.

Johann waited some time until the trio settled down, had something to eat and drink and were beginning to recognise that, for now, they were free but their immediate future was uncertain in the extreme. On top of that, they had very little time to come to terms with the cruel death of little Naomi.

Elise said, 'For tonight, you are very welcome to rest here. We have room to spare and you need some time and space to consider how and when you can find an escape route out of Germany. In the longer term, we know of a safe house where you will be able to stay for a while.'

Eli replied, 'First of all, we are both so hugely in your debt. Clearly, my dear wife, Lea, is as greatly upset as I am. Losing Naomi is traumatic enough, but all this happening at once is too much to cope with in a very short space of time. But I really must thank you again for putting your lives on the line for a Jewish family of total strangers. And you knew full well that your actions would certainly land you in very bad trouble if you were caught. So, we are deeply, deeply grateful to you.'

Mother and daughter nodded, echoing Eli's words and Lea burst into tears again. It was clear that, of the three of them, she was emotionally the most fragile.

Curiously, Ruth seemed to be gathering strength after her traumatic assault at the hands of Leutnant Erpenbeck, but for all three of them, these were very early days and the future still held much peril and uncertainty before they would be able to settle in another country and think about putting down new roots. Then, and only then, could they dare to dream of a better future.

'Now, Eli, if I may use your first name, I am sure that you will have been laying plans of some kind for your escape from Germany. Would it be impertinent of me to ask how advanced those plans are?'

'Not at all. I have drawn up travel documents for all the family and have ensured that sufficient funds are available for us in a Swiss account. It would take only a few days to organise our transport, as I can call upon a private plane to fly us abroad.'

Johann said, 'Until then, we will take you to my wife's sister and her family. They have a large house in the country and have been working with escapees like yourselves for some time now. We will speak to them tomorrow, as you are exactly the sort of people they want to help.'

Elise added, 'Like me, my sister, Ursula, has a Jewish background and she and her husband are both dedicated and compassionate folk.'

'We are so enormously grateful, we can never ever thank you or repay you enough for your courage in helping us. One thing I will promise you, and that is, when we are safely abroad, we will do everything in our power to enable as many Jewish and other families who are in danger to escape to freedom. I shall be happy to provide you with whatever resources you may need to achieve that objective.'

He paused, and then a shadow passed over his face. 'However, there is quite a serious obstacle in the path of our escape, Johann.'

'And what is that?'

'We do indeed have travel and other vital documents including bank codes for accounts in Switzerland and elsewhere, but we were arrested and taken away so suddenly that we had no time to get our hands on them.'

'And where are these documents?'

'In the Nürnberger Landesbank vaults. In a safety deposit box. And my guess is that it won't be long before the Gestapo find out about it. Then, we are well and truly sunk.'

Johann said, 'Who has access to the box and its contents?'

'I do.' Then, suddenly remembering, 'And, of course, so does my dear wife, but I wouldn't dream of putting her at that kind of risk. I'm going to have to try retrieving the documents myself just as soon as the bank opens and hope that no one is yet aware of our escape. I still have my key to the box, which I always wear on a chain around my neck.' He reached into his shirt and pulled it out. 'The other key is held by the bank. And they require a signature too, which they verify before any access to the box can take place.'

They fell silent, puzzling as to what exactly to do next. It seemed that their rescue from the covered wagons in the goods yard was in danger of stalling and their hopes for the future would be dashed. Then, Rudi, who for a long time had been silent, sat up straight, a big innocent smile on his face. Leaning across to Lea, he asked,

'Do you think I might borrow one of your frocks?'

Chapter Eleven

Eli and Lea stared at each other, baffled expressions on their faces. Smiling broadly, Johann explained.

'Rudi, here, is a comedian and quick change artist at the Sommerkabarett in the city centre, and he doesn't just specialise in Nazi military uniforms as he did this evening, he has also been known to dress up as a female, and a very convincing one he makes too. I'll tell you some other time how we met when he showed up on our doorstep with two nasty bullet wounds, looking for all the world like a pretty young thing on a good night out which had come to a very unpleasant end.'

Lea nodded. 'Rudi, surely, you are not really suggesting that you should go to the bank dressed as me?'

'That's precisely what I intend to do. It's far too dangerous for either you or your husband to venture out and visit the bank yourselves because it will almost certainly be under surveillance.'

Eli spoke up. 'We are both very grateful to you for your courage and selflessness. But I really don't want to put you in further danger. After all, you scarcely know us and there's no reason why you should risk your lives again for us.'

'But there is every reason,' insisted Rudi. 'Johann, Elise and I came together to try, even in a modest way, to assist people who fall victim to the Nazi state. We cannot live with ourselves just passively letting the Führer and his gang take over the country entirely unchallenged. Helping Ruth and rescuing you has been our first joint positive act on behalf of human values versus the mindless Nazi machine.'

He paused and looked round sheepishly as if to check that he hadn't been too outspoken.

'Rudi is absolutely right,' said Johann. 'We believe we must do our utmost to achieve something positive, even on a small and personal scale like this. It helps restore our dignity and sense of decency, however bleak the situation appears just now—and probably will be for the foreseeable future. But, try we must, for the sake of our own humanity, if nothing else.'

He too felt awkward for expressing his convictions in such passionate and emotional tones, but Eli and Lea were deeply touched by his words. Oddly, though, it was young Ruth who spoke up.

'I may be only a child still and don't fully understand why my world has fallen apart, but I think I am grown up enough to recognise brave and decent people who put their own lives at risk for the sake of others. I am so heartbroken by the loss of my little sister, Naomi, but what the evil these men did to her and to me pales into insignificance compared to your decent and courageous actions.'

She blushed at her boldness in speaking out, but everyone present commended her words.

Eli nodded, tears in his eyes. 'And I too salute you, all three of you. Especially when those you have helped are Jews, which makes the risks you have taken all the greater. My wife and I—and Ruth too—can never thank you enough.'

Lea spoke up too, 'As you can see, I am so distressed by what has happened to us, especially my beloved Naomi, and I simply cannot put into words my feelings at the way you have helped us so.'

There was an uncomfortable pause after such an outpouring of gratitude from the Birnbaums. Johann pushed his spectacles back on his nose and said quietly,

'But you have encouraged us, simply by the way you have conducted yourselves in a far more dreadful situation than we would ever care to face. The loss of Naomi must be truly terrible for you and poor Ruth has been subjected to a most inhuman ordeal.

'I fully intend to seek out this Leutnant Erpenbeck who abducted and assaulted you, Ruth, treating you no better than a dumb animal, and I can assure all of you that he will get the retribution he deserves. But, for now, we really must concentrate on practical matters, on helping all three of you to safety and assisting you to make your way out of Germany. What we have to do first is to recover your documents and money from the safety deposit box.'

'Thank you so much. What's in that box will gain our passage out of Germany, together with valid documents for entry into foreign countries, and bank access codes which will enable us to survive financially while I take charge of our operations abroad and try and rebuild my business.'

Rudi added, 'And the best way of making that happen is to allow me to pay a visit to the bank disguised as Lea and retrieve the contents of the box on your behalf. All I need is a few minutes of practice with your signature, Lea, and I'll be ready for action.'

'So that's agreed,' said Johann. 'It's way past midnight and you have had a horrendous day, so I propose we all sleep on the plan and discuss it again in the morning?'

They nodded in agreement. Rudi said, 'If it's all right with you, I can bunk down in the consulting room. I believe I have done so before, in slightly different circumstances?'

'If you mean,' laughed Elise, 'going to bed a girl and waking up as a boy, then you're right. It's remarkable what medical science can do nowadays.'

'Thanks to our great German nation and its heroic leader,' said Rudi tartly.

After a breakfast of coffee and rolls the following morning, they all convened around the telephone in the consulting room.

'Can I confirm that we're ready to go along with the plan we discussed last night?' asked Johann.

The others nodded, except for Eli. 'You really are doing far too much for us and putting yourselves at serious risk yet again,' he protested.

'Not at all,' said Johann, 'What you have to do now, Eli, is to get on the telephone and inform the bank that you have asked Lea to gain access to the safety deposit box on your behalf. Can you do that?'

Eli looked thoughtfully at him. 'Yes. Yes, of course, I can.' He looked around for the phone.

Johann pointed to the receiver on his desk. Eli walked over, picked up the handset and dialled. Almost at once, an official-sounding voice crackled in the earpiece.

'Good morning, Nürnberger Landesbank here. Who is calling?'

'H-hullo.' Eli paused nervously, willing his voice to sound normal. 'This is Herr Eli Birnbaum. I'm ringing on behalf of my wife. Unfortunately, I have to go into hospital for urgent treatment and I am ringing to inform you that Frau Birnbaum will be calling sometime today in order to access our safety deposit box.'

'Er, yes, Herr Birnbaum. One moment please.'

There followed what seemed like an overlong pause at the other end of the line, or was it just their imagination? Eli could hear the sound of a typist working away, a man's voice issuing an order and a woman responding deferentially. Time crawled past.

'Herr Birnbaum?'

'Yes?'

'I'm just checking your records.' Paper rustled at the other end of the line. 'Let me see...'

Another agonisingly long pause.

'Ah... here we are. Safety deposit security... Signatories, Eli and Lea Birnbaum can separately access the deposit box number NU3045 on the production of the key and one signature.' Yet another pause, accompanied by a rustling of papers. 'That should all be in order, Herr Birnbaum.'

'Thank you,' Eli said nervously.

The official on the other end of the line coughed. 'Ahem, when did you say Frau Birnbaum might be calling to open the deposit box?'

Eli looked quickly at Johann. A sudden unpleasant thought had occurred to him. He put his hand over the mouthpiece and whispered, 'They want to know exactly what time she is arriving at the bank.'

Johann nodded, a grim expression on his face. He whispered back, 'That sounds very suspicious to me.'

Eli looked anxiously at Rudi, as if seeking his approval. He was growing more and more aware of the terrible risk Rudi could be taking.

'I'll still do it,' Rudi responded in a quiet, resolute voice. Being shot twice has to be far worse than a trip to the bank, he thought. What could possibly go wrong?

Johann raised four fingers to indicate a time that would give them plenty of opportunity to make further plans.

Eli removed his hand from the mouthpiece, took a deep breath, and said in the most authoritative tones he could muster, 'I have just confirmed with my wife that she will be attending the bank at approximately four o'clock today. She will have the necessary customer key in her possession.'

'Thank you, sir.'

Eli placed the phone back on the hook. He looked nervously around the room. 'I'm convinced the SS will be lying in wait for her. So Rudi's great idea of dressing up as Lea and going in her place really isn't going to work. We are well and truly stuck.'

Heads nodded in unhappy agreement. It seemed that their plan to access the safety box was becoming more jeopardised by the second and that would spell the end of the Birnbaum's hopes of escaping to a new life outside the Reich.

'What are we going to do?' asked Eli anxiously, for once at a loss to think of a way forward.

Silence. After several seconds, Johann began to speak. 'I've an idea... ' Then his voice trailed away. 'Forget it. It wouldn't have worked, anyway.'

Another uncomfortable silence. Then Elise stood up brightly and said, 'Anyone for coffee?'

Earnest nods all around.

'Fine. I'll not be long.' She paused, then a grin spread over her face. 'But, before I go, I believe I have a little suggestion that might just work.'

She had everyone's undivided attention. They all anxiously hoped that Elise had come up with a plan which would allow them to secure the Birnbaum's funds and documents after all.

'Johann, we have our business account at the Landesbank, don't we?'

He nodded, 'But we don't rent a safety deposit box, more's the pity.'

'But I could get an appointment at, say, two o'clock, to discuss opening a deposit box account. Rudi,' she nodded in his direction, 'will accompany me dressed as Lea. When we arrive and meet the manager or whoever it is who takes charge of these matters, I could say that I chanced to meet my friend, Frau Birnbaum, and could she take part of my appointment time to quickly examine her box, as she has to visit her sick husband in hospital much earlier than had been arranged.'

Everyone nodded approval at the plan. Lea actually managed a faint half-smile at the thought. It was great to see that she was now gradually beginning to put up a fight in the face of the disasters which had beset their lives and was even starting to take a positive view of their future.

The loss of a child was a searing tragedy, but it was clear that she was now grimly determined to hold the rest of her family together. She still could not bring herself to put it into words, but she felt it would be an insult to Naomi's memory for the rest of them not to go on living and try to make a decent future for themselves.

'But,' said Johann, 'what if the bank official you talk to was the same person Eli spoke with on the phone? And then there's the possibility that all the bank staff have been alerted to the fact that an escaped Jewess was about to visit their establishment.'

Eli spoke up. 'How would they know that we have escaped custody? I bet the SS is mortified at losing all those Jews from the goods yards and they'll have put a lid on the whole affair. I wouldn't like to be in the shoes of those four soldiers who were guarding the wagons, though.'

Johann laughed. 'Good point. Let's assume that there is just a flag against the names of Jewish customers and an alert is to be sent out when one of them seeks to access a deposit box because the assumption would be that they might be trying to escape with money and valuables. The SS would then let them empty their box and arrest them on a pretext as they left the bank.'

Rudi agreed. 'It's a risk well worth taking. And,' he added, looking across at Elise, 'as we are going in that splendid car of yours, we can drop by the Sommerkabarett building so that I can collect a few things which might just throw the SS off the scent. That is after I have borrowed a spare hat and dress from you, Lea.'

The very notion of a man dressing up in her clothes brought a faint smile of embarrassment to Lea's face as she set about opening her suitcase.

'But, now,' Elise said urgently, 'it's up to me to ring the Landesbank and ask for an appointment at two. First, though, I really must get you all that coffee.'

In the hushed, echoing main hall of the Nürnberger Landesbank, the large hand of the ornate clock above the main desk clunked solemnly to the vertical. Two o'clock in the afternoon. People moved about like worshippers in a church, talking in subdued tones and conducting their business reverentially in this temple to wealth and prosperity. At three minutes past the hour, the revolving main door creaked and swung slowly round.

Two expensively-dressed women strode confidently into the building, their heels clacking loudly on the marble floor. Heads swung round and some older folk tut-tutted at the fashionable sound but the younger men stared in admiration at well-tailored costumes clinging to slender bodies. Nor did two pairs of shapely legs encased in sheer silk stockings escape their masculine glances.

The women strode purposefully up to the main counter and pressed the bell for attention. A few moments later, one of the bank's tellers appeared and asked if he could be of service.

'I am Frau Elise Voss and I have an appointment at two o'clock with regard to opening a safety deposit box account,' said Elise without explaining who the woman at her side might be. They had agreed to delay identifying Rudi as Frau Birnbaum for as long as possible.

'Certainly, madam. If you two ladies would care to wait for a second or two, I will ensure that the appropriate staff member comes to attend to you.'

The man swung self-importantly round on his heels and disappeared behind an imposing wooden door. The seconds ticked by slowly, before an older man, balding and somewhat overweight, made an appearance, spectacles glinting in a shaft of sunlight from a window high up in the wall.

'Good afternoon. My name is Müller. Now, if you, Frau Voss, and you, Frau... Er... '

Rudi decided to take the bull by the horns. 'I am Frau Lea Birnbaum, a friend of Frau Voss.'

Herr Müller blinked as if the name was familiar to him, but he couldn't recall why. He opened the low gate to one side of the desk, stepped forward, and motioned the two ladies to follow him. At the end of the corridor, a uniformed attendant stood by the open doors of an ornate lift, which boasted a fitted carpet and mirrored walls. The trio entered the cabin. The official nodded briskly at the attendant and ordered, 'Basement two, if you please.'

The second basement level was decidedly cool but it was not the low temperature that made Elise shiver. She had the distinct impression of being incarcerated in this subterranean place, but made an effort to maintain her equilibrium and said coquettishly to Herr Müller,

'Actually, we ladies do have a small favour to ask of you.'

'Certainly, Frau Voss. And what might that be?'

'Well, I was about to enter the bank when I met Frau Birnbaum here, a good friend of mine, who told me she had an appointment at four today but had arrived early because her husband, sadly, has been taken to hospital and she has to go and visit him before he is taken for his operation.'

Elise's words tumbled nervously out. Rudi looked appropriately apprehensive about Eli's illness and impending operation. He dabbed a corner of one eye with a tiny silk handkerchief.

Herr Müller found himself in something of a dilemma. After an anguished mental struggle, his sluggish brain had just registered the fact that senior staff at that morning's meeting had been informed that, according to the SS, a number of Jews might be expected to appear in the near future to access their deposit boxes. He now recalled that the name Birnbaum was on the watch list but she wasn't expected until around four o'clock.

How was he going to tell the security staff she was here already and would be long gone by that time? He was going to have to do some quick thinking and that was an attribute he sorely lacked. Don't get flustered, he told himself nervously. Something will, surely, turn up.

'I am sorry to hear about Herr Birnbaum's, er, indisposition. I hope his operation is successful and that he will make a speedy recovery. So, er, you wish to access your safety deposit box?' He rummaged around in a desk drawer and produced a sheet of paper.

'Ah, here we are. We just need your signature and date here and then we can proceed.'

At this point, a sudden idea occurred to him.

'But, before we can do that, I must get your key.' He rose in his seat and made to leave the room but Lea stopped him with a gesture. She pointed to a metal wall cabinet opposite, clearly marked 'Bank keys for safety deposit box access. Keep locked at all times.'

'Surely, your key to Frau Birnbaum's box is over there in that cupboard'—she waved imperiously at the far wall—'and you don't have to go elsewhere in search of it?'

She had realised Herr Müller's discomfiture was caused by his belated recognition that the Birnbaum's box was about to be accessed two hours before the original arrangement, and that he was struggling to find some way of informing his masters at the bank that the lady in question was already here. Her name, along with that of the other detainees released the previous night, must have been on an SS list distributed to the banks earlier that day. Elise was grimly determined not to let the greasy little man out of her sight.

'Oh, of course, how silly of me. I quite forgot,' Herr Müller blustered.

Meantime, Rudi had completed a creditable attempt at Lea Birnbaum's signature, scrawled the date with a flourish and stood up. He reached into his handbag and produced the customer key.

'This is my key, Herr Müller. If you would be so good as to get yours... And, by the way, I'd like my friend Elise here to see the safety box room and the procedures for accessing boxes, as I know that she is interested in opening an account herself.'

Herr Müller was well and truly cornered. He sighed, rose and unlocked the cabinet. 'What is the, er, box number, please?'

'NU3045.'

'Ah, yes, of course.' He peered at the rows of keys and lifted one from its hook. 'If you would kindly come this way with me, ladies.'

In the box room, Herr Müller fussed along the rows of rectangular metal drawers until he found NU3045. He turned his key, then stood back to allow Frau Birnbaum to insert the customer key and open the small door. He stepped forward to withdraw the long metal box inside and placed it on the wooden table which stood in the centre of the room. His agitation was almost laughable, but this was a far from amusing situation. Rudi had clearly realised what was going on and was determined to put his acting talents to good use.

'You may leave me now,' said Rudi imperiously, 'I shall not be more than a few minutes.' Herr Müller and Elise withdrew to the office area for a half-hearted discussion on the merits of safety deposit boxes and how to go about acquiring one. Suddenly, a phone rang on the desk. Herr Müller eagerly grabbed the receiver. 'Müller here.'

A short pause as he listened impatiently.

'Yes, yes, I'll deal with that after closing time today.' He looked guiltily in the direction of the safety deposit room. 'And just one other point. You recall the, er, matter which we were informed about at the early morning meeting of senior bank staff? One of those customers is currently here with us. Right now.'

Another pause. Then he put down the receiver, the ghost of a smile on his face and beads of sweat on his forehead. With a sudden panic, Elise realised that Herr Müller had just clumsily succeeded in informing his colleagues that Lea—or, rather, an excellent facsimile of her—was indeed on the premises. My God, she thought, Rudi is caught in a trap. I have to warn him.

She rose suddenly, and said, 'I must have a quick word with Frau Birnbaum about taking her to see her husband in hospital. I forgot to inform her that I would drive her there, as her car is being repaired today of all days.'

Despite Herr Müller's heroic efforts to stall her by standing in her way and waving documents in her face for her to sign, she pushed him roughly aside and swept anxiously out of the room. Herr Müller lost his dignity and his footing and fell back on his chair, which skidded across the room and crashed into a metal cupboard. He ended up in an untidy heap on his backside, gesturing helplessly. Elise shut the door and locked it on the outside with the key which Herr Müller had rather imprudently left there.

I must go down the corridor, she told herself, make a sharp turn to the left and the door to the safety deposit room is on the right. As she hastened along to find Rudi, a rather well-fed young priest strode past and nodded solemnly in her direction. She ignored him and, a moment later, reached the door and pulled on the handle. It was locked. Again, she tugged at it just in case, but the door was well and truly barred against her. Evidently, it locked automatically when it was closed. She panicked briefly, then realised that there was a small round glass pane high up in the door.

She stretched up on her toes and peered through. To her astonishment, the room was empty. The closed box, presumably shorn of its contents, stood on the table. But what had happened to Rudi? And how was he going to make his way out of the bank if it was crawling with SS? They would probably lock the doors and search everybody thoroughly. It looked as if their foolhardy plan was about to fail miserably and the Birnbaum's assets would end up in the hands of the Nazis. And so too would the pair of them.

She swung sharply round and rushed past the office where the florid face of Herr Müller was pressed against the glass, mouthing inaudibly, and towards the lift. The arrow above the door indicated 'G' for ground floor and she pressed impatiently on the call button. It took an eternity for the elderly cabin to crawl down to the second basement.

She dashed into the lift, snapped at the attendant, 'Ground floor please.' She nearly added 'and make it quick', when she realised that the lift could travel no faster than its own very stately pace.

On the main floor, she rushed out into the customer area to find the bank in a state of uproar. SS officers and their men were milling around by the exit, interrogating and searching customers, many of whom were protesting loudly at the unwarranted intrusion. But no one was allowed out of the revolving front doors until they and their bags and briefcases had been thoroughly searched.

Just then, the bank's alarm bell rang stridently. Herr Müller had evidently just realised that it would be a sensible idea to press the panic button in the second basement office where he was well and truly confined. Security, which had already been tight, now became tighter still. The SS had known there was a good chance that an accomplice could have been handed the contents of the safety deposit box and they were now being very thorough indeed. The Birnbaums were seriously wealthy and the SS were intent on getting their hands on as much of the family's possessions as they possibly could.

Elise looked frantically around for Rudi, but he was nowhere to be seen. She made her way impatiently towards the exit but a Gestapo officer halted her. None too gently, he performed a thorough body search and insisted on spilling out the contents of her handbag onto a table. Search over, she swept her belongings back into the bag and stepped quickly through the revolving doors.

Outside, a tangle of official cars and vans blocked the entrance. She forced her way disconsolately through the press of people outside and hastened towards the Adler which she had parked in a side road nearby. With a deep sigh, she flopped down in the driving seat and prepared to depart. Suddenly, the front passenger door was flung open and the corpulent cleric she had briefly seen in the bank stuck his head into the vehicle.

'May I?' he asked and, without waiting for a reply, sat down primly. Elise was too shocked to respond.

'Can I suggest we get going, otherwise the SS will be on our heels, don't you think?' the cleric added in a clearly recognisable voice.

Suddenly realising who it was, she cried, 'Rudi, you rogue!' half angry, half relieved. 'How did you manage to change costume and get out of the bank, and where are the documents from the safe box?'

'Explanations later. Now we really ought to get going.'

When they had cleared the streets immediately surrounding the bank, Rudi yanked off his clerical neckband and turned towards her. 'That was tight,' he said. 'And I don't just mean the collar.'

'Why didn't you tell me you were going to change costume?'

'Sorry. But I did it so that if you saw me you would act naturally and not be tempted to give the game away.'

She had already almost forgiven him, but there was just one matter to clear up.

'And the contents of the box?'

'Here in my portly stomach. Safe and sound. I was stopped at the main entrance by security staff from the bank who poked and prodded me but no one thought of examining my little pot belly. And that's where all the documents and other items are concealed. Now, let's head for your home and pass the good news on to the Birnbaums.'

As Elise drove across the bridge over the Pegnitz, she asked, 'Rudi, what happened to your dress, hat and handbag?'

'Let me put it this way. If the Gestapo insist on opening the Birnbaum's box using the bank's master keys, they are in for a bit of a surprise. Contents: one posh dress, one fashionable hat, one wig, one pair of high-heeled shoes and one expensive handbag—yes, and a rather nice padded bra I use in my Little Marlene routine. I wonder if they'll let me have it back?'

Chapter Twelve

Some days after the harrowing incident of the tram, Thomas Braun found himself sitting uncomfortably in the Voss's sitting room which doubled as the waiting room for consultations with the doctor. Never before had he felt so exposed and vulnerable. For a strong, well-built man, who had always prided himself on his fitness and mental well-being, he was experiencing the uncomfortable sensations of someone who had just lost his footing and was about to fall headlong off a cliff edge.

At least, he told himself, he had the sense to recognise that something was seriously wrong with him, something which was way beyond his powers to manage and defeat without help. That was why he had reluctantly decided to come and consult with his friend and doctor, Johann Voss, whom he and his family had known and greatly respected for many years.

Johann and Elise had helped bring the Braun babies into the world, and they had always been ready at hand to tend to the injuries and ailments which accompany the growth and development of healthy young children. They had been particularly compassionate and caring when Thomas's wife, Gertrud, suffered from a bout of post-natal depression, a serious but little-recognised condition which could have had a long-term corrosive impact on the whole family. That gave Thomas hope that Johann would understand the turmoil raging within him now and find some way to subdue it.

So, here he was, perched on a chair as nervous as a naughty schoolboy outside the headmaster's office, hoping desperately that Johann had a magic wand he could wave and somehow restore him to his former self.

He was so absorbed in his tangled deliberations that he did not hear the door open and Elise say, 'Johann is now ready to see you, Thomas.'

She coughed and repeated the invitation.

'What? Oh, sorry, forgive me. I was completely lost in thought.'

He scrambled to his feet and walked across the corridor to the consulting room. She followed him with a worried gaze. There is something very badly wrong here, she thought to herself.

'Thomas Braun,' she announced, reaching forward and opening the door for him.

The two men shook hands firmly.

'Please take a seat, Thomas. How are your wife and family? Keeping well, I trust. I've not heard from you for some months, so I do hope so.' He shifted in his seat to face Thomas directly and, for a full minute, not a word passed between them.

Johann said abruptly, 'Thomas, you look to me as if you have had the shock of your life and it's had a terrible impact on you. Am I right?'

Thomas nodded and, to his huge embarrassment, burst into tears and sobbed like a child. Johann waited patiently for the crisis to blow itself out and for Thomas to regain his composure, then he picked up the bell on his desk and rang it.

When Elise put her head around the door, he asked, 'Liebling, could you possibly bring us some coffee?'

She looked compassionately at Thomas, smiled briefly and left the room.

'Now, Thomas. Take your time.'

Thomas sat with his head in his hands for a long while, took a deep breath and began quietly and hesitantly.

'I feel so foolish. Like a child. I haven't cried this way since I fell off my bicycle when I was ten and bloodied both my knees.' He paused, smiling ruefully at the memory.

'Don't be embarrassed. You'd be surprised at the sheer quantity of tears that have been shed in this office. Whatever it is that is troubling you so badly, you have my full attention and I have all the time in the world. There are no more patients booked in today, so just take as long as you need.'

He looked round as the door opened and Elise carried in a tray with steaming mugs of coffee, which she gently placed on Johann's desk.

'I had a pot on the go already, as I thought you might be in need of sustenance.'

'Thank you, Liebling.'

'Thomas—black? Sugar?'

'W-white, please, no sugar.'

Johann knew that patients in this fragile state were able to gain better control of themselves if they had something to do with their hands, to help them focus and talk through their problems. Coffee was an excellent means of giving patients something to occupy them and the hot drink itself helped to restore them.

Thomas took a couple of grateful sips, put the mug down and said, 'That was good. Just what the doctor ordered, so to speak.'

A faint smile passed over his lips and Johann responded with an encouraging nod as Elise left the room.

'Well,' said Thomas, 'where on earth do I begin?' Another sip of coffee, then he slowly started to explain what had driven him to come to the surgery.

'It all goes back a long way, I suppose. At least two or three years. As you know, I am a practical man, I work with my hands, but I am also an avid reader and a regular visitor to our museums and art galleries. As far as politics are concerned, I never really took a great deal of notice, until one particular event shocked me into an awareness of the inexorable rise of the Nazis and the increasingly unpleasant nature of their aspirations.'

He stopped suddenly, aware that he had crossed a line by severely criticising the ruling Party. He looked enquiringly at Johann.

'It's all right, Thomas. I fully understand what you are saying and I am no friend of what the Nazis are doing and the direction in which they are taking our country.'

Thomas looked much relieved and continued, 'Let me tell you about the first time it forcibly struck me just how ghastly the situation in Germany had become.'

He began to describe the events of a Wednesday evening back in May 1933 and their enduring impact on him. As he spoke, Johann realised that this man, this mechanic who dirtied his hands and dealt with the repair and maintenance of trams and other civic vehicles for a living, had a real literary talent and could bring the scene he was describing to life in a vibrant and compelling way, like a gifted storyteller relating a gripping tale to an enthralled audience.

'Well, I suppose it was that particular night which made me realise the full extent of what was taking place in our country. I was on my way back from a meeting in the city and had decided to take a tram to the marketplace and then go on to a restaurant. I was hungry and fancied our local favourite, Nürnberger Bratwurst with Sauerkraut. The rest of the family were away visiting an aunt and uncle and I did not relish a plate of cold meat for my supper.

'When the tram stopped at the market square, which had recently been renamed the Adolf-Hitler-Platz, I alighted and was astonished to see a huge commotion of people, most of them young folk and students, and what appeared to be a bonfire blazing away on the cobblestones. I could hear a youthful voice, scarcely broken, declaim a number of words which I couldn't make out and then the mob gave a great shout. The bonfire flared up, and the huge ghostly silhouettes of the dancing, cheering throng rocked and swayed on the facades of the buildings around the square like a gruesome shadow puppet theatre.

'I edged my way closer through the mass of excited bodies towards the bonfire. To one side of it, there stood a large cart, looking for all the world like a tumbril in revolutionary Paris which transported condemned aristocrats to the guillotine, and I soon discovered that what was taking place was indeed a bizarre execution of a sort, not of people, though—but books.

'To begin with, I couldn't figure out precisely what was going on. One by one, a student would step forward, grab a book from the cart, shout out words half drowned in the crackle of the flames and the jeers and ravings of the crowd and throw it onto the fire, sending a jet of sparks up into the night air and whipping the mob into an ever greater state of frenzy.

'There was a sudden shift in the wind and a lull in the noise and fury when one acned youth stepped forward, grabbed at a book and shouted out words which horrified me and chilled me to the bone. I can remember it so clearly, just as if it was yesterday. He cried out in his piping adolescent tones, "Against the literary betrayal of the soldiery of the World War, on behalf of the education

139

of the Volk in the spirit of preparedness for battle, I consign to the flames the writings of Erich Maria Remarque."

'He held the book up high in the air and I could read the title clearly in the orange and yellow flare of the bonfire. It was *All Quiet on the Western Front*, a novel condemning the futility of war which I had eagerly devoured from cover to cover when it first came out four years previously. It had sold countless millions of copies and had captured the imagination of a whole continent weary of wars and conflicts and the scandalous waste of young lives on the battlefield, and it had become an instant bestseller.

'My own cherished copy, dated 1929, had the words "601st-625th thousand" on the title page, and it was well thumbed from frequent reading. It had exerted a huge influence on me, as it had brilliantly savaged the senseless waste of young men in the carnage of the trenches.

'And this pimply youth, on behalf of all the mindless acolytes of Hitler and his gang, was burning my cherished book and all it stood for, seeking to destroy the greatest anti-war novel of a generation and casting it aside before the militaristic hysteria of the National Socialists. I was completely and utterly distraught.

'But what did I do about it?' He paused for a long moment and stared straight into Johann's eyes. 'Nothing. Nothing at all. I just turned slowly on my heel and weaved my way through the jubilant throng with a sense of impotent despair bearing down on me like a lead weight.

'I had just reached the edge of the square, where the crowd was thinning out and the sound of the flames became more subdued, when I caught sight of him, an elderly man with his black mongrel dog, frail and shaking with anger, tears streaming down his face, croaking in a hoarse, querulous voice, "It's an outrage, an insult to our German culture! I tell you, it's a damned insult!"

'For a while, no one paid him any attention, until one student caught his words, looked round and sneered, pulled at the sleeve of one of his fellows, then three or four of them were cavorting round the old man, taunting him and chanting, "You are the past! We are the future!"

'At that moment,'—at this point there was a sudden catch in Thomas's voice, and Johann could see the anguish in his face

—'one of them began to tug at his coat, another spat in his face, a third kicked out at the dog and, suddenly, a mob of a dozen and more of them began to punch and shove him and his pet until he was curled up on the ground, bloodied and weeping at the pain and horror of it all, and the dog, its leg broken, lay whimpering beside him.

'A second later, there came another shout from nearer the bonfire, and the throng of students moved on, leaving the old man and his severely injured mutt lying on the ancient cobblestones. And what did I do while all this was going on? Big, brave Thomas, famed for his boxing prowess, a legend who took on men a weight and more above his own, how did I respond?'

141

He choked again, almost gasping for breath. In a stifled whisper, he repeated, 'What did I do? Once more, I did absolutely nothing. I knew that the gang of young lads would assault me and beat me to a pulp if I challenged them and their arrogant, youthful self-assurance, their bigoted adulation for the Führer, their blind conviction in the supremacy of the German Volk, and God help anyone who stood in their way.'

He paused, then continued in an unsteady voice, 'Was I the only one on that Wednesday evening in May to be shocked to the core by what was happening in our beloved country? And why was I shamefully holding my tongue, afraid to raise my feeble voice above the baying mob?'

He fell silent, and Johann, in an unusual gesture for a man who did not wear his heart on his sleeve, reached out and laid his hand gently on Thomas's shoulder.

'It's all right, Thomas, you are not alone. There are many of us who feel the same, who yearn to cry out against the Third Reich and all it stands for, but who are too timorous and fearful to do so. I am one of them. To my shame, I must admit it. I too am one of them.'

He stood up and paced around the room. As he reached the window, he paused, turned towards Thomas and said in a firm voice, 'But, please, do not let yourself become overwhelmed with despair. I understand very well what you are feeling, and my wife and I share your sentiments. We have become determined to do more than simply stand on the sidelines and silently deplore the present situation. Together with a friend of ours, we were recently able to take some positive action against the régime and its callous disregard for human values. And I am sure that you too might want to take part with us in such undertakings, Thomas.'

Thomas looked up and a brief smile flickered across his face.

'However feeble our protest may be, however limited, ineffectual even, we are firmly convinced that it is essential to keep hope alive and to take action in whatever way we can. Whether it is ensuring that a particularly unpleasant Nazi is punished for his deeds against humanity, or whether we succeed in helping a Jewish family to escape the country—we shall and must do our utmost to keep a candle burning in the darkness, for our sake and for that of future generations. That is, if you'll forgive the rather poetic phrase about the candle my wife came up with.

'As well as being a man of culture and deep convictions, you are very much a practical individual, and the best cure I can offer you is not a bottle of pills or a dose of medicine but the real prospect of taking action yourself against what is happening all around us. You are more than welcome to join our modest efforts, but I must, of course, consult with our friend who has recently joined us. So far, we have had a couple of small successes. However, there is always much more that we can do. Might you be interested, Thomas?'

'Yes, yes, of course, I would. It is such a relief to hear that I am not alone, that there are other people who feel and think as I do. And also that you are prepared to take action rather than just stand on the sidelines and silently complain.'

'That traumatic event, the burning of the books, must have etched itself into your brain and has tormented you for the last few years. It's well nigh impossible for you to shake yourself free from the memory of such a horrendous occurrence. At least, not without support and positive action.'

'It is indeed. And what makes it all the more challenging is the fact that my wife is a great fan of the Führer, can see only the positive things he has achieved and blithely discounts all the "negative stuff and nonsense", as she calls it, of those who dare to raise their concerns. I used to love her dearly, but she is so dreadfully naïve when it comes to anything beyond the domestic sphere, such as matters relating to politics or economics, let alone international affairs. So, I cannot discuss it with her at all and I fear we are drifting still further apart. Her infatuation has driven a huge wedge between us.

'Challenging the might of Hitler's state would be way beyond her comprehension and that's what makes my dilemma all the more terrible. I fear I am on the point of emotional collapse but I cannot explain or communicate it to the one person who ought to be closest to me and offer me support.'

He shook his head sadly. But Johann sensed that Thomas had not finished his confession, that he had something more to reveal, and he waited as he took another sip of coffee and prepared to continue.

'I really thought I was made of sterner stuff, that I was able to manage that painful memory and its consequences by myself. Terrible though that experience was, I did not pluck up the courage to come and see you today because of the burning of the books and the brutal attack on that poor old man.' He paused. 'It was something else which happened just a couple of days ago.'

At this point, Thomas reached into his pocket and brought out a scarf which appeared to hold a small shapeless object. He placed it almost reverently on the desk and unrolled it. Out fell the bloodstained mangled form of Naomi's doll.

'This is what finally drove me here to see you. I know, it's just a rag doll. It belonged to a little Jewish girl called Naomi... '

Johann gave a startled look of recognition but he said nothing and allowed Thomas to complete his narrative.

He told Johann about the Jewish family's arrest, the killing of their daughter and the ghastly task of cleaning the mess of the little girl's blood and bones from the undercarriage of the tram, all of which was to be kept under wraps in order to cover up the involvement of the SS.

'It was a matter of national security, or so they led me to believe. Just as I was finishing my inspection and cleaning up operation, I found this doll which had belonged to the little girl lodged in part of the vehicle's suspension. She had died trying to retrieve it after one of the SS soldiers flung it into the path of the tram. She was profoundly deaf, poor child, and did not hear the vehicle coming towards her. The driver saw it all and he was very badly shaken up by what happened.'

Johann was filled with a feeling of deep sadness at the sight of the muddied, blood-streaked object and the tragic events it represented. His thoughts turned briefly to the Birnbaums, hoping that their escape plans were being carried out successfully. He gave Thomas a look of deep concern and sympathy and asked,

'Do you mind if I ask my wife to come into the consulting room? I have something rather special to tell you, and I would like her to be present.'

Puzzled, Thomas nodded dumbly. Again, Johann rang the bell and Elise appeared in the doorway.

'Please come in. Thomas here has had a terrible experience, and he has found something I want you to look at.'

'What is it, Liebling?' Then she saw the doll on the desk and frowned. She looked at her husband, who mouthed the words 'Naomi Birnbaum' to her. Suddenly, she stared at Thomas and said, in a voice shaking with emotion, 'Is that what I think it is? Where on earth did you find it, Thomas?'

'Sadly, it was found underneath the tram where a little girl died. And when I saw it, I felt I could no longer cope… That is why I am here now, and I am sure that as a nurse, you can understand my feelings… '

'Indeed I can. And I am also certain that Johann will let me tell you'—she looked at her husband, who nodded approval—'that we are more than familiar with the family and what happened to them. The parents' names are Eli and Lea Birnbaum. The little girl who died was called Naomi, and her big sister is Ruth.'

Thomas shot a puzzled glance at Elise, so she told him about Johann's discovery of the elder daughter, Ruth, and their successful rescue of the father and mother from the goods wagon in the marshalling yards alongside the main railway station.

'So that is one of your so-called modest successes,' said Thomas, actually smiling for the first time in days. 'Congratulations. If that's the kind of undertaking you are involved in, do please allow me to become involved with your brave little group.'

They discussed their hopes and objectives at length and Johann told him about Rudi and his many costume disguises. He also spoke angrily about SS Leutnant Erpenbeck who was in charge of the arrest of the Birnbaum family and indirectly involved in Naomi's death and, much worse, his unspeakable assault on Ruth, an utterly unpardonable crime. Something had to be done about the leutnant, insisted Johann, who told him that he was busily putting a plan together to teach the man a lesson he would be unlikely to forget.

'What I'd like to do is arrange for all four of us to meet up somewhere on neutral ground. There's a restaurant in the city centre run by a patient of mine who'd be glad to give us the use of one of his function rooms.

'The only problem,' he continued, 'is that four is a pretty small number for the kind of operations I have in mind. I'd be happier with at least five people, if not more, with a mix of skills and talents, but I am not sure whom to approach. There are also serious considerations of security to bear in mind. In the present climate, it's not easy to be certain that any particular individual really is on our side.'

As Johann explained the situation, Thomas's face had begun to light up at the prospect of being able to do something positive rather than sink into ever greater despair and irresolution. Now, he felt, he could actually begin to face the demons which were tormenting him and seek to defeat them with decisive actions. He spoke up almost cheerfully with his own proposal.

'I believe I know someone who could make an invaluable contribution to the group. He's a bit reclusive, so please let me make the initial approach. In addition, he is in a position of considerable responsibility in the city, so he, in turn, has to be convinced that we really are genuine and trustworthy. There—I am using the word "we" already. I am pretty sure that this man is somehow using his privileged position to thwart the Nazi machine, but how precisely he is doing it I'm not certain. But I know he can and will make a substantial contribution to our cause. Set up that meeting and I'll do my utmost to persuade him to come along. I think you'll be surprised at what he can achieve.'

Chapter Thirteen

Max Feinlein lived a quiet and cloistered existence. In his profession, he would say, he dwelt on an island of tranquillity while the turbulent tide of history swept past him on either side, bearing the debris of humanity and its sufferings along with it. Max was always fond of a well-turned phrase, which was not surprising because he was the Chief Curator of the Nuremberg Museum and Galleries and a man of great erudition.

He had never married, and his colleagues would tell you that he was wedded to his work, his paintings and sculptures, and cared for little else. Max even looked like the epitome of the confirmed bachelor and art connoisseur. He was short, untidily dressed and on the chubby side, with a tangle of grey hair and metal-framed glasses, behind which piercing blue eyes scanned the world with an intelligence that was almost frightening in its power and incisiveness. For all that, he was surprisingly popular amongst the museum staff. Women adored him but he seemed immune to their charms, and the museum was littered with their many failed attempts to seduce him, or at the very least, to persuade him to take a more than a professional interest in them.

The rumour-mongers claimed that there were far more wine stains on his crumpled jacket than he ever had lady friends in all the years that he had worked at the Stadtmuseum. Some folk even hinted unkindly that he was more interested in gentlemen than ladies, but there was no evidence to support the slander, except for one junior staff member who claimed he had recently seen Herr Feinlein in a local restaurant in the company of a thin, artistic-looking young man with long fair hair and what appeared to be an effete manner. They were locked in earnest conversation and showed every sign of being close, if not intimate, with one another.

Not much credence was placed on the report, though, as the young man could well have been a nephew or other relative, and the sighting remained a one-off event which was never repeated, as far as anyone on the staff could determine. Max's social and private life remained a closed book.

In the museum, he treated everyone with the greatest courtesy and very rarely raised his voice, let alone lost his temper. As far as anyone could recall, the last time that happened was when one unfortunate trainee art restorer dropped a loaded crimson paintbrush onto a priceless sixteenth-century miniature of Diana the Huntress. No great loss either, muttered some of the more youthful members of the team, who were closet supporters of the great modern art movements which had swept across Europe and beyond in the early years of the century. But, now, they kept those views strictly to themselves, as did everyone in the museum, because the Nazi diktat defined acceptable art as formal representational works which promoted the aims and ideals of the state.

Heroic warrior figures on black stallions, decorous nudes in bucolic settings and bland scenes of family and rural life constituted the acceptable face of National Socialist art, whilst the supposedly mindless daubs of the Expressionists, Cubists, Surrealists and the rest were derided by the Party establishment as nothing more than a corrosive, subversive and infantile revolt against taste and decency and the very antithesis of true Aryan values. Fortunately, the museum and galleries focused on the works of previous centuries, so there was little to cause offence to their new political masters in the labyrinth of exhibition rooms which housed its highly valuable collections.

About the Nazi takeover of power and their subsequent antics, Max had nothing to say. He simply brushed any questions aside, claiming that his duty lay exclusively within the walls of his beloved museum. What went on outside was the concern of politicians and, for as long as the two co-existed without actually coming into bruising conflict, he was content to let matters rest as they were.

However, there was a darker side to Max's work, one which both saddened and angered him, but which he could not shirk for fear of damaging his career. He persevered in the hope of protecting and preserving at least a fraction of the great artistic heritage which was being pillaged from the homes of local Jews, left-wingers and other alleged enemies of the state, ostensibly to be handed over to public buildings and galleries, although large numbers of the finer works somehow found their way into private collections of the Party nobility.

Ever more frequently, another truckload of paintings, sculptures and objets d'art would reverse up to the service dock of the gallery, to be piled away in a corner of the warehouse facility until the staff could muster the time and inclination to examine it all. Max personally inspected as much of this material as he could and, when he came across a particularly fine work, he carefully catalogued it in his personal notebook with an indication of its provenance and spirited it away in a remote storeroom to which only he held the key.

He told himself that, one day, the Nazi madness would pass, though in all likelihood not until much personal suffering and bloody international hostilities had been inflicted on Europe and beyond, and he might then be able to restore at least a portion of these works to their rightful owners. If, that is, he and they were still alive when that distant day dawned.

One evening, after the museum had closed and most of the staff had gone home, he had wandered down to the storage area where the latest confiscations had been haphazardly dumped by a work detail of soldiers. With a sigh, he determined to spend a little while examining the paintings, to see if any were worth placing in his secret cache.

After looking over a number of pictures containing nothing more interesting than local views and reproduction Albrecht Dürer prints, he was about to abandon his search when his eye caught the flash of a slightly damaged gold leaf frame behind a crate filled with miniature sculptures. Many of the more significant paintings he came across had gold leaf in their frames, but this one sparked a sudden recollection. Surely, it wasn't the painting that he had admired so greatly when he had visited the home of a local businessman some months previously. He looked closer. My God, he thought, it is. But what on earth is it doing here in the basement of the museum?

Of course, he recalled, the family who owned it were Jews and the persecution of the Jewish population in the city was rapidly gathering pace, so it was most likely that the painting, together with the rest of the family's extensive collection, had been forcibly removed from the house and transported here to the museum. Mercifully, no one who had handled it so far had the remotest idea how significant and valuable it was. As he held the gilt-framed landscape up to the light, he reflected on how he had come to see it for the first time almost by chance.

A small part of his work as Chief Curator involved making home visits to people living in and around the city who were notable art collectors, with a view to persuading them to lend one or more of their possessions to a biennial exhibition of privately-owned works at the gallery, which was always very popular and drew considerable numbers of visitors.

He was on one of his visiting expeditions and had just been preparing to take his leave from one of the more substantial houses in the Parkstrasse, where an elderly widow had inherited a considerable collection of important eighteenth-century paintings. She had agreed to lend four of her landscapes to the museum, because, as she dismissively put it, 'I really can't abide the stuffy old things. They just gather dust and, one day, I'll send the whole lot off to auction.'

As he was taking his leave of the old lady, she said, 'While you are in this area, why don't you call on the Birnbaum family at number 49? A couple of weeks ago, they kindly invited me to a reception for some local dignitary or other, and I know they have a large collection which they put on display for an annual charitable exhibition. I particularly recall that there was one very special painting which the master of the house was greatly fond of.'

Of course, Max was aware of the fact that Herr Birnbaum was an established collector and that he had loaned some of his paintings to the museum in the past but he had never met the man personally. The old lady's next words shook him to the core.

'Now, what was the painting called? Death Island, I believe... Something like that. The painter had a name like Brooklyn. Anyway, the family should be well worth a visit. They might be persuaded to lend it to your gallery, you never know.'

Max was barely conscious of the door closing behind him, so excited was he by the name the widow gave to the painting. Surely, it couldn't be one of the famous series Isle of the Dead by the Swiss symbolist artist Arnold Böcklin. It just couldn't be, because all the paintings in the set were well-documented and their current locations known, as far as he was aware. Still, it was worth a try. He hastened to his car, a passionate art historian hot on the trail of a potentially exciting find.

Soon after, he was driving through the gates of number 49 and parking under the portico. As he walked up the steps to the double front door, he suddenly realised that his enthusiasm was running way ahead of his manners. Here he was, on a personal whim and without prior warning, calling on a distinguished member of the local community in his own home. As he hesitated, the door opened and a slip of a girl who looked about fourteen-years-old stepped out.

'Oh,' she said, surprised by the unexpected sight of Max, who did not quite know how to react.

'Fräulein, I'm sorry to call on your family without an invitation, but my name is Max Feinlein. I'm the… ' He was interrupted by a man who emerged from behind the girl.

'I know you well,' boomed Eli Birnbaum. 'You are the Chief Curator at the city's museum and galleries. I heard a lecture you gave some while ago on the works of nineteenth-century painters. Fascinating it was too.'

They shook hands, and Eli said to his daughter, 'Now, run along to your violin lesson, Ruth, and don't be late back.'

'No, Papa,' said Ruth, smiling at the visitor, before she skipped away down the drive.

'My daughter should really have her lessons at home, but her teacher is indisposed so Ruth calls round to see her. She only lives a few houses away.' He gestured Max into the hallway.

'Now,' he continued, 'to what do I owe this entirely unexpected pleasure, Herr Feinlein?'

Max explained that he had been on his biennial trawl for pictures to exhibit at the private collections show in the Stadtmuseum. The old lady he had just visited had told him about a remarkable painting that Herr Birnbaum owned and, on the spur of the moment, he had decided to call on him right away, he added apologetically.

'No need to apologise,' said Birnbaum warmly. 'Yes, I do own a rather special nineteenth-century painting, but it's not one that I would want to leave the house, I'm afraid.'

A pause.

'But I'd be delighted to show it to you. As you'll know, art owners are just as bad as hunters who hang their trophies on the wall and bore everyone to tears with their tales. Do please come and take a look.'

Max gazed admiringly at the spacious entrance hall and its broad pinewood staircase with twin flights of stairs branching down from the mezzanine. In the middle of the back wall of the half-landing hung a small, dark painting peppered with patches of white. His eye was drawn immediately to it, although, from this distance, it was not possible to distinguish more than the general outline.

As they climbed the stairway, Eli explained the picture to him, and as he did so, Max's astonishment grew. If genuine, this painting had to represent a really significant discovery of the greatest importance to the art world.

'It's a Böcklin study for the Isle of the Dead series of paintings,' said Eli, with a note of pride in his deep voice, 'representing a lonely outcrop of symmetrical rock, with tall pine trees in the centre. In a rowing boat, you can make out a coffin and a white figure, who I assume to be Charon, the boatman who transports the souls of the dead to the underworld. The work is complete, oil on board, and particularly striking are the tall slabs of rock which are given a strange reddish hue, clashing with the dark green pines and the steely sea. As he developed his theme, Böcklin changed various elements of the composition, as you will know, some of them quite radically.'

Max was very impressed indeed, both by the fact that Eli owned such a piece which he had no idea actually existed and by his understanding of the imagery and his ability to bring the work to life with his insightful description. Clearly, Eli was an art connoisseur of some considerable knowledge.

Max was aware of five versions of the painting, all in prestigious museums, so far as he knew, and the discovery of a sixth would cause a seismic shock to the art world. First, though, he would have a great deal of research work to undertake.

'With your permission,' he said to Eli, I'd love to look into the provenance of your painting, not least, because the other works in this series are so clearly documented. My guess from a swift examination is that it antedates most of the known existing versions in the series and it may well be a very major discovery indeed.'

Eli took a while to consider his request. 'Of course, under normal circumstances, I'd be happy for you to undertake such an investigation, but,' he continued cautiously, 'circumstances aren't exactly normal nowadays, are they?'

Max nodded in agreement. 'I can understand your concerns and assure you that any enquiries I make will be extremely discreet. I don't want, how shall I put it, to imperil your ownership by confirming that this is indeed an unknown Böcklin worth a considerable sum of money.'

'Thank you for your tactful reply. As for provenance, I have not yet had the time to look into its history, since I inherited it only recently from an uncle who claimed to have had close links with the Böcklin family, and I am anxious to keep my ownership and the painting itself out of the public eye.'

'May I, nonetheless, spend a little while examining the work, Herr Birnbaum? I must admit to being very impressed by the use of colour and the positioning of the various elements of the composition… '

'Please go ahead. I'll stay here and observe, if I may.'

Max gingerly lifted the picture from the wall and examined the back. The reverse held no information about its provenance, except for a small cryptic label with the legend '434D', which probably indicated that it had been hung in an exhibition at some time in the past. The image itself had all the hallmarks of the mature Böcklin, particularly the brushwork, but the overall design did not clearly indicate where in the sequence of paintings it belonged.

After a while, Max thanked Eli profusely for allowing him to examine the work and promised to explore the issue of its provenance with great discretion.

As he now bent down to examine the painting again in the store room, Max sadly recalled the pleasure he had experienced when examining it in the Birnbaums' house. That delight had been severely tempered by the knowledge he had recently gained that one of the versions of the Isle of the Dead series was not in a public gallery at all, but in private hands, and the owner was none other than Adolf Hitler himself, who was a great admirer of Böcklin's work. If it came to be known that this painting was in the possession of a Jewish collector and had recently been confiscated, it would certainly end up in the Führer's possession.

On closer examination, he noticed that one corner of the frame had been badly scuffed, and on the painting itself, there was a long blackish streak across the upper part of the image. It looked as if some idiot had stubbed a cigarette out on the canvas and, when he looked more closely, it indeed proved to be the case.

To Max, that one thoughtless and uncivilised action encapsulated everything he hated about the Nazi régime, but he now faced a real dilemma. If he had the painting restored, it would become known throughout the museum that a significant but undocumented work was in their hands and there were quite a few Nazi sympathisers on the staff who would willingly pass that information on to their masters. If he did not attempt repairs, there was a chance that it might deteriorate further in storage, but that was a much lesser risk which Max was resolved to take.

He carefully wrapped the Böcklin in brown paper and carried it to his office, from where he would later transfer it to his secret cache in a basement storeroom at the museum which, fortunately, was temperature controlled, so that the works he had concealed there should survive relatively well for some considerable time to come.

It was the least he could achieve for Herr Birnbaum. The last thing he wanted was for the painting to fall into the hands of some member of the Party élite and sold on for profit, or displayed as a trophy for fellow looters to envy and admire. Or, worst of all, end up in Hitler's own private collection.

If only, thought Max bitterly, there was more I could do.

Chapter Fourteen

The next day, Max was busy at work when the phone on his desk rang insistently. He reached for it, picked up the receiver and listened.

'Herr Feinlein?' Of course, it is, Max thought irritably. Why the silly girl had to ask every time she rang through to her boss, defeated him. Still, he was very grateful that she continued to be his secretary, despite the Party's national campaign to drive women out of employment and replace them with men.

'Yes, Eva.'

'You asked to be informed the next time Herr Braun visited the museum? One of your security guards tells me he has just entered the nineteenth-century seascapes gallery.'

'Thank you, my dear. I'll be out of my office for a while.' He put down the receiver, pushed back his chair and rose unsteadily to his feet. The force of gravity, he told himself bitterly, seems to get stronger by the day as I get older and crustier. He had been wanting to talk to Thomas for some time and was glad he was paying a visit to the museum that day.

Max made his way into the areas of the building open to visitors, acknowledging the greetings of his staff and smiling and nodding at members of the public. The gallery where Herr Braun had been spotted was one level below his office and it took him no more than a couple of minutes to reach the arched entranceway to the museum's fine collection of maritime paintings from the previous century.

A security guard sitting by the gallery wall half rose from his chair but Max gestured to him to remain seated. ''Morning, Liebermann. How are you keeping?' Max shook his employee by the hand and waited for an answer.

'Arthritis is becoming far worse, Herr Feinlein. I'm not getting any younger, I'm afraid.'

'Sorry to hear that. Do let me know if you require time off work for treatment.'

'Thank you. I will do that, sir.'

Max nodded and moved into the gallery. It was here he had met Thomas by chance, and they had soon formed a close but unlikely friendship. Both shared a passion for the visual arts and what Thomas lacked in academic knowledge he more than compensated for with intuitive insights and boundless enthusiasm.

A solitary figure sat on the circular wooden bench in the centre of the room, contemplating a small painting of some long-forgotten naval encounter between two tall-masted sailing ships which were spitting fire, smoke and cannonballs at each other without either suffering any apparent damage.

Max walked up to the man and touched him lightly on the shoulder. Thomas jerked nervously around, but smiled broadly when he recognised his friend. He rose to his feet and the two shook hands warmly.

'How are you, Thomas? It's a delight to see you again.'

For a little while they exchanged pleasantries, then Thomas said in earnest tones, 'Do you think we could discuss a matter in private? Actually, I was sitting here plucking up the courage to come to your office and talk to you.'

Max looked curiously at him, wondering what it was that could be of such concern to his friend.

'Of course. Come this way. As it happens, there is a matter I wish to discuss with you, too That's why I asked my gallery staff to keep an eye open for you when next you visited us.' They strolled together to Max's office.

Seated in comfortable chairs in one corner, Max said, 'I can ask my secretary to get some coffee... '

'No, thanks, I'm fine,' said Thomas.

He looked nervously at Max, took a deep breath and addressed his friend. In the politically charged atmosphere of the Nazi years, it was not difficult to detect when people began to touch on a potentially dangerous subject matter, because they used coded language to test the waters. This Thomas set about doing, trying to tease out from Max the extent of his disenchantment with the Nazis, when his friend raised a hand to stop him.

'Let us both be clear, Thomas. I appreciate your discretion and tact, but I think we have known one another long enough to be candid about our views on matters political. Let me put my cards on the table, as this is precisely the delicate matter which I wanted to raise with you. So, let me tell you first about my own increasing disgust for National Socialism and all it stands for.'

Thomas nodded, a relieved look on his face. Then he settled back in his chair to listen. Max began by explaining that he had been particularly dismayed at the duties imposed on him in dealing with the confiscation of paintings, sculptures, furniture and objets d'art from Jewish families and other so-called enemies of the state. He told Thomas that he and his staff had to sift through the incoming loads of material and determine their value and catalogue them. Then, it was up to a Party representative to take any further action.

Certain artists and works were to be set aside for onward transport to regional reception centres, notably Berlin, so that the Party bigwigs could make their selections. That much Thomas was also aware of, but then Max lowered his voice and continued.

He explained that, in his own small way, he had been subverting this process ever since confiscated art first began to make its way into the storage rooms of the museum. He would secretly remove a particularly fine painting, attach to it a note of its owner and the address, where known, and conceal it in a remote storeroom to which only he had access. But this wasn't possible if a

Party representative was likely to be aware of the existence of such a painting, so sometimes tricky situations could arise. Thomas smiled to himself as Max confirmed what he had suspected about his political sympathies and his actions against the Nazi plunder of works of art and other artefacts.

More recently, Max continued, he had also been employing a far more sophisticated approach to preventing works either held by the museum or brought in after raids on homes of 'enemies of the Reich' from getting into the hands of the Party élite. A few months previously, he had been taking a walk through the galleries of the museum when he chanced across what he described as the most amazing artist he had ever encountered.

A thin, poorly dressed young man with long fair hair and an ill-fitting grey raincoat was sitting in front of a landscape by Caspar David Friedrich, apparently sketching it in coloured pencils. Artist's oil colours were banished from the galleries because of the potential damage to the wooden parquet flooring.

Max walked up quietly behind the young man and was so astonished by the quality of the drawing which, within the limitations of the materials used, was such a stunningly accurate copy of the painting before him that he blurted out, 'My God, that is wonderful.'

At which, the young man protectively closed his sketchbook, rose to his feet, head bowed, and prepared to make his way out of the gallery. Max restrained him gently and said, 'I mean no harm or disrespect to you. I was simply lost in admiration at your skills.'

The young man made a half-hearted attempt to shake himself free but Max continued to talk to him gently, trying to reassure him that nothing was amiss. Quite the contrary, in fact.

'I am the Chief Curator of the Nuremberg Museum and Galleries,' he told the young man. 'And I have never seen a copy of such remarkable quality as you have made here. I'd like to talk to you in greater detail, to find out more about you and your painting skills. I think I might be able to put some important work your way. By the way, my name is Max Feinlein. May I ask what yours is?'

'Kaspar Schröder,' the young man replied in a very quiet voice, almost a whisper.

'So, Kaspar, if I may use your first name, come with me to my office and we'll have a little talk. I promise you there is nothing to be alarmed about. Are you happy to do that?'

Max went on to describe how he had spoken to Kaspar in great depth, gradually teasing him out of his shell until he gained a clearer picture of the young man and his extraordinary talent. He had a wild idea that he could put his incredible gift to practical use. It depended critically on what Kaspar's political leanings and sympathies might be, though.

Gradually, Kaspar opened up about himself and his circumstances. He was a solitary individual who rented an attic room at the top of a tenement block not far from the museum where he eked out an independent living from a small inheritance.

When he was seven-years-old he had fallen seriously ill and had been near to death. During his long convalescence. his sister lent him her set of paints and easel simply as a means of keeping him occupied. Almost at once, he began to paint with great skill and fluency.

The family were astonished at his newly-won facility with the paintbrush which he continued to develop over the following years. Then, when he was sixteen, a brutal tragedy struck the family. His parents and sister died in a house fire started by Brownshirts who mistakenly believed that the building was occupied by Jews, and he only just escaped with his life.

From that day on, Kaspar was consumed with a deep hatred of the Nazis and all they stood for. He became obsessed with painting as a means of easing the pain of the loss of his family and of healing the wounds of his bitter memories. Over the years, he had made copies of many of the pictures in the museum from memory, he added. He would often visit the galleries and make initial sketches of the more challenging works before going home to recreate them. This is what he had been doing with the Caspar David Friedrich painting when Max chanced to meet him.

'And,' concluded Max, 'to cut a long story short, I took him out to dinner, as he looked as if he hadn't enjoyed a square meal in ages. Afterwards, he invited me to his apartment, where I was truly astonished by the quality and accuracy of his work. I then told him that I was trying to preserve a number of paintings from being pillaged by the Nazis, and he gladly undertook to assist me by making copies of these works.

All he would need, he said, was a few minutes to imprint the painting in his mind and he would be able to make an exact copy. But he was lacking money for materials, which I was glad to supply for him. I have also helped him generally with his finances.

'He was as good as his word, and there are quite a few Nazi collectors who are now the unsuspecting proud owners of Kaspar's work. There are one or two paintings in the museum galleries too, which I have exchanged for copies and hold the originals in my storeroom.'

He gave an impish smile. 'By the way, what do you think of the Encounter at Sea you were closely examining when I came to meet you?'

'Surely, it isn't... ' said Thomas incredulously.

'Indeed it is. I have had word that a high-ranking local Party member who is a collector of naval paintings intends to force me to hand the canvas over to him in the near future and I will, of course, do so with a convincing show of the greatest reluctance. I don't like my Kaspar Schröders being removed from the museum. Not one little bit.'

Thomas laughed. 'I can see that you are doing your utmost to protect important works of art from falling into the wrong hands, although it must be a pretty daunting task. Now, let me tell you why you found me here in the maritime gallery today. I was actually taking a moment or two to think through what I was going to say to you before asking one of your staff if I could call on you.'

He revealed that he too had become increasingly appalled at the way in which the Nazis were imposing their rule on the country. He described his horror and shame when he witnessed the burning of the books episode in the market square and the impact it had made on him. And he told Max how dealing with the aftermath of young Naomi's death had traumatised him to the point that he was finding it almost impossible to function. When he mentioned the family name, Max looked shocked and told him of his own meeting with Eli Birnbaum, the Böcklin painting, and how it had just turned up in the museum storeroom in a sorry state.

Swallowing his pride, Thomas explained that he had been to see Dr Johann Voss for medical help with his deep-rooted anxieties and fears and discovered that the doctor and his wife were of like mind. Johann, together with his wife and a friend, had already undertaken a successful rescue attempt of the Birnbaums who would otherwise now be languishing in a concentration camp.

They were only a small group, four members in all for the present, and they were about to come together for their first meeting. Thomas very much wanted Max to join their number. Max hesitated, but it was the link with the Birnbaums that persuaded him that the group might well be capable of positive action which he would be glad to support in whatever small way he could.

'We are due to meet next Thursday at the Castle Room of the Mautkeller restaurant at around seven-thirty. Shall we see you then?'

'Indeed, I trust you will,' replied Max.

Chapter Fifteen

'Could you tell me where the Castle Room is?' The chubby middle-aged man in a scruffy jacket and trousers blinked through his metal-rimmed spectacles at the head waiter of the Mautkeller as he shook the rain from his coat and stamped his feet.

'Down the corridor to the right, sir. The Castle Room is at the end.'

'Thank you.'

The man walked slowly along the corridor, cautiously twisted the door handle and entered the room, only to find it in darkness. He looked around, uncertain what to do when he saw the head waiter nodding and gesturing to him to turn on the switch by the door.

The man fumbled for the switch, and a chandelier bathed the small wood-panelled room in a golden light. Oak benches lined the walls and a refectory table dominated the centre of the room. A half dozen beer glasses were lined up, together with bowls of nuts and snacks. A small bar stood in one corner.

The man walked slowly up to the table and picked at the nuts. He was still not entirely certain that he should have come to this place, since his presence would indicate that he was prepared to make some kind of public stand for the first time in his life. Yet, for all his trepidation, he knew that it was right and necessary for him to do so because he could no longer stand to one side and pretend that the momentous events that surrounded him did not concern him in his ivory tower. And, to be honest, as he had already been working behind the scenes to impede the Nazi Party's determined efforts to loot and plunder works of art, this was really not such a great step for him to take at all.

He had always been a loner who valued his art more than anything else and dedicated his waking hours to its advancement and preservation. But he could no longer pretend that his precious paintings and artefacts were somehow immune from the world outside the doors of the museum and that, if he did not take all possible steps to protect them, he would not be able to look himself in the mirror any more.

A loud click of the door interrupted his reverie. He swung round nervously as Thomas strode confidently into the room.

'Max, I am so pleased that you have come.'

'Thomas, my friend, I must confess that I struggled with myself long and hard before I finally resolved to do so.'

They shook hands warmly and Thomas gestured to the Curator to sit down.

'I can assure you,' said Thomas earnestly, 'that you will not regret your decision.'

In the awkward silence that followed, the door swung open again and the waiter came into the room. 'Beers for you two gentlemen?'

Both nodded, and Thomas reached out for a handful of nuts from the table. Drinks served, the waiter slipped quietly out.

'Now, Thomas, you must tell me more about Dr Voss and his wife.'

'Well,' he said, struggling to swallow a mouthful of nuts, 'I've known Johann and Elise for many years. They've been our first port of call for all the family's health needs, and they are a splendid young couple. I am sure you'll like them very much.'

Another handful of nuts, smaller this time. 'But, with life under the Nazis becoming more and more regimented and restrained, it's very difficult to start talking to anyone about disaffection with the régime, when potential betrayal seems to lurk around every corner and a careless word, written or spoken, can end you up in one of their concentration camps with a life expectancy approaching nil.'

He reached for his beer glass and took a long drink. 'That's better. Now, I had no clear idea that Johann and Elise were both extremely unhappy about the way things were going politically, until I was faced with a personal crisis which culminated with having to clean up the mess after the brutes who caused that poor little girl's death.'

He moved his chair a little closer to Max.

'When I poured out my heart to Johann, he responded by telling me what he, his wife and a friend had been doing to try and make a practical difference, however small, a means of keeping the spirit of decency and freedom alive. It was as if a huge burden had been lifted from my shoulders. At last, I could not only talk openly about my feelings and views on the way our country has been going but, more than that, there was the promise of an opportunity to do something practical about it.

'As I told you in your office, I thought of you as a potential member of the group, because I had heard strong hints from you in the past that you too shared our disenchantment with the Nazi state, and I have long suspected that you were using your eminent position to seek to undermine their efforts. And, so—here we both are. I'll let Johann tell you about the fifth member of our little group when he... '

Just then, the door of the Castle Room swung open again, and Johann and Elise swept in.

'So sorry we are a little late,' said Johann, 'but the SS set up a roadblock in the city centre, as they like to do from time to time, and the queue of traffic tailed back over the bridge and into the market square.'

He turned to speak to Max. As he shook his hand, he said, 'You must be Max Feinlein, Max, if I may use your first name.'

'Of course. I am delighted to meet you both.' Max's voice was a little hesitant because he was not confident in the company of people whom he did not know well.

'So, Max, may I introduce my wife, Elise.'

Greetings and handshakes over, they all sat down at one end of the refectory table to discuss the purpose of the meeting.

The waiter poked his head around the door, organised beers for Johann and Elise, and left, indicating that they should feel free to serve themselves with further rounds of drink.

Johann began by thanking them all for coming, then continued, 'As for the fifth member of our little group, he sends profuse apologies as he has to work this evening and won't be able to join us. But we shall arrange a further meeting at a time and place which suits us all.'

He sipped at his beer and took a deep breath.

'We are here because we share a common disgust, to put it mildly, at the direction this country has been taking since the Nazis seized power. I won't elaborate on that further, because all of you know where you personally stand. I am also confident that the five of us can trust each other and be prepared to take whatever actions we all consider to be practical to challenge and impede the onward rush of National Socialism without risking our own lives in the process.

'Each of us round the table is eager to do something, but it would be pointless if, say, we walked down the Lorenzstrasse in the middle of the city in broad daylight holding up banners attacking the Nazis. That would simply result in our being taken out of circulation and facing the prospect of incarceration and almost certain death at the hands of the SS.

'But we have already proved that we can take actions which are positive, in that they support and assist the oppressed in our nation, albeit on a fairly small scale. I hope, in the future, to be able to put together our first significant project which will seek to exact an appropriate measure of retribution, in this case against a particularly unpleasant SS Leutnant whose activities we have had the misfortune of experiencing. And I am convinced that our group has the mix of skills and talents which I'm sure will complement one another in our future activities.'

Johann paused and scanned the pensive faces of his listeners. Max raised a tentative hand.

'As the newest member, can I applaud all you have said, but may I ask about… '

His words were interrupted by a loud authoritative knock at the door. They looked at one another in alarm, wondering what the cause of this unwarranted interruption might be.

Johann half raised himself in his seat when there a further succession of blows hammered on the door of the Castle Room.

Suddenly, the door swung open and a short figure in military uniform, with black hair and a toothbrush moustache, stomped into the room.

Thomas and Max took one look at the intruder and nearly passed out.

'Oh my God', said Max. Thomas just stood there with his mouth wide open in horror.

Chapter Sixteen

'What is the meaning of this conspiracy? A secret gathering of enemies of the state challenging the Party and our great nation? Are you Jews, or Communists—or both? Why am I not invited to supper with you?' The staccato accent and tones of the man were frighteningly recognisable, the body language and gestures all too familiar from countless radio broadcasts and cinema newsreels.

Thomas muttered under his breath, 'Gott im Himmel, that cannot possibly be the bloody Führer, can it?'

'Speak up, man! Explain your conduct, Herr Braun. Yes, I am the Führer and I have come here for supper. I know all about you, Thomas Braun, and the loving Voss couple, and our learned man of art here, Max Feinlein.'

The man identified as Hitler took a step into the room, paused, gave the famous salute, right elbow crooked, hand pulled back almost to the horizontal. He fixed those present with a long, penetrating stare. The tension in the room was almost at breaking point and Max in particular looked extremely fearful.

Then, suddenly, the intruder erupted into laughter and plumped down in a chair. The expressions on the faces of

Max and Thomas were a sight to see, a blend of incredulity, fear and a sudden dawning recognition that this must, surely, be some kind of bizarre set-up.

'Well,' said the Führer, 'Dr Johann Voss, aren't you going to tell me who these people are?'

Johann and Elise both burst out laughing. 'Sorry to frighten the lives out of you, Max and Thomas, but we couldn't resist introducing our fifth member in a really dramatic fashion. It was his cheeky idea to demonstrate just how valuable a member of our group he can be with his considerable talents.

'As you can see, Rudi Fischer here, comedian and impressionist from the Sommerkabarett, makes a very fine Hitler. And that's just one of his transformations. We thought the best way to showcase the substantial contribution that Rudi can make to our little group was to let him hop into one of his uniforms and put on a brief show for you,' said Elise.

'In fact,' added Johann, 'he also made an excellent SS officer when we successfully rescued the Birnbaums from the railway sidings at the Hauptbahnhof.'

'And you,' Rudi said, 'were a pretty terrifying Gestapo agent.'

Thomas and Max, now sufficiently recovered from their shock, walked over to Rudi and shook him by the hand.

'A pleasure to meet you, mein Führer,' said Thomas. 'If you were the real thing, it would not be your hand that I would want to shake.'

Max added, 'A bravura performance, Rudi, if I may call you that. I'm sure we will find more than one part for you to play in the future.'

'I believe,' said Johann, 'that we're all agreed on first name terms? Good. Now, let's all take a seat, organise ourselves some more drinks and get down to business.'

There was a shuffle of chairs and Rudi drew himself a large glass of the local beer. As they sat down, Johann continued, 'Can I begin by saying how particularly honoured we are that Max Feinlein has agreed to join us, as I know he will have a great deal to offer our group.

'In his role, Max is obliged to oversee the disposal of art, sculpture and other objects confiscated from the homes of so-called enemies of the state, and a disagreeable and unpleasant task it is too. I'm sure he will not mind me mentioning that, as Thomas has told me, you, Max, are also responsible for spiriting away as many of these art works as you can, in the hope of, one day, restoring them to their rightful owners, or unfortunately, it will more likely be the heirs or surviving relatives of those owners. He has also recruited a young man of amazing talents, Kaspar Schröder by name, who is brilliant at forging paintings, which means that many of the significant works which the Nazi bigwigs believe are in their possession are actually locked away in a storeroom in the museum.'

An approving murmur came from the rest of them, and Max said, dismissively waving his hand, 'What I have done is hardly putting myself in grave danger unless someone finds out where I have concealed these works, and I am honoured to have been asked to join your group.'

Johann countered, 'What you are making, Max, is no small contribution to challenging the might of the Party. Thomas, too, is a substantial addition to our membership. He plays a key role in the transport system of Nuremberg and has good cause to be shocked and horrified at what our Nazi friends have been getting up to. Recently, he had the truly unpleasant task of clearing up, after an SS gang caused the death of poor little Naomi and is very keen indeed to seek retribution against those responsible. We were fortunate in being able to help her sister, Ruth, and her parents escape from a desperate plight in a concentration camp.

'Like all of you, I have been growing increasingly distressed, frustrated and embittered at the disastrous régime which has taken over our much-loved country. Our homeland has been usurped by a band of bigoted thugs and hooligans who are bent on destroying every civilised value.

'Also, like you, I have felt the stinging pain of humiliation when called upon to pay our obeisances to the Nazi state. We all face impossible choices: to make a stand and be spirited away to a concentration camp, or pretend to fall in with the rest of the population, shout an enthusiastic 'Heil Hitler!' at all the right moments, and, generally, let the filthy tide of National Socialism wash over us.

'I have been desperate to find some way of striking back without bringing about my imprisonment and death, and the harder it becomes to do so, the more I am convinced that I am permanently damaging my own self-esteem by my very inaction. We must do something, we must find a way of fighting back, however small and however limited the impact of what we do. Our recent successful attempt to rescue the Birnbaums has given us confidence to believe that it is indeed possible to strike back.

'My wife came up with a phrase which precisely summarises our situation and contains a kernel of hope that even the slightest achievement is in itself worthwhile. It not only keeps our sense of morality and decency alive, it gives the hope of a future in which the Nazis and all they stand for are expunged from our land and a new and humane society will emerge from the ruins.

'Her saying, which she tells me she read from the quotations of an American politician's wife, is that we should each try and light a candle. However black the night, don't rage against the darkness, because one candle, however feeble its flame, is better than no light at all.'

All of those round the table were greatly moved by his words, none more so than Max.

'Thank you, Johann, for expressing your feelings so eloquently. In my work, I should be dealing with objects of beauty, representing the very best of our civilisation, but I feel myself sullied by the disgusting tasks the Nazis force me to undertake. You are right. Anything is better than sitting in the dark complaining about the absence of illumination.

'We may light only a few candles, but however inadequate our efforts may be, we shall, at the very least, be keeping alive our own humanity, and with it the hope and conviction that, one day, Germany will re-emerge from this darkness of its own creation into a brighter and more civilised future.'

Johann nodded. 'We have already achieved more than a little, and I'd like to briefly tell those of you who are not familiar with our efforts more about our little undertakings so far.'

He briefly described Rudi's vengeance on a particularly nasty Brownshirt who attacked his sister, his own encounter with Ruth, the rescue of her parents from a train destined for the concentration camps, and the escapade in the Nürnberger Bank from which Rudi managed to spirit away vital family documents, money and passports and, so, prepare the way for the Birnbaums to leave the country.

'Which, I am delighted to report, they have recently done, with a firm promise from Eli Birnbaum that he will support and fund subsequent attempts by Jews to escape from Germany,' Johann continued. 'Now, about our future undertakings. I have one special project in mind, and I'll need all of you to assist in its execution. By the way, money in general will not be an obstacle to anything we decide to do. I inherited a large sum from my parents and

I am happy to commit considerable resources to our undertakings.'

Johann went on to explain that he intended to teach SS Leutnant Erpenbeck a lesson that he would never forget, and how each of them could contribute to the plan, which he set out in three stages. First, the Leutnant will have to be heavily sedated and taken to a secure location which he had located on the outskirts of the city. Next, the actual retribution would take place, which he guaranteed would shock the man to the core, and, finally, the Leutnant, again sedated, would have to be transported back to his apartment.

The rest of the group applauded Johann's plans and they all declared themselves fully in support of the enterprise.

The waiter, smiling broadly, knocked and entered, pushing a trolley loaded with plates of Nuremberg Bratwurst and Sauerkraut. The Führer had wanted to take supper with them, and that is precisely what was going to happen.

As the waiter left the room, Rudi said, 'Don't worry about that young man. He smuggled me in here and I told him I was springing a birthday surprise on one of you.'

As they were eating, Johann continued. 'Now, a few ground rules. We must do what we can to ensure that we are not identified by the Leutnant, nor by anyone involved in our future plans, so I propose that we continue to act with great caution to preserve our identities.

'If we need to meet again, it can either be here in the Mautkeller or at our home, where you will be very welcome indeed. Now, let's consider in detail how and when to abduct Leutnant Erpenbeck and give him an experience he'll never forget. As I said, I think I have found the ideal location, so let's get down to business. By the way, Thomas, do you know how to rig up a telephone to ring as if it's taking an incoming call?'

Chapter Seventeen

One corner of the room had been curtained off in hospital drapes and the walls freshly distempered. A single bulb in a white shade hung from a crossbeam, casting the metal framed bed in a garish yellow light. To one side, a chair stood at an angle, a neatly folded SS uniform, gloves and cap perched on the seat. Underneath, a pair of polished army boots stood to attention. A Luger pistol lay on the bedside table and, next to it, a small glass bottle.

In the bed, a flaxen-haired young man, head swathed in a bandage, slept peacefully, his arms resting on the top sheet. Unusually, his wrists were bound together and held firmly in position with bandage strips tied to the frame of the bed. His right leg, encased in a plaster cast, was held up in traction by a rope and pulley mechanism.

A fly buzzed tiredly against a small window set high in the wall behind the bed. For a medical environment, the window was surprisingly dirty, so mired in dirt and cobwebs that the thin early afternoon sun barely penetrated the space. Outside, a distant church tower chimed the hour. Three o'clock. Exhausted, the fly ceased its efforts and silence fell again except for the faint sound of the man's steady breathing.

In the shadows beneath the window, a shape seemed to shift and move. The figure of a nurse in a starched white apron, dark blue uniform dress and hair drawn back in a fierce bun, slipped quietly forward. She wore a surgical mask and a stethoscope hung limply down over her breasts. She stopped by the bedside, touched the patient lightly on the arm. There was no response. Another prod, this time, less gentle. The young man stirred, moving his head slowly from side to side before gingerly opening his eyes. He blinked vaguely into space, then, focussing on the nurse, spoke in a harsh whisper.

'Where am I?'

The nurse looked down at him. 'The Stadtklinik. A private hospital.'

The patient frowned. 'How... how in God's name did I get here? What happened to me?'

She reached out to smooth down his sheets and said, 'Don't you remember anything?'

The patient shook his head, still befuddled by the anaesthetic. 'No idea, nothing, nothing at all... '

Just then, he caught sight of his right leg in its plaster cast and bent his head forward to inspect it.

'What has happened to my damned leg?'

At the same time, he tried to gesture with his hands, but the restraints prevented him from moving.

'And my arms—why are they tied down?'

'Calm yourself down, please.'

The word 'please' was uttered more in the tone of an order than a gentle request. 'Don't agitate yourself. Your leg is in traction and your movements are restricted to help prevent you from doing further harm to yourself.'

The patient paused for a moment, his mind clearing a little as he became gradually aware of his hospital surroundings and the bizarre and alarming situation he found himself in. He was still badly disorientated by the drugs he had been given to sedate him.

'Broken?' he croaked.

'We're not sure. Doctor will be here to see you soon, and he will be able to explain your condition fully to you. For now, just lie back and relax.'

'But... '

'No buts, just kindly do as you are requested and you will be on the road to recovery in no time.'

'But I really have to... '

The voice trailed away as the patient struggled to express the embarrassing nature of his predicament.

He pleaded with his eyes, and the nurse immediately recognised what his urgent need might be. 'You need to urinate?'

The patient reddened and nodded.

The nurse bent down into the shadows, retrieved a porcelain bedpan and drew back the sheet. As he relieved himself, he noticed her staring at his genitals but, because of the manner in which she had lifted the sheet, he could not see for himself if anything was amiss. Perhaps she was simply admiring his manhood. She wouldn't have been the first to do that, he thought smugly through the fog of medication.

The nurse picked up the bedpan, pulled up his pyjama trousers and folded the sheet back with deft impersonal movements. She turned on her heel and swept out through the curtain.

A long silence ensued, broken only by the occasional attempts of the fly to escape through the skylight window. Suddenly, brisk footsteps approached and stopped outside his cubicle. Voices spoke in an undertone for some moments, then the curtain was brusquely swept back and the nurse re-emerged, followed by a doctor.

He was a tall, bespectacled man with sharp, intelligent eyes and a thinning mop of dark hair. The lower part of his face, like that of the nurse, was covered by a surgical mask.

'Now,' said the doctor, pushing his spectacles up on his nose and examining the patient's notes, 'you are— Leutnant Wilhelm Erpenbeck.'

A nod from the patient.

'Do you remember how you sustained your injuries?'

With an effort, the patient cleared his throat and uttered a single word. 'Nein.'

Doctor and nurse exchanged worried glances. After a whispered discussion, the doctor closely examined the notes again and continued, 'You must be suffering from a form of temporary amnesia as a result of the concussion you received.'

He shuffled his notes. 'What I can tell you, Leutnant Erpenbeck, is that you were involved in a violent altercation outside the Mautkeller restaurant at around ten o'clock last night. According to witnesses, you were set upon by four youths armed with wooden clubs. Apparently, you snatched one of the clubs and wielded it against all of them to great effect. Unfortunately, one of them managed to strike a heavy blow to your head before he could be stopped.

'The local police arrived just as the last of your four attackers cracked you across the shin. That's why your leg is in traction. It appears that this was an unprovoked and savage attack in which you defended yourself with great courage. Your assailants were identified as local Communist revolutionaries and, as you can imagine, they will be feeling the full force of the law.'

The doctor cleared his throat.

'For the next little while, complete bed rest is essential, not least because of the head injury you have suffered. It will be a day or two before we can be certain that you really are on the mend. As for your leg, that too requires further investigation.' He looked down at the notes again. 'Temperature and heart rate are fine. You're a healthy young man and I'm sure that, in due course, you will make a complete recovery. The military authorities have been apprised of your injuries.' Doctor and nurse turned round in unison and left the cubicle before Erpenbeck could respond.

Shortly after, a telephone rang just outside the curtain. Three rings, then someone picked up the receiver. A couple of squawks from the earpiece and the nurse could be heard saying, 'It's for you, Herr Doktor.'

'Stadklinik here. Whom am I speaking to?'

The vague muffled squeaking continued for a full minute. Silence for a while, then...

'What?! Er... I mean, you can't be serious... ' More muffled squeaks. 'Gott im Himmel... '

The patient strained to hear what was being said, sensing that something significant was going on.

'Visit? Today? Are you really sure?—I mean, yes, of course, he can... We would be greatly honoured... Three o'clock, did you say? We'll be ready.'

The patient could hear the nurse and doctor whispering frantically to each other. Then the curtain was drawn aside and both appeared, still wearing their face masks.

'You may have heard the telephone ringing just now. We are a little overwhelmed by the honour we are about to receive. We've just been informed that the hospital is to be visited shortly by a very special guest.' A pause. 'No less a person than SS-Obergruppenführer Gottlob Berger himself, Commander of the SS Central Office in Berlin.'

The patient stiffened with pride. Who? Berger? The Chief? That would indeed be a singular honour. But why would he want to pay a visit to Nuremberg and to this hospital of all places?

The doctor said, 'The Führer is presently in the city to lay the foundation stone of the Kongresshalle near the Dutzendteich lake and the Party parade ground and, on occasions like this, he always sends officers from his senior staff out to local hospitals, especially if they include amongst their patients military personnel and others who have become injured in the course of their duties for the Reich. I understand the Führer's office was informed of your bravery earlier this morning.'

The patient tugged against his restraints, tried to sit up, winced, then subsided back onto his pillow. 'Here? Mein Gott, the Commander himself... What a great honour... '

The patient's voice was strong and resolute despite his ordeal, and the doctor nodded approvingly.

'Yes, Leutnant. You are a shining example of our Aryan youth defending the Volk against the enemy within. And we shall ensure that you are properly introduced to the great man.'

'But I still don't really remember what happened to me... '

'No matter. Your courage in defending yourself against enemies of the Reich ensures that you will be the star attraction during this august visit.'

The doctor swept out of the cubicle, leaving the nurse behind to fuss around the bed, ensuring that everything was tidy for the VIP visitation. Erpenbeck followed the nurse's movements with his eyes, leering appreciatively as she bent over to tuck in the sheets at the side of the bed. She glared at him and strode smartly out.

Three o'clock arrived and, soon after, there was a distant flurry of movement. Doors swung open and slammed shut, military footsteps pounded their way along the corridor outside. They halted as they reached the cubicle. A muted conversation took place, punctuated by repeated responses of, 'Jawohl, Herr Obergruppenführer'. Suddenly, the curtain was drawn aside and the Obergruppenführer himself appeared, accompanied by an aide, both in full dress uniform.

For one who bore such high office, Gottlob Berger cut a pretty undistinguished figure. Clean-shaven and of medium height, his severe features were faintly reminiscent of the Führer himself. His bearing was that of a man accustomed to being obeyed without question, although his military posture was at odds with his well-fed midriff which strained against a stiff black leather belt. The aide, a tall, well-built individual, stood to one side, clutching an important-looking sheaf of papers.

'Ach, ja,' said Berger to the aide, seeking to adopt an informal tone, although both men were clearly uncomfortable in a hospital environment. Still, duty was duty, and the young man lying in the bed had clearly suffered for the Volk and the Reich. A quick exchange of words, a shake of the hand and a photograph should suffice, and then Berger could be on his merry way to deal with more important matters of state. 'Photographer!' he barked. Leaning over the patient, he said, 'Now, Leutnant, er… '

He turned swiftly to his aide and glared at him. The man cast a nervous eye down the first sheet of paper and stuttered, 'Er… er… Erpenbeck, Herr Obergruppenführer.'

'Of course, Leutnant Erpenbeck.'

The curtain twitched, and a tubby, middle-aged bespectacled individual in an overcoat wielding a press camera with a flash unit attached peered into the cubicle. The aide waved him in.

'It is a great honour, Herr Obergruppenführer,' replied the Leutnant huskily. The patient was clearly embarrassed at having to lie flat on his back in the presence of such an important superior officer. And, given the restraints on his hands, a Hitler salute was pretty well out of the question.

Berger said stiffly, 'The doctor here has been telling me of your single-handed efforts to face down a band of Communist hooligans in defence of the honest burghers of Nuremberg.'

Erpenbeck opened his mouth to respond, but thought better of it, not least because he still couldn't remember a single thing about what he was supposed to have achieved.

'On behalf of the Reich, I must congratulate you on your conduct which, er, matches that of our finest young officers, and wish you a speedy recovery and a rapid return to your duties. Courage and self-sacrifice, you... er... are a fine example of our proud military and a credit to, er, all our young men of today.'

Berger stuck out his hand, realised that the Leutnant was not exactly in a position to shake hands with him, so he stood uncomfortably by the bed and stared at the photographer. Erpenbeck lifted his head up as far as he could, there was a loud pop and a brief blaze of white light, the cameraman nodded, turned on his heel and departed, followed by the aide, who first whispered briefly to Berger.

Left alone with his superior officer, Erpenbeck was clearly ill at ease. Berger leaned closer to him and said in a conspiratorial whisper, 'My understanding from my briefing papers is that you, er, have been entrusted with confidential duties relating to the... er... resettlement of members of the local Jewish population?'

'Jawohl, Herr Obergruppenführer.'

'Keep up the good work, young man. We in the leadership of the Party recognise that this kind of task is not perhaps part of the main thrust of the obligations a soldier might be expected to carry out... er... but it is greatly valued nonetheless. Don't let the great circumcised Jewish hordes get the better of you, eh? We Germans are proud to retain all our manhood, are we not? Every last little bit, eh?'

A forced laugh and the patient nodded furiously, Berger stepped back, saluted him with a perfunctory 'Heil Hitler!' and marched off, entangling himself with the curtain in his haste to leave.

From outside, the aide pulled the curtain out of the way and the pair stomped off, presumably in pursuit of the next suitable patient for a quick handshake and a photograph. Leutnant Erpenbeck lay back, basking in the afterglow of the distinguished visit and the prospect of a publicity photograph in the local Nürnberger Zeitung.

The curtained-off cubicle lapsed back into silence. A few feeble buzzes from the fly, now caught in a web in the high window, which quickly ceased as it seemingly resigned itself to its fate. Flushed with pride at the words of the leader of the SS, the patient smirked in self-congratulation. Phrases like 'courage and self-sacrifice' and 'credit to all our young men' rattled around in his head and he eagerly looked forward to boasting to his fellow officers about his heroic single-handed battle against the forces of Communism and the sincere words of praise from his highly distinguished visitor. A half-an-hour or so passed and the patient drifted off into a light sleep.

Suddenly, he was disturbed by the sound of the doctor and nurse engaged in an earnest discussion outside the cubicle. Then, the curtain was jerked roughly aside and the two of them stood earnestly observing the patient.

'Shall we tell him?' whispered the doctor in a sombre tone. The nurse raised a hand to her face and replied conspiratorially, 'Sooner or later we'll have to. No time like the present, is there?'

Erpenbeck struggled to make out what they were saying. The gravity of their tone caused his volatile mood to switch instantly from self-congratulation at the Obergruppenführer's words of praise to a nagging apprehension. What were the doctor and nurse so concerned about? Something must, surely, be seriously wrong with him, but he hadn't the least idea what it might be.

Perhaps his injuries were more severe than they had led him to believe. Maybe that was why he was restrained in the bed in this unusual manner. Perhaps his leg had been crushed or, God forbid, amputated. Or was it something even more sinister? He cast his mind back to the strange reaction of the nurse when he was relieving himself. She seemed to be seriously worried about something. Surely, he had not been damaged in the region of his manhood during the fight with the Communists. The mere thought terrified him. One unpleasant possibility after another whirled around in his head until he could restrain himself no longer.

'Doctor, what in God's name is wrong?' he half shouted. 'Why are you looking at me like that? What has really happened to me?'

For a second or two, the doctor and nurse ignored him and continued to whisper anxiously to one another. Then, as if suddenly making his mind up about a disagreeable duty, the doctor looked severely at Erpenbeck.

'Please do not raise your voice so, Leutnant Erpenbeck. Remember that there are many other patients here who are resting and trying to recover from injury or illness. Do please try to be calm.'

Calm? That was the last thing Erpenbeck felt. He waited anxiously as the doctor turned to the nurse and spoke to her in a grim undertone. She nodded and gestured to him to continue.

The doctor cleared his throat anxiously and said, 'Very well. We have some good news for you, Leutnant, but also some bad news.' He picked up the patient's notes from the bedside table and looked through them slowly.

'The good news is that your head did not suffer any serious damage in the affray last night.'

He paused, and Erpenbeck almost shouted, 'Then tell me what the bad… ' Remembering the doctor's injunction about the other patients, he lowered his voice and continued, '… what the bad news is, doctor.'

'First, though, to continue with the good news,' the doctor persisted, 'while you were asleep, you were taken to our state-of-the-art X-Ray department and your knee was examined from various angles.'

'And the results?'

'Results? Oh, the results. They were negative. Sorry to have misled you earlier. A suspected fracture of the tibia and fibula was actually nothing more than severe bruising and the nurse here will remove the plaster cast quite soon. We left it in place to impress your distinguished visitor.'

Doctor and nurse stood looking uncomfortably at their patient. When he could endure their silence no longer, Erpenbeck spoke up again.

'A-and the bad news?'

'Ah, yes, the bad news. Well, according to your notes'—the doctor closely examined the sheets of paper on the clipboard before continuing—'you were involved in an altercation with a group of Communists who decided to confront you. The heated exchanges ended up as an ugly brawl in which you distinguished yourself and earned yourself a moderate concussion as a result.

'While you were unconscious, an ambulance was called and you were transported here to the hospital.'

Another long pause. Erpenbeck was hanging on his every word as it was clear that the doctor was doing his best to delay informing him of something seriously unpleasant but, for now, he forced himself to remain silent and wait.

The doctor took a deep breath, then continued. 'However, in this place, nothing is quite as it seems. I have to tell you that the story of your courage and heroism in defending the Volk and the Reich was—a complete fabrication. There was no gang attacking you and your heroic deeds were entirely manufactured.'

Erpenbeck stared in astonishment. What did the doctor mean? A fabrication? If it was all made up, then what did happen and why was he here in a hospital bed?

'What actually took place was that you were so busy trying to seduce a young woman in the Zum Schwarzen Kater bar last night, that you did not notice that she had, how shall I put it, dropped an additional ingredient into your shot glass of schnapps. When she asked you to toast her as a prelude to taking her around to your apartment for fun and games, you tossed back the liquor and passed out on the spot. We had arrangements in place to assist you from the bar and transport you to where you find yourself now.'

The nurse stepped forward and, in a lecherous, thick sing-song Bavarian accent far removed from her previous clipped, professional tones, she taunted him, 'Remember, big boy, knock back your schnapps like a good little lad and we'll soon see what you are made of?'

Erpenbeck paled at the sound of her voice. The nurse was the girl in fishnet tights and the breathtaking split skirt who... Now, he began to hazily recall something of what happened the previous evening. He vaguely remembered chatting her up in the Zum Schwarzen Kater bar... or was it the other way around? Perhaps it was she who had picked him up instead.

'And you were brought here'—the doctor swept a hand round the cubicle—'to sleep off your potion, but not until after you had undergone a certain medical procedure.'

What is the man talking about now? Procedure? What procedure? Erpenbeck tried to force himself upright, but the room began to spin around him and his head collapsed back onto the pillow.

'That's probably the result of another little injection we gave you a while ago,' said the doctor, whose voice had suddenly switched from being serious and concerned to a much more severe and sinister tone.

'Before we go any further, Leutnant Erpenbeck, I must inform you that you are actually alone in this part of the hospital. This is a specially isolated ward and you can make as much noise as you please, because no one will hear you. No one at all.

'Now, you will listen to me very carefully and in total silence if you wish to leave this place in one piece. Any attempt to become violent towards us and there are a couple of very well-built security guards behind the curtain who are just aching for an excuse to teach you a lesson. Do not speak. Just listen and move your head in response. Do you understand me?'

Erpenbeck nodded dumbly. This crazy situation was going from bad to worse and he could not begin to comprehend what was going on. A few minutes ago he was a local hero, and now he was being threatened with all manner of unpleasantness. A host of disagreeable thoughts swirled around in his head as he tried to comprehend what exactly was happening to him.

'Right. Let us get down to business.' The nurse touched the doctor's arm as if to remind him of something. 'Oh, yes, before we go any further, I understand that a small group of your colleagues are on their way here to visit you soon and celebrate your alleged bravery, so we must not waste any time.' He gave the patient a steely look from behind his surgical mask.

'You are SS Leutnant Erich Wilhelm Erpenbeck?' A nod.

'Part of the SS team charged with the rounding up and transit of Jewish families to the Hauptbahnhof sidings for relocation elsewhere in the Reich?'

A second bemused nod.

'Four weeks ago, you were responsible for the work detail who evicted the Birnbaum family, father, mother and two daughters, one fourteen, the other just five, from number 49 Parkstrasse? During which, things went tragically wrong?'

Puzzlement mingled with a sense of dread and premonition. Erpenbeck looked pleadingly at his captors.

What was happening here? Why were they referring to that unfortunate incident in the Parkstrasse? What were they going to do to him? Was it some kind of mad act of vengeance? After all, he was only obeying orders like a loyal soldier of the Reich. And Berger himself had applauded him for his work.

'I asked a question,' demanded the doctor. Erpenbeck nodded again in reply.

'The younger daughter's name was Naomi. I am told that it means "pleasantness", although what happened to her was far from pleasant. Naomi, poor child, was profoundly deaf and, when one of the soldiers under your command grabbed her doll and flung it in the path of an oncoming tram, she tore herself free from her mother and rushed after it, unaware of the tons of metal hurtling towards her frail little body.

'Let me tell you that the tram didn't just kill her. It ripped her apart until the mess of blood and bones remaining was completely unrecognisable as human body parts. Fortunately for you, Leutnant, I cannot show you what the actions of your soldier did to that child. But her doll is a different matter.'

Out of the corner of his eye, Erpenbeck saw a blur of movement as the nurse threw a small object onto the bed before his horrified gaze.

'This doll was recovered from the undercarriage of the tram, missing an eye, one arm torn off, and covered in its owner's blood. Still, it's in a far better state than poor Naomi. Look at it, Leutnant. Just look and consider.

Directly or indirectly, you see before you the consequence of your brutal actions.'

Erpenbeck visibly shrank back from the grotesque, twisted, bloodstained object before him, which had once been an innocent child's beloved plaything.

'But, of course,' continued the doctor harshly, 'she was only Jewish. And Jews don't matter to you, Leutnant, do they? You and your soldiers just laughed when she was crushed under the tram wheels, didn't you? One less Jew, one less subhuman in our pure Aryan Reich!'

To his complete shock and embarrassment, Erpenbeck heard himself beginning to sob, as if something inside him had snapped, some part of him had collapsed and fallen apart. Where did these damned emotions come from, he demanded of himself? I am a soldier of the Reich, simply obeying orders. Sometimes, matters do get a little unpleasant, but that is all part of the sacred duties which I am called upon to perform and which I carry out gladly. But, in spite of himself, the tears were coursing down his face and he could not understand why.

Suddenly, a vivid, compelling image flooded into his tormented mind, of a bright sunlit day years before, in the orchard of his parents' garden. His sister was riding back and forth on a swing his father had made for her and had suspended from an apple tree branch. As she did so, she sang quietly to herself. One second, she was happily suspended in the warm summer air, her skirts billowing in the breeze, the next, there came a loud crack like gunfire, the branch snapped and his sister hurtled through the air, dashed bloodily against a tree trunk—and then the vision went blank as it always did at that instant.

He could not save her, he wailed as he had then. He could not reach out and save his little sister.

The doctor waited until Erpenbeck had calmed down. The man seemed to be having a serious bout of conscience at the pitiful sight of the broken doll which must have triggered painful memories from his own past. So much the better. It took several minutes for the patient to regain a measure of composure. The nurse reached forward, gathered up the doll and held it in her arms.

'But, Leutnant,' the doctor continued even more severely, 'that isn't why we brought you here and hospitalised you. No, your involvement with Naomi's death was grievous enough, but we turn now to consider someone else and her fate.'

At that moment, the nurse slipped out through the curtain, leaving the doctor alone with his patient.

'This part is just between you and me, Leutnant Erpenbeck. I want to spare the nurse a repetition of the unpleasant details of what I have to tell you next. Late that same evening, I was taking my regular walk through the main streets of the city. It was a chilly night and the air was fresh after a long shower of rain. I was deep in thought about the current situation in our country, how the Nazi Party was threatening to destroy everything of value, all sense of humanity and decency in the mad pursuit of a deranged ideology, when I suddenly heard someone crying softly.

'It was a raw, rasping, deeply distressing sound. Looking down an alley, I saw what looked like a bundle of rags in a doorway. Rather like Naomi's doll, I suppose. But it wasn't a doll at all. It was a young girl of fourteen who had been brutally raped, beaten and abandoned for dead in an alleyway by none other than'—he pointed severely at the patient—'you, Leutnant Erich Wilhelm Erpenbeck.'

The patient was utterly motionless, transfixed by the doctor's words. How in God's name did these people know about that harmless little episode? And who the hell are they? What did they want of him? I only took what was mine by right. She was just a little Jewish bitch, after all.

The doctor continued, 'Doubtless, the girl had caught your filthy eye when you were rounding up the Birnbaum family. Later, you ordered one of your men to fetch her from the wagon in the goods yards of the Hauptbahnhof and bring her up to your apartment. In fact, I know that's exactly what happened, because that's what she told me herself.'

During this narrative, Erpenbeck's face displayed a kaleidoscope of indignation, shame, fear, bewilderment and sheer terror. Part of him demanded, What of it? She was only a worthless Jewess, just a bit of fun. She'd have been dead in a few days or weeks at the most. The other half burned with the image of his sister swinging from the apple branch in her billowing skirts, then flying through the air and falling, falling…

'I don't suppose a young man like yourself can begin to understand what it is like for a girl to have intercourse for the first time. It should be a special occasion, marking the transition from girlhood to full womanhood, filled with apprehension, certainly, but also of the promise of maturity and the expectation of adult life and love.'

The doctor stopped for a moment and looked the Leutnant straight in the eye.

'Which you shattered in a few brief moments of lustful gratification, Leutnant. Or to call it by its proper name, rape. You acted like an animal, destroying her dreams, her aspirations, her faith in humanity. A young girl is now appalled beyond words at what happened to her, horrified that anyone could commit an act so ghastly, so barbaric, against any human being—even a Jewess. Imagine that happening to your own sister.'

The words shot through the Leutnant like a bolt of lightning. How in God's name did this man know he had a sister and how she had died? The situation was becoming utterly unbearable. He almost cried out for the doctor to stop, but he recalled the man's strict admonition that he be silent and listen.

The doctor had paused. He too was caught up in the emotional trauma of the moment and needed a few moments to regain his own composure. He took a deep breath and continued.

'Did you know—or care—what her name was?'

Despite himself, Erpenbeck shook his head. How was he to know what the wretched girl was called?

'Then, I'll tell you, Leutnant. Her name was—and still is, thank God—Ruth. And let me tell you what the meaning of her name is. It signifies "friend". But you certainly offered no friendship to poor Ruth. It is a credit to the remarkable strength of character of someone so young that she is gradually beginning to recover from the nightmare you inflicted on her. In God's name, Leutnant Erpenbeck, are there no vestiges of humanity left in your miserable body?'

For a long time, the doctor allowed the words to hang in the air, giving the man ample time to absorb what he had been told and to ponder what more might happen to him as a result of his actions.

'Now, comes the really interesting part. After my nurse and I had treated the poor girl, I wondered what, if anything, could be done to go some little way towards ensuring that you made amends to Naomi and Ruth. And, being a doctor, there was one little possibility which came into my mind as both an appropriate punishment and a means of constantly reminding you of what you did when you simply "obeyed orders", and when you treated a human being like a disposable toy, something for you to play with and then discard. Like Naomi's doll.

'It involved taking you on a little detour to my home, where my nurse and I have a consulting room in which I can perform minor surgical procedures. Now, I wonder what that particular procedure might be? Maybe one that would be particularly appropriate for a man who raped a Jewish girl?'

Again, the doctor paused, allowing Erpenbeck to come to terms with what he had been told and for him to try and puzzle out what manner of punishment had been meted out to him.

It took him several minutes to do so, but then a sudden connection clicked in his mind. When he was peeing earlier, the nurse had looked strangely at his manhood. She was clearly concerned about something. He realised that her expression, half hidden behind her mask, was not one of admiration, but of anxiety. Hers had not been the impersonal touch of a nurse performing a routine procedure, but that of one seeking to avoid inflicting pain on a very tender part of his body, which had just been operated on. And, then, the doctor had stressed that his supposed offence was against a Jewess. There was a long silence, then...

'No!' shrieked Erpenbeck. 'No, no, no!'

He tried to reach out to inspect his lower regions, forgetting his hands were still firmly tied.

The doctor said, 'You will see that, on your bedside table, there is a little glass bottle. In it, I have thoughtfully preserved a little circle of flesh which, until very recently was attached to you. The operation, as you will know, is called—circumcision, in other words, the surgical removal of the prepuce from the penis.'

Erpenbeck's face went grey with utter horror as he turned to examine the bottle.

'Normally performed on male babies of the Jewish faith, the procedure with older children and adults can, unfortunately, be quite painful. Recovery time may well be counted in weeks, and the penis will probably become inflamed and painfully itchy. However, that should make an interesting talking point with your colleagues in the showers after gymnastics or swimming.' The doctor checked his watch.

'Nurse!' he called. The nurse duly re-entered the cubicle. 'When did you say the Leutnant's visitors were due?'

She looked at her watch. 'Sometime in the next half hour, I believe, doctor.'

'Then that will give our SS officer here more than enough time to think things over. And we must not forget to tell his friends what the little procedure was from which he is recovering.'

'Come on, nurse, we do have other patients to attend to.' He looked back towards Erpenbeck. 'Oh, and by the way, the distinguished visitor you received, Obergruppenführer Berger, was not for real either. An actor friend from northern Germany was here on a visit, so I invited him to try out his skills as an impersonator. But the photograph which was taken—that was genuine enough. I'll be keeping it as, how shall I say, part of an insurance policy. The other part'—he stepped forward and picked up the glass bottle—'I'll take that with me, just now, if you don't mind. Unless you want to show it off to your friends?'

Erpenbeck gave a meaningless, despairing gesture.

'And, nurse, could you just undo his wrists? He may now wish to inspect the affected part of his body.'

The nurse duly obliged and the two of them left.

Rage alternated with terror in Erpenbeck's mind as he tried to come to terms with everything that had happened since he had regained consciousness in this damned cubicle. He clawed at the bedcovers, tearing them back to reveal his private parts neatly covered in a surgical bandage, on the end of which bloodstains were clearly visible, doubtless caused by the operation.

He shook his head from side to side as if to try and cast out from him the experiences of the past hour or so, to dismiss them as some kind of nightmare from which he would wake up and find himself in bed in his own apartment. The whole thing just had to be unreal, it must, it simply must.

Then, in the distance, he heard a door open and close and the sound of subdued male voices. Footsteps drew ever closer until they reached a crescendo outside the cubicle.

'Stop,' the doctor's voice could be heard saying. 'Are you gentlemen the visitors Leutnant Erpenbeck is expecting?'

A muttered reply.

'Then, I am sorry that I must disappoint you. He is very distressed right now because of the news I have given him about the nature of his injuries. He'll be making a full recovery in time but, for the immediate future, he is too weak and upset to receive visitors. I can, however, give you some details of his condition.'

More mutterings, followed by expressions of shock and surprise, and the footsteps clattered hastily away down the corridor. Again, a distant door opened and shut, then silence.

Erpenbeck was beside himself with terror and humiliation and, as he twisted abruptly from left to right as if trying to shake the whole nightmare out of existence, he caught sight of his Luger pistol. Impulsively, he reached across and grabbed the weapon, his fingers scrabbling to grasp the trigger. He took one more horrified look at the blood-stained bandage covering his penis, then he slowly and deliberately lifted the gun to his mouth.

In the window, the fly, still tangled in the spider's web, had regained the strength to buzz again frantically as the sticky threads wrapped themselves ever tighter around its tiny body. Then the sound swiftly died into silence.

Sitting rigidly to attention, tears streaming down his bronzed features, SS Leutnant Erpenbeck cried out, 'Heil Hitler!' and pulled the trigger.

Click.

Another shout of 'Heil Hitler!', this time more of a croak than a soldier's proud salutation, and he pressed the trigger a second time.

Click.

One last feeble buzz from the fly.

A third, fourth frantic pull of the trigger. Click. Click.

Incredulous, the patient dragged the barrel of the pistol out of his mouth and checked the weapon. Empty. Bloody empty. With an angry despairing cry, he flung the useless gun to the ground and broke down into choking sobs.

When the patient's outburst finally began to subside, the curtain parted once again. Doctor and nurse came into the cubicle. The nurse moved swiftly to the side of the patient, looked at his face, then at the bloody bandaged member. She looked at the doctor with a gesture of confusion.

'What is going on here?' demanded the doctor. 'What is the cause of all this uproar?'

At first, the patient did not speak, but pointed despairingly at his bandages.

'What have you done to me?' he finally croaked, the tears continuing to trickle down his cheeks once more. 'What have you done to... me... '

'That,' said the doctor, 'you must judge for yourself. And you should ask yourself instead what you have done to Naomi and Ruth. And probably many others as well.'

The nurse moved closer to his side and reached forward to undo the surgical dressing.

'No, stop, don't... '

With a practised movement of the hand, she pulled the dressing away. Erpenbeck shut his eyes, not daring to witness the sight of his bloodied and mutilated manhood. After a long silence, the doctor spoke softly to him.

'What have we done? Why, Leutnant, all you have to do is to take a look for yourself.'

Erpenbeck still held his eyes firmly shut. But, after a long moment of indecision, he opened a cautious eye and saw—a perfectly normal uncircumcised adult penis, untouched by the knife, but at its most pathetically flaccid.

'And, whenever you take an admiring look at your genitals again, Leutnant, remember this day, remember that I took pity on you and did not circumcise you, but you, by contrast, did not show a shred of pity for that young girl. Never, ever again conduct yourself towards any of your fellow creatures as you did Naomi and Ruth. Even though they were mere Jews. By the way, the bottle contains a little ring of pigskin, not your own precious flesh. And the friends of yours who were trying to visit you? That, Leutnant Erpenbeck, was another piece of playacting for your benefit. In fact, this whole episode has been put together in order to teach you a painful lesson you will never forget.'

As Erpenbeck coughed and frantically tossed his head from side to side, the nurse moved swiftly forward. Years of practice had taught her to anticipate when a patient was about to be violently sick, and a bedpan appeared magically in her hand.

Erpenbeck heaved and heaved until his throat ached and his whole body shook. Images of his sister on the swing merged with his shameful recollection of the little deaf girl running towards the tram, his assault on Ruth, the dignity with which she stared into his twisted features as he brutally penetrated her. He hardly noticed the needle pricking his arm and the injection which sent him into the instant, merciful release of unconsciousness.

Outside the cubicle, the five shook each other by the hand. Johann and Elise were still quaking at the emotional roller coaster ride they had just experienced, but they too felt the exhilaration and relief of the moment. Rudi congratulated them for playing a couple of brilliant roles, which he had carefully tutored them to perform. Johann had acted his part to perfection.

Max held up his camera and threatened to take a photograph of all present. And Thomas, who played the aide to the SS Chief, applauded them all.

'Shame about one thing, though,' Thomas said with a half smile. 'You shouldn't have emptied the bullets from his sidearm. Then he really wouldn't be able to act like an animal ever again.'

Johann nodded thoughtfully, then he held up the small bottle to the light and said, 'Talking of an animal, what a waste of a perfectly good piece of pigskin I have here. Oh, dear, I think I'm about to throw the wrong bit of Leutnant Erpenbeck away!'

His words were greeted with laughter, and a huge sense of relief that their undertaking had gone so well. Now, all they had to do was remove Erpenbeck from his bed, transport him back to his apartment before he regained consciousness and remove all traces of their presence there.

Extract from the Nürnberger Zeitung June 1935,

Last night a blaze gutted a disused factory and warehouse on the Vorwärts industrial complex in the east of the city. The fire was evidently started deliberately. It is believed that petrol was used as an accelerant and that this act against German society was the work of a disaffected group of Communists who apparently used the warehouse as a hideout, because the burnt-out remains of a metal bed and an army issue pistol were found near the seat of the fire. Arrests are currently being made and punishments will be severe.

Chapter Eighteen

'Herr Feinlein, there's a telephone call for you from a Herr Leopold Bucher. I understand he is the Deputy Mayor. Shall I put him through?'

Max thought for a moment or two, then said, 'Very well, Eva.'

What on earth does he want? Where had he heard that name before? It must have been somewhere in the pages of the local press, where the Nazi leadership of Nuremberg featured prominently.

There was a click, and a self-important voice came on the line. 'Am I speaking to Chief Curator Feinlein?'

'Indeed you are, Herr Bürgermeister. It's a pleasure to talk to you.'

Max hoped his warm words did not have too cynical a ring about them.

'I am calling to ask you for your assistance and support in an undertaking I am planning for a charitable cause.'

Max did not reply but waited for Bucher to continue. From his tone of voice, this was clearly not a man to come with a begging bowl asking nicely, but one used to people obeying his orders without question.

'I recently moved into number 49 Parkstrasse.'

I know that address, thought Max. That's the Birnbaums' home I visited where the Böcklin painting used to hang. This Nazi must have requisitioned the place, and I bet he wants to continue the tradition of the annual exhibition and social evening for charity.

'I understand that the previous owners used to hold a much admired social event,' continued Bucher, clearing his throat. 'It involved an informal gathering with wine and hors d'oeuvres, together with a viewing of the previous owner's personal collection of works of art in the long gallery which runs the length of the rear of the building. I'd very much like to ensure that the tradition is continued on an annual basis, with the Winterhilfswerk as the charity, but I face something of a problem. When I moved in, the contents of the house had naturally been completely cleared out.'

I know, thought Max, I know. Nearly all of the paintings and objets d'art from the house ended up in my storerooms and I had to decide what to do with them. And I personally wouldn't use the bland phrase 'cleared out'. How about 'looted'?

'If I wanted to hold an exhibition I would have to start more or less from scratch. However, I do own one or two modest paintings myself.'

I bet you do, thought Max.

'So, I want to host a display of the kind of art which the Party seeks to promote, as a showpiece of National

Socialist creative painting, but I would need your assistance in doing so.'

As Bucher continued expanding on his plans, Max's brain started to work overtime. This man had expropriated the house and now he had the gall to try and step into Birnbaum's shoes as an art collector and benefactor. And, to add insult to injury, Bucher wanted him to put together a collection of paintings, largely pilfered from the homes of 'enemies of the Reich' and set him up with an exhibition of art which conformed to the National Socialist view of what was culturally acceptable.

As Bucher rambled pompously on, the germ of an idea was beginning to form in Max's mind, a possible means of exacting retribution against Bucher. He would have to contact Johann and the others in order to put a proper plan together but he was sure that this could represent an outstanding opportunity for the group. If they managed to engineer Bucher's downfall, it would have a huge impact on the city itself and possibly way beyond the local level too.

'So, what do you think, Herr Feinlein? Could you assist me in this matter? I should be most grateful.'

'What? Yes, of course... yes.' For a second or two, Max was caught off-guard by his question, which was little less than an order dressed up as a polite request, but he swiftly regained his composure.

'Certainly, Herr Bucher. Let me see... Perhaps the best course of action would be for me to inspect our holdings of contemporary and historically approved art and make some appropriate selections. As you will understand, our main focus here is the art and sculpture of previous centuries but, as you may know, large numbers of works come under our guardianship from time to time and I am sure that I can assemble a reasonably representative collection.'

Guardianship, thought Max bitterly. Now who's peddling euphemisms?

'It will enable you to present an exhibition within a relatively short space of time. I would like to propose that you place the mounting and choice of pictures in my hands and those of my staff. We would be able to hang the works in your gallery in good time for the exhibition and would be happy to be on hand during the event in order to render any assistance or support you may need. Naturally, there would be other matters such as a catalogue and a description of each work to attend to, and that is certainly something we can undertake on your behalf.'

Bucher sounded delighted. 'Well, I must say I am very pleased indeed with your cooperative response, Herr Feinlein. I should be delighted to take up your offer and look forward to meeting you in due course.'

Max had a sudden thought. 'One further matter, Herr Bürgermeister. Would it be impertinent for me to suggest that you and your staff give us the freedom of the long gallery until such time as the opening of the exhibition takes place? That will allow us to prosecute our work as efficiently as possible, and also I am anxious to surprise you with our expertise in mounting an exhibition such as this. Oh, and one further matter: I'd prefer my contribution and that of my colleagues to be anonymous. Otherwise, we should be overburdened with similar requests from all and sundry.'

Bucher was only too eager to concur. The poor man clearly had no knowledge of art and cultural matters and had probably been propelled into the project by a pushy wife anxious to show off her new status and possessions to other members of the local Party aristocracy.

'Certainly, certainly. I shall ensure that my staff put the keys to the long gallery at your disposal. There is a rear entrance so that you need not disturb us during your preparations. Once again, thank you so much, Herr Feinlein.'

As he put down the receiver, Max heard a double click on the line. Odd, he thought, that sounds as if my secretary is listening in on my conversations. I wonder if it's just nosiness on her part, or something more sinister. He needed to contact Johann and decided that it would be prudent to determine whether Fräulein Eva was still at her listening post as he did so. He picked up the receiver.

'Eva, you may go to your lunch now. I may be out of the office when you return. I have to put together arrangements for a planned out-of-house exhibition in the near future.'

'I... I'll do that, Herr Feinlein. I'll switch the phone line directly through to your desk.'

'Thank you, Eva.' Was he being paranoid, or was her hesitation an attempt to avoid a slip of the tongue? Was she about to say, 'I know', which would have given the game away? When he heard the door to the outer office close, he picked up the receiver and dialled Johann's number.

'Hello?' It was Elise's voice.

'Max Feinlein here. There's a little matter I'd like to discuss with you, Johann, and the others too, and I think we should all get together for a meeting.'

'Certainly. Johann was going to suggest a gathering at the Castle Room next Thursday evening at the usual time, just for an update on our plans.'

'I'll be there. Goodbye.'

Max replaced the receiver, rose painfully from his desk and made his way to the outer office. He had another person to contact, but his young artist friend did not possess a phone so he would have to visit him in person.

As he entered the outer office, he was surprised to see Eva still standing by her desk, nervously reaching into her handbag.

'I thought you had left for lunch,' he said.

'Oh, yes, er, Herr Feinlein. I came back because I had left my spectacles on my desk somewhere... Ah, here they are. Silly of me. I must rush now. Goodbye, sir.'

Max nodded. As she left, he wondered if she had slipped back to listen to his call. No, I really mustn't become paranoid, he told himself, otherwise, I'd be looking over my shoulder all the time. She is probably telling the truth, but it does no harm to be extra prudent.

He picked up the phone on Eva's desk. Listening to the dialling tone, he realised that she hadn't set the line to direct calls to his office as she had claimed. Perhaps it was just an oversight on her part. After all, she was only a silly young slip of a girl. Come on, Max, you really are beginning to see danger lurking around every corner. Or are you just imagining things? I'd better inform Johann and Elise about this, just in case.

The public phone booth in the café across the road from the museum was empty, and Max dialled the Voss's number. This time Johann answered and Max began by apologising for troubling them twice in ten minutes.

'No problem at all, Max. Is it about Thursday's meeting?'

'No... well, yes, I suppose it is. I have a strong suspicion that my personal secretary is listening in to my phone calls. I don't want to sound unduly suspicious but I believe we should be extremely careful not to risk our conversations being overheard.'

'What makes you think she is eavesdropping?'

Max explained what had happened a little earlier and Johann pondered for a moment.

'I don't think you are being overcautious at all. You are an important figure in the local art world and the Nazis are keen to ensure that confiscated art is handled according to their demands. They may have a hold of some kind over your secretary. Their surveillance, if it's taking place, may be purely precautionary on their part, but let's try a little experiment.'

He explained to Max that he would arrange for the meeting to be held at his house instead and that he would ask his friend at the Mautkeller to let him know if any official enquiries had been made about a private gathering there at the same time.

Max thanked him and then added, 'The reason I asked for a meeting is that I believe we have a real opportunity to topple a seriously unpleasant local Nazi Party chief from his perch.'

He went on to describe the phone call from Bucher and, before he could complete his first sentence, Johann cut in excitedly.

'It's an open secret that his wife desperately wanted that house, and there is a strong rumour doing the rounds that Bucher arranged for the arrest of the Birnbaums just so he could get his hands on the property. He sounds like an excellent target, but do you have any suggestions on how to go about causing his downfall?'

Max replied that indeed he had the beginnings of a plan, but he would rather wait until their meeting, which would give him time to think the whole matter through more thoroughly.

After spending some time in the museum storeroom, Max unearthed a small selection of pictures which he was sure would serve his purpose in the exhibition Bucher had requested. Now, he needed to visit Kaspar and talk through with him the kind of images he wanted him to paint. It would involve Kaspar coming to the museum and examining the originals, but he was sure he could organise that without attracting undue attention. The plan was rapidly maturing in his mind and he could hardly wait until the following Thursday to explain it to the others.

Chapter Nineteen

It had been a long, rowdy evening in the Sommerkabarett and there would be many sore heads the next morning. The build-up to the autumn Party rally in Nuremberg was just beginning and trainloads of high-ranking officials and functionaries were in the city making initial preparations for the annual event. The streets were to be decked out with banners, special seating had to be arranged, guest lists drawn up and a thousand and one other things had to be organised so that everything could run like clockwork. But, for the most part, the planners and organisers were free in the evenings, and the Sommerkabarett was packed out as it had a growing reputation as the place to go for political satire, top acrobatic acts and dancers with the longest and shapeliest legs in Bavaria.

Rudi had been on top form and the audience had roared its approval of his quick change acts and his comic routine. Little Marlene appeared to be a particular favourite of the crowd, as did his Hitler impersonation. The jokes went down pretty well too. He began with a classic, 'How do you start a German joke? Answer: First, you look over your shoulder... ' After that, as he said to himself, the audience would laugh at the instructions on a jar of Sauerkraut. After all, they were Nazis and seriously drunken ones at that.

He left the stage to a standing ovation and a budding riot in one corner, where two inebriated officers were fighting over a girl. The stage manager even gave Rudi a pat on the back and, from him, that was praise indeed. But it was an exhausting way of receiving plaudits too. Rudi collapsed into his chair in the tiny cubicle which served as his dressing room with a huge sigh of relief. He stared at his cracked image in the dirty mirror, that of a sad-faced clown, the persona he adopted for the climax of his act, a tragicomic figure lamenting the departure of the Weimar Republic and the advent of the Third Reich.

As he leaned forward to begin removing his bright red lipstick and the black tears from his cheek, he heard a slight movement behind him but, before he could react, his whole world went dark as a hood was slammed down over his head and tied tightly. A second later, his hands were securely cuffed behind his back. He began to protest, but a harsh, sinister whisper forced him into silence.

'Not a word, otherwise you will be in serious trouble, my friend.' He received a sharp prod in the ribs to reinforce the message.

Oh no, panicked Rudi, they must have found me out. God help me—and my friends too, if these people know about them. He felt himself being roughly jerked to his feet and the harsh voice snarled, 'Is he ready to go?'

A second, equally unpleasant voice snapped an affirmative answer and Rudi was bundled out of the door.

He was half dragged, half frog-marched down the narrow corridor which led to the back of the building. His captors forced him down a flight of stairs to the basement exit, well away from any fans who might be waiting for him, and out into the street. He had scarcely a second or two to savour the fresh night air when he was yanked to an abrupt halt and bustled into the back of a car. One of his captors shoved him across the seat and slid in alongside him.

The driver's door slammed shut, the engine started and the vehicle sped away with a grinding of gears over the rough cobbles of the alleyway and out into the busy main street which ran through the heart of the city. Rudi was soon completely disorientated and frightened out of his wits.

After about twenty minutes, the car swerved sharply left with a squeal of tyres and stopped. The driver wound down the window, spoke a few words which Rudi couldn't catch, and the car jerked forward again. When it came to a standstill a few moments later, he was pulled out, dragged across a gravelled area, up a flight of steps, through a set of doors into an echoing marble-floored space, then down another set of steps, along a carpeted corridor and into a side room. He was forcibly shoved into a chair and he could hear his captors turn on their heels and march away. The door banged shut, then, total silence.

Rudi determined to put on a show of calmness and courage and just sit quietly and wait for whatever was going to happen to him. But, after ten minutes, his resolve was beginning to weaken and he was becoming increasingly fearful and restless. Suddenly, he heard his captors return. The door swung open and a voice sounding like that of an officer ordered the other two men to take up position behind him. There was a scrape of a chair and a long silence. Then he felt the sudden heat of a bright light being switched on. The hood was roughly dragged off his head and, for several seconds, he sat there blinking half-blind in the harsh glare.

On the edge of his vision, he became vaguely aware of rich curtains, flowered wallpaper and a thick grey and blue patterned carpet and wondered if all Gestapo interrogation cells were decorated in a similar fashion. Or was this some device to trick him into a sense of false security?

A minute or so later, the light was pushed a little to one side, and his attention was grabbed by the unwavering emotionless stare of two intense blue eyes across the narrow table from him. He blinked repeatedly, trying to make sense of what his own eyes were telling him. His heart pounded violently as the uniformed figure sitting opposite him gradually resolved into a sinister and terribly familiar shape.

No, no, he said to himself. This is not possible. It cannot be true. I must be in some kind of nightmare from which I will, surely, soon wake up. He shook his head again and stared across the table. Oh God, he thought. It really is him. I am well and truly done for.

Chapter Twenty

The man facing him gave the terrified Rudi a long, penetrating stare. Then, in that familiar, grating, staccato voice he snapped, 'I witnessed your pathetic so-called performance this evening from the back of the auditorium at the Sommerkabarett. I came incognito to see for myself if what I had heard about you is true.' A nerve-wracking pause.

'Did you think I would find your antics amusing? Mocking the leader of the German Reich? Demeaning my character and my ability with women? Scorning the achievements of the Party? And venturing to express sympathy with Jews and gypsies and Communist scum of the earth? And, then, you top it all by dressing up like a clown and actually lamenting the passing of the Weimar Republic? Are you totally out of your senses, man?'

Adolf Hitler beat an angry fist on the table to underline his words and, for a long while, maintained his hypnotic stare.

Rudi was fearfully preparing himself for the very worst that could happen to him, from agonising sessions in the Gestapo torture chambers to a long, lingering death in a concentration camp. And God knows what would happen to his friends if they too were captured by the Gestapo. All their aspirations would end in nothing but suffering and tragedy, and the Nazi Reich would march on regardless, crushing them beneath its jackboots. He was beginning to experience a wave of the most intense despair when the most extraordinary thing happened.

Adolf Hitler grabbed his cap, threw it on the table and roared with laughter. His two companions, who had been standing behind Rudi, joined in with the merriment.

Rudi, comedian, quick-change artist and Hitler impersonator extraordinaire, had never experienced such a welter of contradictory emotions in his life: total bewilderment, an overwhelming sense of relief and incredulity, all tangled up with a burning desire to slap himself very hard and wake up from what must be the most bizarre fantasy imaginable. He could not believe what happened next.

Hitler tore off his moustache, stood up, still vainly seeking to subdue his eruption of mirth, and said, in the most un-Hitler-like deep voice, 'You should see your little face, Rudolf Fischer. Here, let me shake you by the hand and welcome you to the club.' He reached across the table with his arm outstretched. Rudi's arms were still bound and the man ordered their release.

Rudi nervously shook hands, still utterly bewildered. 'C-club?' he stuttered. 'What club?'

'First of all,' said the supposed Führer, 'let me introduce myself. Like you, I am an actor, and my name is Hans Castorp. Secondly, you will want to know what on earth I am doing here and, even more important, why you have been brought here.'

Rudi was gradually beginning to calm down but was still totally mystified by what was happening to him.

'What I am about to tell you,' continued Hans, 'is top secret, and now I am deadly serious. One word of this to anyone and you will find yourself in serious trouble. And, nowadays, you'll have a pretty fair idea of what "serious trouble" means?'

Rudi grinned with relief and nodded. 'Like dead, or being torn limb from limb in a Gestapo cell? Or both?'

'Precisely. I can see that we are going to get on very well indeed. But, first, let me give you some background to our activities. Around five years ago, before Herr Hitler came to power, there was a serious attempt on his life which very nearly succeeded. A disaffected ex-soldier had managed to get close to him at a Party rally, but an SS officer wrestled him to the ground, getting shot and wounded for his bravery. Just imagine how terrible it would have been if the ex-soldier had succeeded.'

Rudi was enough of an actor to detect the faintest note of irony in that comment and he responded in kind with the ghost of a smile.

'So, it was decided that a secret unit, codenamed Double Eagle, be established which would provide a very special kind of protection for the Party leader on occasions when his safety might be considered at risk.'

Rudi let out a huge sigh of relief. The penny, to coin a phrase, had dropped. His heart rate began to return to something approaching normal and his breathing was coming under control.

Hans said, 'I see that you are quick to understand what our unit is charged with, and also why it is you are here.

'This isn't an interview, by the way. You have got the job. I have watched your impression of the Führer at the Cabaret several times in the last couple of weeks. You have the talent, the flexibility and, above all, the sheer bravado to take on this role. Of course, you'll need some additional voice training, as Hitler's verbal delivery has quite different qualities when speaking to a small political or social gathering than it does when addressing the nation from the Party rostrum. By the way,' he added, reaching in his pocket for a large handkerchief, 'you'd better wipe off that clown's face right now, as you wouldn't want to be walking the streets in bright red lipstick, would you? People might get the wrong idea.'

Rudi took the cloth and rubbed his face vigorously.

Hans nodded to the two men behind Rudi. 'You may leave us now.'

The two men crossed the room, opened and closed the door, and Hans and Rudi were left alone.

'As you may have gathered, this isn't Gestapo Headquarters but a private house which acts as our main base in Bavaria and whose previous occupants had the misfortune to display overtly left-wing tendencies. They were summarily dispatched to an unknown location and won't be heard from again. I'm sorry if my two subordinates were a bit rough with you. They do like to indulge in a bit of playacting themselves, all as part of, what they're pleased to call, the softening up process of potential candidates and others in their tender care.

'I have acted as Hitler's double on many occasions in the past and I'm convinced that you are more than capable of joining our team. I cannot tell you how many of us there are but it's only a handful, and some of them specialise in standing in for other members of the High Command.'

Rudi felt bold enough to venture a comment. 'I bet it's not easy to find anyone who would even want to be capable of being Goering... '

Hans gave a short, humourless laugh. 'We do have one unfortunate individual who is pretty convincing in that role. So good, in fact, that he is once rumoured to have gone to the Goering estate at Carinhall and... but I mustn't betray state secrets, must I?'

Rudi smiled and nodded in agreement. After a pause, he said tentatively, 'May I speak openly?'

'There are no witnesses here, as you can see,' said Hans carefully.

'I am not the Führer's greatest fan,' Rudi admitted. He might as well be honest, as there was no way he could act as a double unless it was clear on what kind of terms he would consent to play the part. 'In fact, quite the contrary.'

Hans held up a hand. 'As you may have gathered, neither am I. I sent my two security guards out of the room, not least, so that I could explore this rather sensitive issue with you because I did pick up on your reaction to my observation on the assassination attempt on our beloved leader. I also have other very good reasons to believe you are not exactly one of the Party faithful.

'I too have mixed feelings about what I do, but I have discovered—how shall I put it?—that I can exploit my acting role in positive ways which the Party would be horrified at if they found out about them and, if they did, I'd be on the next train to Dachau.'

Rudi looked thoughtfully at him, then said, 'In that case, I volunteer. Although I do have the impression that my options are fairly limited.'

'Indeed they are,' said Hans, 'especially after one of your recent exploits came to my attention.'

Rudi stared at him, a worried expression on his face.

'In fact, you owe me something of a favour. Remember how dark and cold it was in the local goods yard when you last paid it a late-night visit?'

The question shocked Rudi to the core. 'How did you... '

'Find out about your subversive and successful rescue attempt on the Birnbaum family? Because, quite simply, your acting was too convincing for your own good. The guard whom your co-conspirator put to sleep, so to speak, was a regular fan of the Sommerkabarett and he was convinced he had recognised you.

'Fortunately, I have friends in the right places who quickly responded to his unwise assertion and, soon afterwards, the man was sworn to secrecy and offered two options: a promotion and relocation for himself and his family to a comfortable post as a security officer in our

Buenos Aires embassy, or—well, the alternative was too unpleasant for him even to contemplate.'

Rudi gave a huge sigh of relief. 'That could have been disastrous for me and my friends.'

'Indeed,' replied Hans. 'And the Birnbaums? What happened to them?'

'They are safely out of the country and settling down very nicely, thank you.' Rudi paused for a moment. His brain had been working in overdrive for the past few minutes and he was convinced that he had come up with a plan which would enable him to test out his ability as Hitler's double and, at the same time, advance the cause which he and the other group members so earnestly believed in. He decided to risk putting a proposal before Hans.

'Might I make a suggestion? It would involve my closest friends knowing that I would be playing the part of the Führer, but I can swear on my life to their discretion because they have put their own lives on the line more than once to promote our cause, if that's not too grand a name for it.'

'It certainly isn't,' replied Hans thoughtfully. 'And your proposal is?'

'We are putting together a plan to try and topple one of the local Party grandees from his pedestal. His name is Leopold Bucher… '

'Say no more,' Hans cut in abruptly. 'That man is one of the worst examples of the most unpleasant and downright evil creatures who have managed to insinuate themselves into positions of power in Bavaria.'

'Well, he caused the Birnbaums to be arrested so that he could expropriate their house which his ghastly wife, Marie, had lusted after for years. He has arranged, with another friend of mine, the Chief Curator of the Nuremberg Museum and Galleries, to reopen the private art gallery at the rear of their house with a splendid exhibition of pro-Nazi art, and the one gap in our plans was to find a suitable guest of honour from the Nazi aristocracy to perform the opening ceremony. At which, I might add, he is in for a very nasty surprise, which should bring his glittering political career to a crashing and very ignominious halt.'

'When are you considering holding this special occasion?'

'In a month or two.'

'During which time, Hitler will actually be in Nuremberg making final preparations for the annual Party rally. I can arrange for the Führer to retire in seclusion for that particular night, so long as you can get the information to me in good time. Our dear Adolf always loves to take a few hours out of the public view to pursue his own—how shall I express them—private interests.

'A couple of vehicles and three or four security personnel should meet your requirements. I will be happy to provide you with whatever support you need and we should have ample time to offer you the necessary training.

Let's regard it as your first professional appearance. I'm sure you'll make a great success of it.'

Hans paused.

'I should add one important point, and that is, Hitler himself is privately horrified at some of the excesses of the truly awful monsters he has unwittingly created, despite his own pretty ghastly policies, particularly towards Jews and political opponents. This means that he is prepared to give tacit support to attempts to unseat people like Bucher, although he would never admit this publicly. As a result, I am sure I can throw all the necessary resources your way to enable you to make a success of your project. Let me have more information about the proposed downfall of Bucher as soon as you and your friends have worked out your plan in detail.'

Rudi nodded enthusiastically at Hans's words.

'Also, as you will discover, Hitler's personal and private passions do not exactly match the ascetic persona he presents in public. He enjoys making use of his doubles to ensure that his desires are, so to speak, regularly satisfied. But that is, and must remain, a dark secret.

'Now, let us begin to put in place some practical details. We need to be in close contact with each other and we must arrange your training sessions. Not just for voice and body language, you'll have to be familiar with a range of names, places, and much more besides. You'll also require uniforms and regalia, and there are many other little details we need to attend to. Finally, you will be placed on the duty roster for taking the starring role in quite a few little jaunts on behalf of our great Führer, and you will get extra training for them. Welcome aboard, and Heil Hitler!'

Rudi nodded enthusiastically. Then a sudden unpleasant thought struck him.

'What if someone actually succeeded in assassinating Hitler?'

Hans laughed. 'Then those of us appointed as doubles would have to fight it out among ourselves, wouldn't we? Unless, of course,' he added wickedly, 'it has already happened.'

Chapter Twenty-One

For the first time in her employment as Max Feinlein's secretary, Eva was late. Not excessively so, but sufficiently behind time for Max to be already seated at his desk when she knocked and opened his office door. Clearly flustered and still wearing her outdoor coat, she apologised for her tardiness.

Max handed her a folder of signed correspondence from the previous afternoon, together with some documents for filing and, as she made to return to the outer office, she gave a sudden little cry and, without any warning, dropped the lot on the floor. He forced himself to his feet, edged around the table and helped her to gather up the scattered papers.

'Are you all right, Eva? Is there something bothering you?'

Eva shook her head silently. Unusually for her, she would not look him in the eye.

'Are you absolutely sure? Is it to do with your lateness today?'

'Of course not, sir, no, sir… '

'And how are your parents doing?' he asked, hoping to distract her from whatever was troubling her, but his words had the opposite effect. Eva burst into tears and rushed from his office. Hard on her heels, Max followed her, to find her slumped over her desk sobbing her heart out.

He walked over and stood by her side, took out a large red handkerchief from his top jacket pocket and handed it to her. At first, Eva waved it away, but he insisted and she gingerly took it and vainly attempted to wipe away her floods of tears.

It took several minutes for Eva to calm down sufficiently to attempt to speak, and Max gently told her to go back into his office where they would have greater privacy. Still very tearful, she removed her coat and followed him. He gestured her to one of the comfortable chairs reserved for visitors, and she sat down, head bent and clearly in great distress.

After closing the office door, Max went over to a glass-fronted cabinet in one corner of the office and poured a large brandy into a balloon glass. He took it across, proffered it to her and said,

'Take a drink. It will help to steady your nerves.'

Eva did so, coughed at the bite of the strong liquor and placed the glass on the low table between them. Max settled down in the other chair and looked compassionately at her.

'Is this really something to do with your parents?' he asked.

She shook her head, paused, then nodded. Her movements would have been comical if she had not been so distraught.

'Anything said between us here stays in this office and will not affect you or your employment in any way,' said Max slowly, ensuring that she understood what he was saying. Suddenly, she raised her head and the flood of tears was swamped by a torrent of words.

'He told me they would be taken to a premier old people's home and given special treatment but, if I did not help him, they would be thrown out of their house and deported to a concentration camp,' she blurted out. 'He'd befriended me and, very quickly, we became—extremely close.'

She blushed but Max encouraged her to continue with a wave of his hand. 'Silly me, I thought he was just being a kind man, who actually said he thought he was falling in love with me. And, then, he started making demands about me reporting on you and what you do, who you speak to, and things like that. I feel I have utterly betrayed you. You have always been so kind towards me, Herr Feinlein. I am so, so desperately sorry.'

Eva was a picture of utter wretchedness. Max let her sit undisturbed for some time, while he tried to unpick what she was saying and decide how to respond.

Then, he said softly, 'Take another sip of that brandy.' She obeyed, knocking the glass against the side of the table as she put it down. She began to apologise when he stopped her.

'Don't worry about that. You've only spilled a couple of drops. Use my handkerchief to mop it up, Eva.' She complied, still sniffing and evidently very frightened.

'You refer to someone as "he". Who is this man you are talking about?'

Eva looked nervously at him. 'His name is Erpenbeck, Leutnant Erpenbeck of the SS.'

Max nearly had a heart attack. 'What?' he shouted, quite unable to prevent his shocked reaction.

In reply, Eva burst into tears again. Max hastily sought to calm her but, for a while, she was completely inconsolable.

'It's—it's just that I have heard that name before, on more than one occasion,' said Max, seeking to calm her down, 'and he's a particularly nasty piece of work. I'm sorry, my dear, I really didn't intend to frighten you. Far from it. I feel truly sorry for you. You evidently fell victim to his blandishments and he's exploited your elderly parents ruthlessly.'

More floods of tears. The poor girl was plainly in a terrible state and not far short of breaking point.

'I'm going to ring a good friend of mine to ask if he will see you right away. You clearly need his help. He is a doctor, his name is Johann Voss, and… '

'Johann?' she gulped. 'You phoned him the other day and I told Leutnant Erpenbeck you referred to that name and were having a meeting and… ' Her voice tailed away miserably and she reached again for the red handkerchief.

Max waited patiently for her to regain her composure a little, reached out and held her hand.

'Eva, you have been the victim of a cruel and manipulative individual who viciously exploited your inexperience and your devotion to your parents. I cannot blame you for the huge pressure you were placed under, but I honestly do believe you will recover from this situation and that everything will be fine in the end.'

His words of comfort only caused her to burst into tears once more. Max looked down, realised that he was still holding her hand and reluctantly let go of it. Eva was clearly in a pitiful state. Max looked thoughtfully at her, then he asked, 'Tell me, Eva, what made you confess to me today? It must have been an awful secret for you to bear, but something must have happened to cause you to break down and speak out.'

Eva took a deep breath and said, very quietly, 'This morning, I could stand it no longer. I expressed my concern about what he was forcing me to do for him, and he struck me. Hard. On my... ' Embarrassed, she touched her left breast.

'Carry on, my dear,' said Max, almost in a whisper.

'Then he pushed me against the wall and threatened me with a thorough beating. So, I told him I just couldn't do any more spying for him, and he replied by threatening to punish my parents. He forced me out of the apartment, telling me to damned well go to work and think matters over, or it would go very badly for all of us. For me... and my parents too.'

She fought to maintain a semblance of self-control. 'I—I suppose I am going to have to go and make my peace with him, otherwise, mum and dad will… '

Her voice trailed away once more.

Max paused to consider what to do next, then he elbowed himself up from the easy chair and returned to his desk, where he began making notes.

'What are you going to do, sir?' asked Eva tremulously.

'I'm working out a plan of action for you,' he replied.

'But all I can do is go back to him and grovel and hope he will forgive me… '

'Stop. Stop, Eva. No more tears, I beg of you. For your sake and your parents', just sit there quietly, take a couple more sips of your brandy and give yourself a moment to steady your nerves.'

'But, sir… '

'Eva, please. Have I ever let you down in the past?'

She shook her head dumbly, wondering what on earth he could possibly to do rescue her from the huge hole she had dug for herself, especially since she had betrayed him so badly. After some note-taking and muttering to himself, Max finally put his pencil down and looked at Eva. 'Are you feeling a little better now?'

She nodded nervously, not trusting herself to speak. 'Come and sit in front of the desk, like you do when I give dictation.'

She moved slowly across the room, perched on the edge of the chair, smoothed her skirt and stared at the floor.

'Now, as I see it ,there are a number of issues for us to resolve. Top of the list is your parents. Where are they now?'

'They are still at their apartment in the city centre. Wilhelm—I mean, Leutnant Erpenbeck said arrangements had been made to move them into a home for privileged Party members the week after next. My parents think it's my idea for them to leave the city and go into pleasant sheltered accommodation. They are quite unaware of the real reason.'

'Are they in good health? Fit to travel, for example?'

'Oh, yes, they are both reasonably well, considering their age.'

Max looked solemnly at Eva. Then he added quietly, 'Do you really think he would put them in a special home just to drag a little more information out of you?'

Eva shook her head wretchedly, as he continued, 'Of course not. I believe that they are in grave danger of being transported to a concentration camp rather than a retirement home.'

Eva looked horrified at his words.

Max paused, then said gently, 'Have they ever been to the seaside?'

'No, sir, that would be too far away and too expensive for them. They've never been out of Bavaria. W-why do you ask, sir?'

'Let me answer by asking you another question. I presume you have a means of contacting Erpenbeck during the day?'

'Y-yes, sir.'

'Right. What I'd like you to do is to get in touch with him and tell him that you are very sorry you had words with him. But you have just heard that an aunt is gravely ill and that is what has upset you so greatly. Explain to him that I have given you leave to go and visit her for a week. Can you manage to do that?'

Eva nodded tentatively, still very puzzled.

'I am a single man with no dependants, I have an income most people would envy and an art collection at home which is worth rather a lot of Reichsmarks. My needs are modest and I am almost embarrassed at the financial means at my disposal. All of this puts me in a very good position to help you and your parents.

'As you know, I have a small cottage on the Baltic coast where I spend my time during the summer holidays. It's late in the season now but I'm sure that your parents will love the place. You can accompany them there and, in the meantime, I will work out what is to be done with Erpenbeck. If you are visiting an imaginary aunt for a week, that will give us some breathing space to consider what to do next.'

'But, sir, how… '

'How can the travel tickets and so on be organised? Quite simply. You are my secretary and arranging such things is part of your job. I suggest you contact your parents, tell them to pack for an extended holiday because you are in some kind of trouble with a prominent local Nazi, then organise first-class rail transport from

246

Nuremberg to Kuxhaven. From there, you can arrange a taxi to take them to the house. I shall contact my housekeeper who calls in regularly to keep everything in order, and she will see to it that fires are lit and ensure there is plenty of fresh linen and food in the cupboards.

'As for expenses, I shall provide you with sufficient money to tide you over the days and weeks to come. And, when this unpleasant matter is finished and done with, I can and will find a way to enable you to return here to your job and to allow your parents to go back to their apartment.'

Max spoke with a confidence he did not personally feel. He was not sure how Erpenbeck could be silenced a second time, but he was hopeful that the other members of the group would be able to come up with a plan of some kind. Johann had shown himself to be most resourceful and imaginative when dealing with Erpenbeck the first time around, but the immediate issue was to try and resolve Eva's present predicament.

The poor girl burst into tears again and, this time, they were tears of overwhelming relief and gratitude. She impulsively rose to her feet, walked around the desk, placed her hands on his shoulders and kissed him full on the lips. Max felt a sudden strange combination of embarrassment and pleasure surge through him at her spontaneous gesture.

'Now, now, Eva. I am just so pleased to be able to help you,' he said, not a little flustered. 'I can tell you in confidence that a small group of friends of mine and myself are dedicated to assisting people who fall foul of this ghastly Nazi régime. So I am only too delighted to be in a position to help you. Please sit down again and we can begin to consider the practicalities of your relocation. I presume you will be able to persuade your parents to move north?'

Eva nodded enthusiastically. 'Yes, indeed. They are finding the political atmosphere in the city increasingly oppressive and unpleasant, and when I explain to them in general terms what has occurred and how generous you have been to us all, I am sure they will be delighted to escape for a while and enjoy some sea air and spend time with me too.'

She reached forward and touched him lightly on the arm. 'I don't really think I need to see a doctor though, sir. You have been so generous and helpful, and you've made me feel so much better already. Here, sir, have your handkerchief back. You'll need it to wipe my lipstick off.'

She flushed, looked up and smiled warmly at him. Once again, that unaccustomed sensation flooded through him and caused him to redden and move his head away.

'Now,' he said, clearing his throat and trying to sound businesslike, 'let's work out a plan of action for you. My first task is to put some funds together and yours is to get on the phone with Leutnant Erpenbeck and tell him a couple of little white lies.'

Chapter Twenty-Two

Johann stood up in his sitting room and said, 'I had called this meeting to keep ourselves up to date on what has been happening and also about how much we should be concerned about our own safety, but I understand that Max has two important announcements to make on that very topic. So let's give him the floor.'

As Elise poured more coffees, Max looked earnestly around at the other members of the group. 'I must start with what I hope isn't bad news, although I fear it may well be.' He paused as they anxiously waited for him to continue.

'You may know that I have a personal secretary called Eva. She's an excellent worker, if rather reserved and insistent on doing things just so, and she has been with me for a little over three years now. She's extremely shy and undemonstrative, but I have nothing but praise for her work. As for her personal life, I know next to nothing about it except that it appears she had a very unfortunate relationship a long time ago and, since then, she has kept very much to herself. Until recently, that is.

'The other day we were about to deal with the normal office routine—letters to file, calls to make and the like—

when she suddenly burst into floods of tears and dropped her papers all over the floor. She was clearly totally distraught. It took me quite a while to settle her down and persuade her to confide in me but, when she did, I must admit to being horrified at her words and their very serious implications for all of us.'

His eyes swept around the room, and he took a long drink of coffee before continuing.

'It appears that she had been forced into spying on me, listening to my phone calls, noting the contents of my correspondence and the like and reporting what she found. She was greatly distressed that she had allowed this to happen to her. Now, I wasn't entirely surprised that someone might be keeping an eye on me, not only because of my position in the local art and culture world but also because I have resolutely refused all attempts to lure me into becoming a member of the Party.

'What shocked me most of all was that the poor girl had been seduced—quite literally, as it happens—into becoming an informer by threats to the safety of her elderly parents. And the really bad news is the identity of the man who had taken such cruel advantage of her. That man,' Max continued solemnly, 'was SS Leutnant Wilhelm Erpenbeck.'

There was a horrified gasp from the others. Max raised a calming hand before continuing.

'I'm fairly sure that this is no more than a ghastly coincidence. It seems to be part of the man's job description to keep tabs on local high-ranking officials and others of similar standing, and Eva just happened to be a convenient target for him. As we are already well aware, he rather fancies himself as a ladies' man, and he certainly knew how to play on Eva's weaknesses.'

Another pause for a mouthful of coffee. The others were listening intently to his narrative and trying to evaluate the implications of his words.

'Now, I am pretty well convinced that she has not passed on any critical information about us as a group. It seems, though, that she had told Erpenbeck about a brief phone call I made, requesting a meeting at the Mautkeller. I did take the precaution of ringing Johann later from an outside phone to propose that we do indeed meet soon, but here at his house rather than at our usual venue.'

'And that I, of course, agreed to,' Johann intervened. 'I also called my friend who runs the Mautkeller restaurant to ask him if he would let me know if any suspicious-looking individuals dropped by this evening to enquire about a private meeting. I am convinced that we must redouble our efforts to be cautious about what we say and do, but I don't believe that we are in any immediate danger. Max here spoke to me briefly about this matter before the meeting, and I understand that he and Eva have already worked out some appropriate misinformation to put Erpenbeck off the scent for the time being at least.'

A pause. Max nodded in agreement.

'But, now, Max, I believe that you have something more positive to tell us.'

'Indeed I have. In fact, I'm sure that you will genuinely welcome the proposal I am about to put to you. It will be a unique opportunity to cause serious social and political damage to an individual who has been responsible for much suffering and distress in his hitherto unstoppable rise to one of the key power positions in local society.

'As you may be aware, the Birnbaums were very well-known in local art and cultural circles, and it was their custom to organise an annual gathering in their home, a social event combined with a showing of Eli Birnbaum's private collection of paintings, at which large sums would be raised for a nominated local charity.

'Now that the Birnbaums are no longer on the scene, an extremely nasty piece of work named Leopold Bucher, a deputy mayor no less of our fine city, has taken possession of the house at number 49, Parkstrasse. There is good reason to believe that he engineered this acquisition because his dear wife was desperate to own the place and he saw an opportunity to evict the Birnbaums and requisition the building for himself and his charming consort. Herr Bucher was evidently familiar with the annual event the previous residents used to hold and he is now determined to continue the practice, with the Winterhilfswerk as his designated charity. How very noble of him to support that fraudulent Nazi cause.'

A pause, and another sip of coffee. The rest of them were hanging on his words in total silence.

'Unfortunately for Herr Bucher, being basically a thug who has wormed his way up the local Nazi hierarchy by employing the most ruthless and unpleasant tactics imaginable, he has no feeling for culture and no paintings of his own worthy of the name. So he telephoned me and asked if I could be of assistance in setting up an exhibition. Well, I say he asked—his words were, in reality, nothing less than commands dressed up as polite requests.

'As he talked about his shameless plans to step so blatantly into the shoes of a civilised, decent man like Birnbaum, it began to occur to me that if we could find some way of humiliating Bucher very publicly at the opening of the exhibition, that would be a real triumph for us, as well as a powerful act of retribution for what he has done to the Birnbaums. The house will be swarming with the high society of Nuremberg and the upper crust of the local Nazi Party, and such a splendid occasion presents a unique opportunity to cause him to fall spectacularly from grace.

'And, so, I put my thinking cap on and, after a while, came up with the following idea, which will require all of us to work together to achieve our objective. Of course, at some point, I may have to pretend that I was forced out of my role as designer of the exhibition and some nameless dark forces or other took everything over and deliberately perverted and destroyed my plans. Now, this is what I propose.'

Max spent the next twenty minutes expounding his plan in great detail, including his idea of asking Rudi to seek out the name of an appropriate visiting Nazi dignitary to open the exhibition and then to act out the part. He had already outlined this aspect of the plan to Rudi, who had eagerly agreed to look into the matter.

By the end of his narrative, not only did the group have before them an excellent well-conceived proposal which they all applauded, but they had also received a free tutorial on early twentieth-century art thrown in for good measure. Max told them more about the young man, Kaspar Schröder, whom he had taken under his wing and who had the incredible gift of being able to make brilliantly accurate copies of existing paintings, as well as creating new works in the style of any painter he chose. He explained briefly how he would make use of Kaspar's talents in his plan.

Max sat back and was immediately congratulated by Thomas, Rudi, Johann and Elise, who all spoke over each other in their enthusiasm for the project. When the hubbub had died down, Johann asked,

'Is there anything else we need to add to Max's excellent idea to topple Herr Bucher?'

Elise leaned forward. 'It would be a really sensational coup if we could ensure that the exhibition was opened by a really top figure in the Nazi Party.'

They all nodded and turned towards Rudi. 'Is there any particular character you'd like to play?' asked Johann.

Rudi looked glumly around the room, paused for effect, and then an impish smile crept slowly across his features. 'Maybe. There is one little announcement I'd like to make myself which might just contribute positively to Max's enterprise. Max has told you that I had agreed to look into impersonating an appropriate Nazi bigwig to open the exhibition and, after what occurred to me recently, I believe I've come up with a suitable name. Let me tell you how it happened.'

He explained to them how, after a hectic night on stage at the Cabaret, he'd been abducted in fear for his life and taken to an unknown location just outside the city. Rudi, as everyone knew, loved to tell a story, but this one topped the lot when he revealed to them who it was that faced him across the table.

'I recalled the little trick I played on you when we met at the Mautkeller for the first time, but I can assure you that being on the receiving end of a similar ploy was no laughing matter. And so,' he concluded his account, 'I am now officially a double for Adolf Hitler himself and other leading Nazis, and I have already proposed what my initial assignment might be. By the way, all this is seriously top secret, and I had to gain special permission to reveal my new role to you. So, now, we have someone to open Herr Bucher's spectacular exhibition.'

They all looked at him questioningly.

'And that someone, meine Damen und Herren, is our Great Leader, the Führer himself, who has magnanimously agreed to be present at the opening of Herr Bucher's autumn charity exhibition event!'

They all loudly applauded his words.

'Well done,' said Thomas, 'but I bet you were more than a little worried when you were abducted in the middle of the night.'

'Me?' said Rudi. 'Certainly not. I managed to cope with the whole experience with great confidence, dignity and courage. But, if any of you know of a washerwoman who undertakes to clean very dirty underwear, I'd be most grateful for her name.'

Laughter greeted his admission, and he continued, 'I should also add, that the man who runs the small unit of doubles for Hitler and other senior Nazi leaders has given the proposal his full support, and will supply transport and some additional staff for added authenticity. He will even ensure that the real Hitler, who will actually be in Nuremberg on the night in question, is kept out of the limelight, but it's more than my wretched life is worth to tell you how he intends to do that.

'The unit, which goes by the ingenious name of Double Eagle, has a great deal of latitude in the way it performs its tasks and disposes of official funds. But, I must stress, once again, that everything related to my acting as a double is strictly confidential.'

Elise was all smiles. 'Am I glad I asked who could be persuaded to open the exhibition. That really puts the icing on the cake. If we could humiliate Herr Bucher in front of the Führer himself, that would make a huge and lasting impact. It would be absolutely brilliant.'

Max seldom became emotionally excited and, from him, a smile was as rare as a heatwave in the Arctic. But, now, he was beaming from ear to ear and delighting in the way his proposal was being received.

'I know what I want to select as the subject of the key pictures in the exhibition,' he said. They all waited for him to tell them, but he shook his head mysteriously. 'You'll have to wait and see,' he added. 'But I can promise you—and Deputy Mayor Bucher—a really big surprise.'

At that instant, the telephone rang. Johann went into the consulting room and lifted the receiver. He listened to the voice at the other end of the line, uttered a brief word of thanks and replaced the instrument. He returned to the group with a worried expression on his face.

'That was my friend, the owner of the Mautkeller. He says he had a couple of rather unpleasant visitors this evening asking about a private meeting. He told them that there must have been a misunderstanding, as none of the function rooms were booked for this evening. And that demonstrates that we really must redouble our efforts to ensure that our identities remain confidential and our security is kept watertight. But, now—let's get our preparations underway for the grand opening of Leopold Bucher's exhibition.'

Chapter Twenty-Three

It was a glittering occasion, the social event of the autumn. All Nuremberg society was there, from Party dignitaries and local politicians to prominent businessmen and their wives. Many of the menfolk had donned their dress military or Party uniforms, weighed down with medals and regalia, and the leaders of the business community were all attired in formal evening dress.

The women were decked out in the finest and most glamorous long evening gowns. Their necklines plunged daringly low to reveal sculptured bare flesh adorned with necklaces encrusted in precious stones set in gold and silver. There was a lively hum of conversation, almost drowning out the ten-piece orchestra playing familiar classical melodies in one corner. Burdened with trays of champagne and hors d'oeuvres, waiters and waitresses in black-and-white uniforms weaved their effortless way amongst the large throng of guests.

Attendance was further boosted by a well-organised whispering campaign, quietly but efficiently masterminded by members of Hans Castorp's Double Eagle unit, that a very senior member of the Party indeed would be addressing the assembled revellers and would declare the new exhibition gallery open. Everyone who was anyone was present, desperately eager to be there, and determined to see and be seen on this exclusive gala occasion. The only absentees were, of course, those members of the Jewish community who had patronised the auspicious event in past years. But, in this august gathering of the nobility of the New Germany, they would hardly be welcome.

It was just a few short months since the Birnbaums had been evicted from their home, but now all traces of their occupation had been obliterated. The interior had been redecorated at great expense, and the new owners and hosts on this prestigious occasion, Leopold Bucher and his wife, Marie, were the focal point of attention. Marie was truly in her element, as the house which she had always yearned for was hers, and her status as a leading figure in the local Nazi hierarchy of fiercely competing wives was now totally assured.

Bucher had been shoehorned into a specially tailored formal evening dress which did its utmost to disguise the fact that its owner was becoming seriously obese. His face had fattened unattractively in recent months, and his dewlap overhung the stiffly starched collar which threatened to strangle him.

Marie wore a hideously expensive electric blue gown and far too much jewellery, none of which could mask the fact that she was no raving beauty, and her plunging neckline was wrinkled rather than pleasantly revealing. Her mean, pinched features and inelegant posture betrayed her very modest origins, which the display of outward wealth and affluence singularly failed to conceal.

In the main reception rooms, the house was ablaze with light, the main illumination supplemented by large candelabras standing on tables around the room. Their flickering candles gave out a warm orange glow against the plush dark brown velvet curtains and imparted an ambience of warmth and domesticity, despite the formality and grandeur of the occasion.

The driveway was lined with expensive motor cars which spilt out onto the roadside beyond. At one corner of the drive, in front of the outbuilding which housed the garage, an outside broadcast van from the Reich Broadcasting Service was parked. Cables snaked from it through one of the side windows and into the house. Directly under the portico, a space was marked off for the vehicles of the guest of honour who, it was said, was due to arrive around nine that evening.

In the area leading to the exhibition gallery, last-minute preparations were under way to ensure that everything would run smoothly. A gold-plated ceremonial key to the exhibition was resting on a plump purple cushion. Behind the double door to the gallery, Thomas was making final checks to his equipment, and Johann, Elise and Max were all busily in attendance. Unsurprisingly, Rudi was not among their number.

A podium had been set up in one corner of the main reception room. A lectern and microphone sat on a small table and, behind the platform, a huge swastika banner was draped from ceiling to floor. According to the rumour mill, the opening ceremony and the speeches which preceded it were due to be broadcast live on national radio.

As nine o'clock approached and all but a few stragglers amongst the guests had arrived, Leopold Bucher fished an expensive hunter watch out of his top pocket, noted the hour for the twentieth time that evening and strode self-importantly through the crowd and up to the podium. Earlier that day, he had been informed in the strictest confidence of the identity of the guest of honour, and he could hardly contain his pride and self-satisfaction. With an effort, he disciplined his emotions, planted himself in front of the lectern and tapped the microphone, which obligingly generated a loud clicking noise and a mild electronic squeal in the loudspeakers. He cleared his throat and prepared to speak.

'Meine Damen und Herren,' he began and waited for the din of conversation to subside and the audience to pay attention. The small orchestra abandoned a polka in mid-flow, but it took a little longer to persuade those present who overly enjoyed the sound of their own voices to interrupt their monologues, and one elderly deaf gentleman had to be sternly admonished into silence. Bucher slowly cast his eyes around the room, cleared his throat noisily and prepared to launch into a short opening speech. Just wait, he thought smugly, just wait until I tell them. When at last the babble of conversation died down to an expectant hush, Bucher continued.

'Meine Damen und Herren, it gives me very great pleasure indeed to welcome you to our humble home on the occasion of the first of a new series of annual viewings from my modest private exhibition in the long gallery behind me.' He gestured stiffly towards the double doors.

There was a brief scattering of applause. He cleared his throat again and pursued his theme. 'As you know, this is a charitable event, and our chosen good cause on this occasion is none other than the Winterhilfswerk, the Winter Relief Fund, which is organised nationally by the Party. It is the sacred duty of those of us who enjoy the benefits of financial security to give generously to those of our fellow citizens who find themselves in reduced circumstances through sickness or some other adversity.' He paused for effect. 'And, now, I have a very special announcement indeed to make.'

Slowly and deliberately, he scanned his audience. He had their full attention, the whole room hanging on his every word. They were aware that someone very important was about to appear and officiate at the opening ceremony of the exhibition but, who that was, nobody could guess. Most of the senior Party members were either here in Nuremberg or on their way for the annual rally the following week, so there would be no shortage of distinguished names to choose from. It would be an honour indeed to be present in the same room as any one of the Party nobility, and it would make a riveting talking point at dinner parties for many months to come.

'I am delighted to inform you that this part of our little gathering is being broadcast by the Reich radio service, especially in order that our honoured guest's words can be carried across to every corner of our great nation. This is a hugely special occasion indeed, and one which I can assure you will remain in your hearts and memories for a very long time.'

He paused to allow a flurry of excited anticipation to ripple around the room. Who was the mysterious guest of honour? Surely, it wouldn't be some Gauleiter or regional functionary? Or has Bucher finally overstepped the mark and blown the whole evening entirely out of proportion? Scarcely a handful of those present were endeared to their host, and few tears would be shed if the evening turned out to be something of a damp squib. The tension in the room was electric.

Bucher glanced across to the front door. There was a nod from one of the Gestapo officers in the doorway. A large black saloon car had drawn up outside and its passenger was just alighting. Behind it, another two cars discharged a small selection of aides and security officers.

'And so, meine Damen und Herren, it is my duty and very greatest pleasure to introduce to you our guest of honour who has so generously consented to open the proceedings of this very splendid evening. May I ask you all to welcome none other'—at this point the emotional break in his voice made the introduction all the more dramatic, as it should have done. He had been practising it all afternoon with his speech writer. '… er, none other than the Leader of our great Reich and our great Party, the Führer himself, Adolf Hitler!'

An astonished gasp went up from the assembled dignitaries and some of the ladies were close to swooning with shock and delight. This was, surely, going to be a once-in-a-lifetime occasion and everyone present deemed themselves fortunate indeed to be able to boast to their friends and colleagues that they had seen the Führer close up and in the flesh—and maybe, just maybe, some of them might be fortunate enough to shake the great man by the hand. Bucher really had pulled off a coup this time, and the doubters were forced to concede that this would inevitably strengthen his position in the local and regional political landscape.

There was a sudden commotion at the door and the leader of the Third Reich with his intense, staring blue eyes, dark hair swept down over his left forehead and the famous toothbrush moustache strode swiftly into the room to the accompaniment of popping flashbulbs from the press and official photographers and loud applause from those present. Adolf Hitler was wearing an SS uniform, the Iron Cross Second Class prominently displayed on his chest, and a peaked military cap which he removed as he entered the room and neatly tucked under his left arm. He nodded and waved to acknowledge the applause. Then, dramatically, he raised his right arm in its characteristic crooked pose, the hand back flat like a waiter manoeuvring a tray across a crowded restaurant, and clicked the highly polished heels of his military boots, as the small orchestra struck up the opening bars of the National Anthem, Deutschland, Deutschland über alles.

A thunderous response of 'Heil Hitler!' threatened to rattle the windows and blow out the candles in the candelabras. What happened next was like the Biblical parting of the Red Sea. A passageway magically opened up across the diagonal length of the room, as men and women retreated to stand aside for their Führer. With exaggerated dignity, Bucher stepped down from the podium and took several stiff paces forward. Then, he stopped, snapped his right arm up in the formal stiff-armed salute and shouted 'Heil Hitler!' The entire audience repeated the greeting once more in deafening unison.

Hitler was evidently delighted with his reception. He smiled warmly and reached out his hand to Bucher. The two men shook hands and exchanged a few private words. More flashbulbs popped. Bucher intimated to the Führer that he might wish to greet some of those present personally and the two men moved slowly along the lines of enthusiastic guests, switching from one side to the other, shaking hands and bestowing a few brief words on each of them as they processed slowly towards the podium, where Marie had been prompted to take her place at one side of the lectern.

When the two men reached her she was almost beside herself with pride and awe. 'Might I introduce my dear wife, Marie, mein Führer?' Hitler nodded politely, took the lady's hand and said,

'You have organised a truly splendid gathering this evening. I am sure it will be a considerable success.'

Marie blushed like a fifteen-year-old and accepted the compliment graciously, although her only contribution to the night's proceedings had been a four-day trawl through the exclusive emporia of Nuremberg in grimly determined pursuit of the electric blue dress she was now wearing. Greetings over, Hitler mounted the podium, Bucher at his heels. The parting of the Red Sea came to an abrupt end as waves of guests surged forward towards them.

Bucher cleared his throat. 'Meine Damen und Herren and listeners to the Reich radio, it is with the greatest pleasure that I invite our guest of honour to speak to this distinguished assembly in our beautiful city of Nuremberg on the occasion of the opening of my exhibition of National Socialist art and paintings and for the charitable purpose of supporting the Winterhilfswerk. Please will you give the warmest Bavarian greeting to our beloved Führer, Adolf Hitler!'

There was a loud and prolonged burst of rapturous applause, peppered with shouts and salutes of 'Heil Hitler'. Bucher stepped to one side and Hitler took to the lectern where the text of his speech had been strategically placed a little earlier. Afterwards, hardly anyone could remember exactly what he said, for a variety of reasons, but he expertly trod his customary path of attacking Jews and Communists and praising the hard-working and loyal citizenry of Bavaria in particular and the Reich at large. He devoted a section to the crucial importance of the visual arts in underpinning and promoting the values of the Party and lavished praise on the significance of this evening's gathering, both culturally and in advancing the cause of social cohesion through their charitable donations. Finally, he held out the promise of a golden future for the Reich when their enemies would be crushed and all their dreams fulfilled.

On the whole, it was a relatively relaxed and informal performance, targeted at this gathering of a hundred people as well as the radio audience in their homes, more intimate and direct than the bombastic and inflated rhetoric of his major speeches at the Party rally parade ground in front of tens of thousands of supporters, and it was received with rapturous applause.

The ovation went on for several minutes until Hitler raised both hands and said, 'Thank you so much, meine Damen und Herren. I do not want you to wear your hands out as I understand you will soon have to put them into your pockets to make generous donations to the Winterhilfswerk.' A gale of laughter and applause greeted his words.

'And, now, we come to the second high point of the evening,' said Bucher, leaning forward into the microphone to be heard over the continuing applause and buzz of excited conversation. One of the waiters, who had been assigned the task, came forward, raised up the purple cushion on which reposed the golden key to the double doors of the exhibition gallery and nervously presented it to the guest of honour, bowing as he did so.

Hitler solemnly took the key, thanked the waiter with a curt military nod, and marched forward towards the doors. There was an excited hush. Someone threw a switch and the main lighting dimmed, leaving a flickering ring of candlelight around the room to enhance the dramatic effect of the moment. A second later, Hitler and Bucher were picked out by two spotlights which were directed across the room towards them.

The Führer moved forward and inserted the key in the lock. It turned smoothly and, as he stepped back, the double doors were eased open from within the gallery which was in almost total darkness. The spotlights were extinguished and, in the gloom, there followed several seconds of expectant silence as they all waited keenly to see what would happen next.

Suddenly, three more spotlights were switched on which cast their pools of light directly into the entrance of the gallery. A gasp went up and instantly the entire room broke into rapturous applause. A trio of substantial paintings were revealed, each standing on its own easel. The centrepiece of the display was an almost life-sized full-length portrait of the Führer himself posing on elevated ground, gesturing to the distant horizon in a Napoleonic pose with the flags and banners of his armies waving loyally beneath him. In the sky above him, red-grey and intensely theatrical clouds lowered, and the entire composition created a dramatic and darkly atmospheric impact.

No less impressive but more modest in scale, the two paintings on either side depicted characteristic scenes of Nazi-approved art. On the left, a positive image of family life was portrayed, with father, mother and two children sitting around a table, gazing admiringly at the eldest son in the doorway who was proudly showing off his brand-new military uniform.

On the other side, a scene of country life was displayed, of a farmer and his workers who had been bringing in the harvest, and were now resting from their labours and being served food and drink by a bevy of well-built young maidens. The whole scene spoke of richly deserved repose after hard and fruitful labours.

The applause was long and heartfelt. Hitler pointed approvingly at each painting in turn and caused much merriment when he imitated the pose in which the central portrait had depicted him. Bucher swelled with pride. The city's art gallery staff had clearly achieved nothing short of a miracle and, for him and his wife, this evening was going to be the crowning success of a triumphant—and lucrative—year.

He was relishing too, the reflected glory of having his personal exhibition opened by none other than the Führer himself, which would do no damage at all to his prospects for the future. He bent stiffly to his left and smiled at his wife, whose eyes were brimming with tears of joy and self-satisfaction. Nothing, he told himself, could possibly spoil this magnificent occasion.

But, as the applause became more ragged and began to fade, all the spotlights suddenly cut out as if a fuse had blown in the building. In the renewed semi-darkness of the flickering candlelight, people looked anxiously at one another, wondering what was happening and how they should react. A couple of security officers edged cautiously nearer to Hitler, ready for any eventuality. But they could not possibly have prepared for what happened next.

Just as suddenly, the three spotlights were switched on again and another gasp went up. This time, though, it was an outburst of absolute horror and disgust. Somehow, each of the dignified and noble paintings had been mysteriously exchanged, to be replaced by the most vile and disgusting display that anyone present was ever likely to witness.

The cosy family scene on the left had been translated into an orgy, in which the son in his military uniform was copulating vigorously with his mother as the family looked on, applauding his lustful antics and themselves preparing to indulge in similar activities. The farming idyll had mutated into a tangle of naked, thrashing bodies with exaggerated genitalia, penetrating one another with eye-popping lust against the background of a purple, lurid skyscape rent with jagged streaks of lightning.

But the greatest abhorrence of all was reserved for the central painting. Instead of a heroic leader surrounded by his adoring armies and scanning the distant horizon with a promise of future challenges and triumphs, Hitler was caricatured as a grotesque homunculus with a patch over one eye, sporting a tin helmet adorned with a skull and crossbones and a parrot on each shoulder.

Between his shrivelled legs, his huge engorged penis was being serviced by a buxom wench whose buttocks were thrust out towards the audience, legs splayed, leaving nothing whatsoever to the imagination. On her left rear cheek was tattooed the flag of France, and on the right, the Union Jack, clearly depicting her conquests achieved and yet to come.

She was pleasuring the giant organ in an oral manner which not many of the gentlemen present had experienced personally and which a goodly number did not realise was even a sexual possibility. The ladies squealed and shrieked their horror and revulsion, although quite a few of them found it rather difficult to detach their prurient gaze from the lecherous visions before them.

Several seconds later, all the lights in the room came back on. In the breathless, ominous silence, every eye was fixed upon the Führer, fearfully seeking to determine his reaction. He had seemingly turned to stone, so horrified was he by the lewd and grisly spectacle before him. It was everything that National Socialist German art despised and condemned, the very worst manifestation of degenerate modernism and moral turpitude like that due to be exhibited the following year in the Degenerate Art exhibition in Munich. However, it was far worse than even the most extreme excesses of artists like Egon Schiele or Georg Grosz, and it was calculated to cause the most terrible insult to the sacred person of the Führer himself and all that he represented.

Having drunk her fill of the paintings, Marie gave a horrified squawk and collapsed in a dead faint at the feet of the Führer, who jerked back with a disapproving snarl. He swung furiously round on his heel and snapped an order to an adjutant. Far more abruptly this time, the Red Sea parted once more to allow their Führer, livid with anger and disgust at the humiliating visions before him, to stomp rapidly out of the room and down the steps, as his retinue scrambled after him. Doors slammed and the large black Mercedes surged down the drive, scattering gravel to left and right.

The room exploded into a cacophony of horrified voices as everyone sought to express their revulsion at once. Bucher bent over his wife, anxiously patting her hand in a vain attempt to console her. All about him, a torrent of excited voices avidly debated the disgraceful scene and the Führer's reaction. The more calculating among them were already beginning to work out the impact of Bucher's inevitable fall from grace on their own Party careers and prospects, as the members of the ten-piece orchestra rapidly packed up their instruments and slipped out through a side door.

Two security guards who had remained in the room marched up to Bucher, grabbing him by the arms, dragged him from his wife and forced him through the tangle of guests to the front door. Moments later, van doors slammed and an army vehicle drove rapidly off with Bucher inside.

In the semi-darkness of the gallery, Max, Thomas and their companions could scarcely contain themselves. But their task was only half done, as more was yet to come. The double doors of the exhibition gallery had, in the meantime, been gently closed and locked from within, while the crowd in the room milled about in a swirling maelstrom. No one wanted to leave without witnessing the bizarre spectacle to its bitter end.

Suddenly, the loudspeakers began to blare out strident orchestral chords. Shocked, the din of outraged speculation swiftly died down to a murmur. What was happening now? Why this emotional surge of dramatic music? What did it signify?

One exclamation, then another, then a babble of voices uttered the one word: 'Wagner'. More mutterings, then a solitary man's voice called out, 'It's playing the Liebestod from Tristan and Isolde!'

It was the final, crowning scene of the great tragic opera, when Isolde sings of the ecstasy and ultimate fulfilment of love through death, culminating in majestic, orgasmic chords denoting her immolation and blissful union beyond the grave with her lover, Tristan. It was also one of Hitler's favourite pieces.

Realising the symbolism of the music and its bitterly ironic commentary on what had happened to Bucher's hubristic aspirations as a patron of the arts and a man close to the centre of Nazi power, the room burst into sporadic guffaws of laughter, which drained some of the tensions and apprehensions of the moment in Isolde's solemn final words,: 'Breathe away my life... to drown, to founder, all-knowing lost, in utmost rapture!'

Then, in the hysterically laughing, volatile crush of people, someone must have pushed hard against a side table. The candelabra wobbled, its candles smoked and guttered as it crashed back against the dark brown velvet curtains. For a second or two, nothing happened. There was a sudden whooshing sound as the drapery dramatically caught fire. Those nearest the sheet of flames scrambled frantically away to escape the blaze, but their passage was blocked by the press of people in the centre of the room.

Moments later, another table toppled over and a second column of flame shot up towards the ceiling. As a third candelabra and table fell, the sound of fire engines could be heard in the distance. No one thought to ask how it was possible that the fire service had been alerted before the flames had even begun to take hold.

As the fire started to spread, the laughter faded and a wave of panic set in. Some joined the increasingly mad rush towards the front door, others fled along side corridors and out into the night at the rear of the building. Within a few minutes, the room had all but emptied, leaving a trail of broken Champagne glasses, military caps, and discarded ladies' shoes and handbags.

Smoke swirled down from the ceiling and shrouded the space in a shifting curtain of grey murk. The Liebestod had become transformed into a fearsome parody of the Twilight of the Gods as the last stragglers made their frenzied exits and the fire engines drew nearer. The music climaxed and faded in a final, dramatic series of chords.

Outside, car doors opened and slammed shut, frantic voices shouted, tyres screeched and angry horns honked as the guests struggled to put as much distance as possible between themselves and the lurid glow of the flames flickering in the ground floor windows.

Amidst the murk and the crackling of the fire, the faint sound of a woman sobbing could be heard. It came from behind the lectern in gasping, racking, anguished tones. Hunched on the floor, her electric blue dress torn and besmirched, Marie bewailed the brutal and instantaneous destruction of her dream.

In a brief cruel fragment of time, her world had fallen apart. Her husband had just been dragged away by two of Hitler's security guards, she had been humiliated in the very presence of her beloved Führer—and her vastly expensive curtains had burst into sheets of flame. She was almost oblivious to the fires licking ever closer across the room and of the air becoming stifling hot and starved of oxygen. Almost oblivious, but not quite.

A small voice began to whisper in her head which quickly tempered her lamentations of self-pity. It urged her insistently, 'Stop bewailing your lot, woman, and make the best of what you've got. Remember, you must survive. Leopold is probably on the next train to Buchenwald. Do you want to join him? Get upstairs, grab your expensive jewellery, open the safe, empty it of Reichsmarks and get the hell out of here. Now!'

She stumbled to her feet, vision still blurred by tears, and made her tottering way across the room to the entrance hall and its double staircase which led up to the private rooms of the house, to the master bedroom and the safe.

Much later, when the flames had been extinguished, it was possible to begin to assess the damage. The main reception areas had borne the brunt of the flames and smoke. The ceiling was smudged with sooty deposits, the walls streaked with smoke and water damage. The wall-to-wall carpet was almost unrecognisable, like the muddy surface of a football pitch after a mid-game downpour. Many of the windows had shattered, leaving jagged glass shards with fragments of blackened curtain snagged on them.

As can happen in any fire, some parts of the room remained relatively unscathed, while others were reduced to a smouldering ruin. The double doors to the gallery were almost like new, golden brown burnished oakwood only slightly smudged by the smoke and, when a pair of firemen managed to force open the lock, the doors swung smoothly outward, to reveal—three paintings, a triptych perched on sturdy easels, each marking a significant facet of National Socialist cultural aspirations. On the left, a family scene with the young man parading his new military uniform, on the right, a bucolic idyll, farmworkers taking a well-deserved break from their labours. And, in the middle, the splendid, charismatic figure of Hitler the warrior-king, broodingly contemplating his troops. Of the ghastly parodies of those splendid tableaux, there was no sign.

Later, as the firemen were ensuring that no pockets of smouldering material remained, which might threaten to burst into flame if caught by a draught or gust of wind, one officer spotted a charred table leg in a corner of the room which appeared to have a rope of some kind attached to it. The rope had almost burned away in the conflagration and, tied to it, at an odd angle, lay the twisted remains of a candelabra.

It looked almost as if the falling candelabras were no accident. For a couple of seconds, the fireman was tempted to report the matter but, when he considered the bureaucratic flurry of incident reports and paperwork it would generate, he looked rapidly around him, kicked the candelabra aside and moved busily away to inspect the rest of the room.

Chapter Twenty-Four

The plain black van drove slowly down the narrow driveway at the back of the house, through the tradesmen's entrance and out into the night. After a little while, the vehicle's lights came on and, if anyone had been nearby, they could have heard loud shouts of merriment and sheer delight from inside. The plan had worked, brilliantly. No one had been seriously hurt. Bucher had been utterly ruined and totally humiliated. And, albeit a bit late in the day, the Birnbaums had been accorded a measure of vengeance for the loss of their home and their younger daughter, Naomi.

Johann was driving with Elise beside him, her arm lightly resting on his knee. In the back, Thomas and Max perched uncomfortably on wooden boxes.

Johann called out, 'But the real belle of the ball was our dear Rudi, who is, without doubt, the Führer of our little band. His acting was nothing short of perfection. Heil Rudi!'

All present loudly echoed his parody of the salute to Hitler. 'And,' added Max, unusually animated by the evening's riveting chain of events, 'I must put in a word for the consummate skill of my little painter friend,

Kaspar, who lovingly created those vile and brilliant travesties of our beloved Führer and his faithful subjects.' He gestured in the darkness at the paintings in question which were propped up against the van walls.

'Three cheers for him, and for all of us too,' echoed Elise.

They drove on in silence for a minute or two, then Max called out to Thomas, 'Where did you get that crazy idea of tying the candelabras up so that they fell over one after the other?'

'Probably from the same dark corner of my mind that you came up with the notion of soaking the curtains next to them in premium vodka. Lovely flames, but what a waste of good Russian liquor,' added Johann with a smile.

They turned a corner onto the main road leading into the city centre and were beginning to accelerate away when Elise suddenly called out, 'Look, there he is.'

By the roadside, Hitler's Mercedes car was parked, its engine ticking over almost silently. As they drew up behind it, Rudi stepped out of the vehicle, spoke briefly to the driver and the other passengers, and walked across, every inch a leader of his people.

As the Mercedes whispered away into the night, Rudi clambered up into the back of the van to the plaudits of those inside. It had indeed been a night to celebrate, a culmination of their efforts and an achievement to savour. Only Johann among them felt the first creeping fingers of doubt in his mind. Was this the most they could achieve?

Were their increasingly high-profile undertakings actually leading them into serious danger and risking their lives?

At his side, Elise squeezed his knee and said quietly, 'Cheer up, Liebling, we have all done well tonight. Don't look so gloomy.'

Johann forced a smile but his thoughts were filled with misgivings and anxieties about the future. It was almost as if they had become too successful and, as his father used to tell him, pride comes before a fall.

Chapter Twenty-Five

Johann walked slowly up the steep cobbled roadway towards the castle. It was late evening with a wintry bite in the air. The first eddies of the heavy snow which would soon blanket the whole of Bavaria for the coming months danced and sparkled in the street lights. He forced his hands deeper into his overcoat pockets and leaned against the stiffening wind.

He still loved to walk at night over the Pegnitz bridge to the medieval market square, where he let his feet take him through to the upper part of the old town and along the castle walls. The brisk walk still helped to clear his head and prepared him for a good night's rest and another day caring for his patients. And, now, much more than ever, he felt he was actually doing something positive against the deprivations of the Nazi Party, although he could not shake off his concerns and worries for the future. His diary entries too were now reporting on actual achievements rather than vague aspirations.

As he approached the timber-framed Albrecht Dürer house, a crescendo of laughter and raucous singing blasted out from a bar across the road. The front door opened and two drunken figures staggered out. The Brownshirt duo stuck their right hands in the air and bellowed, 'Heil Hitler!' at no one in particular and made their uncertain way down the steep hill towards the city centre. Johann experienced a profound sense of relief that they had not directed their attention at him and demand that he too, should salute the Führer. For all their achievements, he and countless others were still at the mercy of thugs like those Brownshirts, and a whisker away from humiliation or far worse.

He turned left, parallel to the castle walls, and continued on his way, thinking back, as he did so, over the hectic events of the past months. His original wild notion of fighting back against Nazism and all it stood for seemed to have been surprisingly successful, but he was becoming increasingly anxious, seeing Gestapo agents hiding around every corner and behind every lamppost, and fearing that unwitting security breaches in the group would cause serious trouble for them all in the future. He stopped, suddenly, and looked behind him, but the street was empty, at least as far as he could see. Maybe, though, it wasn't all paranoia, especially because of Max's secretary, Eva, and her predicament with Erpenbeck.

He walked back quickly to his car and drove home. Elise saw that he was close to exhaustion, and urged him to go to bed early so that he could get as much sleep as possible. He took little persuading and followed her up the stairs.

The dream came less often now but, that night, it invaded his slumbers with greater savagery than ever before. The spectators at the Party meeting were not just beaten by the Brownshirts, they were pummelled into a pulp and dismembered. Bloody and broken bodies were scattered everywhere. In the dream, Johann himself only escaped by playing dead and waiting until the marauding Brownshirts had torn everyone else limb from limb and had departed, leaving the hall echoing to the sound of dripping blood and the anguished cries of the injured.

The location switched again to their bedroom and the sound of knocking at the door was like the hammering of a pile driver, brutally thundering on and on until he woke in a sweat—and he suddenly realised that, once again, this was no mere dream. The insistent battering at the door persisted, so he dragged himself out of bed and made his way towards the stairs.

Elise, wakened by the din, pleaded with him not to answer, but he said very quietly, 'If they are coming to get me, whoever they are, they will do so regardless of whether I open the door or try to run and hide.'

Still half asleep, he staggered down the stairs into the hallway and opened the door.

'Johann Voss?'

The Gestapo officer snapped impatiently at him. Johann nodded, too fearful to ask why they were battering down his front door at two in the morning.

'Come with us.'

'Couldn't I just get dressed and... '

'Come. Now.'

Behind the officer, he could see three other figures in uniform and, at the roadside, a covered army lorry, its engine ticking over noisily. He could almost sense the other residents of this quiet suburban road peering anxiously through the curtains to see what was happening. They would be fearful for their own safety but guiltily relieved that, this time, the Gestapo had not come calling on them. The officer grabbed Johann by the elbow and marched him forcibly towards the back of the lorry.

As he was being roughly shoved up into the interior of the vehicle, he looked up at the house and saw Elise's white face in the bedroom window, mouthing words he could not make out. Then a hood was pulled roughly over his head, the driver's door slammed shut and the vehicle drove off into the darkness.

For several minutes, Elise was so severely shaken by the speed with which Johann had been snatched and taken away that she could only sit sobbing on the bed, trembling with fear. One second, they had been safe and asleep, the next, her husband had been thrown into a truck and brutally abducted. Gradually, she managed to calm down and, as she did so, she began to ask herself what, if anything, she could possibly do to help Johann.

For some moments she was too distressed to think clearly but, at last, she resolved to call Thomas, despite the fact that it was after two o'clock in the morning. She hurried down the stairs into the consulting room and picked up the telephone. After several rings, a sleepy woman's voice said, none too cheerfully, 'Who is this?'

Elise had sufficient presence of mind to recall that Thomas's wife was unaware of his membership of the group and was an ardent supporter of Herr Hitler, so she chose her words carefully, despite her desperate need to help Johann.

'Frau Braun? I'm sorry to disturb you in the middle of the night. There is a crisis situation at the central depot and we need to speak to your husband immediately.'

'Very well,' came the tart response.

After a longish pause, Thomas's voice came on the line. 'Hello? What's the problem?'

'It's me—Elise. I'm desperate and I don't know what to do. I told your wife it's the tram depot on the line with an emergency, but what's actually happened is that the Gestapo came battering our front door down and dragged Johann away, presumably to their damned headquarters. I'm out of my mind with worry and you were the only person I could think of who might be able to find a way of doing something.'

Thomas pondered for a few seconds, then said in his best managerial tone to an imaginary subordinate, 'Right. It sounds as if your problem at the workshops can't be fixed without me coming in personally, so I'll be on my way to deal with it immediately.'

'Thank you so much, Thomas. I understand what you are saying and I presume you'll be contacting Max and Rudi.'

'I certainly will. Now, I must go and get myself dressed.'

A door was flung open, boots clunked across the floor and the hood was whipped roughly from him. An SS officer stomped to his desk and sat down. Johann blinked rapidly and shook his head. A purple bruise covered his right cheek, and a nasty gash on his forehead oozed a dark ribbon of blood.

A bright table light was pointed straight at him, nearly blinding him. He peered at the figure behind the desk, but he was unable to make out more than a blurred outline. Shivering half with cold, half with fear, he waited nervously. Suddenly, the SS officer sat up, removed his cap and placed it on the table before him and stared intently at his prisoner.

'Don't you remember me, Herr Doktor?'

Johann stiffened and an electric jolt of fear shot through him. That voice, which had trembled with terror the last time he heard it, was now supremely arrogant and powerful. He recognised it instantly. It was that vile Leutnant Erpenbeck, clearly now intent on exacting vengeance and on forcing him to reveal the identities of his comrades. Up until now, Johann had never experienced utter fear and helplessness, but now despair swept over him like a relentless tide. He slumped in the chair. Oh God, he thought, how did we ever believe we'd get away with it?

Erpenbeck stood up and moved round the table towards Johann, clearly relishing the situation.

'Did you think you could inflict that humiliation on me with impunity? She was just a little Jewish bitch, a totally worthless chunk of juicy flesh and you felt you could play the part of God and punish me, a National Socialist Gestapo officer, for taking what was my right? Damn you, Dr Voss, you and the rest of your nasty little gang are all about to regret the day they were ever born.'

Erpenbeck signalled to the two Gestapo men who were standing by the wall. They stepped rapidly forward, grabbed Johann by the arms and dragged him across the room. He was brutally gagged and hooded again, and one wrist was tied to a rope which was thrown over a butcher's hook hanging from the ceiling.

A violent yank on the rope nearly dislocated his arm and he was dragged upright, feet just touching the floor. One of the officers stepped up on a chair to tie his other wrist to the free end of the rope so that he was left half suspended from the ceiling, arms high above his head. If he relaxed his feet, the pain of his twisted outstretched arms would rapidly force him to stand again on his toes until he could no longer endure it.

Erpenbeck, sitting at the desk, quietly observed him for some considerable time.

'If you are making yourself nice and comfortable, Dr Voss, I think we'll begin.'

He cracked the whip and the tip licked across Johann's belly, leaving an ugly welt. The hooded figure twisted in agony and uttered a muffled howl of pain.

'Not hard enough for you, Dr Voss? Remember, we are only just beginning to get under way. Further down the road, there's a little procedure waiting for you, without benefit of anaesthetic, of course, as we are somewhat underfunded and cannot afford to throw Reichsmarks away on such luxuries for proven enemies of the German nation.'

He paused, then flicked the whip across Johann's midriff again. The searing pain was unbearable and he jerked and contorted his body in a vain attempt to escape the lash.

'Now, what was it you called that procedure? Ah, yes, that was it—circumcision, I do believe.'

Once again, the hooded figure twisted and turned and fought to shake itself free.

'But, before we go that far, though, do let me tell you how it was that I found you out, Dr Johann Voss,' sneered Erpenbeck. 'You and your little gang were very clever in covering your tracks and keeping well out of the limelight, but I managed to hunt you down via a certain Herr Feinlein.' Johann groaned inwardly at the mention of Max's name and wondered in his anguish if he too had been taken prisoner.

'More of him in a moment. I had already assumed that my tormentors included a trained medical doctor and a nurse. So I acquired a list of general practitioners in Nuremberg and noticed that at least twenty of them employed their wives as nurses. Clearly, I did not want to go through official channels as that would involve explaining how our first little meeting came about and expose me to further ridicule. So, as I was, so to speak, freelancing and trying to hunt you down in my spare time, it took a while for me to work my way down the people on the list. Fortunately for you, it was in alphabetical order, so your name had yet to be checked out.'

He paused to take a sip of water from a glass on the table and to lash Johann once more with a practised swish of the horsewhip. Johann twisted in agony, but he was efficiently bound and any evasive movement only served to increase his suffering.

'Now, where was I? Ah, yes, doctors with nurses for wives. I was beginning to wonder if you weren't from the city but had been brought into Nuremberg from elsewhere in Germany to assault an officer of the Reich in that appalling fashion when I got lucky.

'As you may know, I am quite a success with the ladies and I make good use of those skills in my work for our Party and the Reich. We keep a watchful eye on senior figures in our local society, particularly those who are not Party members, and Curator Max Feinlein fell into that category. Purely as a precautionary measure, you understand.'

Erpenbeck was clearly relishing every moment of his revenge and Johann told himself through the fog of pain that his one consolation was that, for every minute Erpenbeck kept speaking, that was one minute of real torture inflicted on him postponed.

'It was drawn to my attention that his secretary, Eva, was a lonely mousey little woman stifled by a lack of male companionship, if you follow my drift. It was not difficult to strike up a conversation with her and, well, one thing led to another until we became, how shall I put it, the closest of friends.

'I soon discovered that she had elderly parents who were not in the best of health. They were living in relative poverty and she was trying to support them as best she could, so I told her I would arrange for them to be transferred to one of the premium homes the Reich normally reserves for the ailing elderly relatives of top Party members, on condition, of course, that she kept a watchful eye on her boss, listened in on his telephone calls, and regularly reported back to me. She particularly enjoyed that last bit, because I was able to offer her a rather delicious reward on each occasion. Completely uncircumcised too.

'Pity about her parents though, as they are actually due to be carted off on one of the next trainloads to a concentration camp, along with other undesirables.

'Anyway, for a while, Eva, the secretary, couldn't offer much more than tittle-tattle and the dull daily routine of museum work. Herr Feinlein kept very much to himself and seemed to be a paragon of virtue, until just recently, that is, when she recently told me of an urgent call he made to the wife of someone called Johann, requesting a meeting at the Castle Room of the Mautkeller.'

Johann bitterly recalled making light of Max's fears about Eva reporting on their meeting, but it now appeared that those concerns were fully justified. Erpenbeck, clearly revelling in the situation, continued his account after taking a generous slug of schnapps from the bottle on his desk.

'Now, that sparked my curiosity, and I was casting my eye down the rest of the list of doctors married to nurses when I saw the names Johann Voss and his wife, Elise Voss. Now, Johann's a common enough name, of course, but then I happened to pick up a photo of Herr Feinlein from his file and, on close examination, it triggered a faint recollection in my mind. I know I was befuddled and rather fearful at the utterly deplorable situation you had placed me in when you exacted your so-called vengeance on me, but I managed to recognise a slight resemblance between the Feinlein in the photo and the little man who came to take a picture of me with the supposed Commander of the SS.

'Two plus two, as my maths teacher used to say, always add up to the same total, and—here you are, about to pay a very heavy price indeed for what you perpetrated against me. As for your friends, I will deal with them at my leisure. But you have always been my top priority. Eva has become something of a burden, but she's coming to the end of her usefulness anyway, so I'll be eliminating her in my own good time.'

Another sip of schnapps, another flick of the horsewhip. Another twitch of the hooded body, the stomach now streaked ugly red with blood oozing from multiple welts.

'There is one other little matter which I'll need you to sort out for me. I believe that you were implicated in aiding the Birnbaum Jews in their unlawful departure from this country. That little enterprise involved someone sneaking into their bank and emptying their safety deposit box containing assets that should have been forfeited to the state. However, when I forced the bank manager to open the Birnbaums' safety deposit box, this was all I found.'

He swept his hand over a small pile of clothing on the desk.

'Of course,' he said in a parody of an apology, 'you can't see what I'm showing you, but we do have to keep a hood on your handsome head for now. It helps to increase the fear factor, not being able to see what is about to happen to you next. Perhaps, Dr Voss, you will also be able to assist me by explaining how anyone would want to use a safety deposit box to store items of women's clothing, including'—he hefted up the offending object—'a padded brassiere.'

Erpenbeck waited for a while. Then he continued cheerfully, 'So, we have plenty to discuss and there is a great deal of information in that hooded head of yours which, one way or another, I shall extract from you. What happens thereafter depends on the level of your cooperation. You can either die fairly swiftly and not too excessively painfully, or—but I assume I do not have to spell out the alternative. So, shall we get underway with our little question and answer session?'

It was then that Johann knew the real pain was about to begin. How was he going to be able to tolerate it? How long would it be before he gave away the names of the rest of the group? Had Elise contacted them and warned them off? Should he have ever begun this crazy attempt to challenge the Nazi state at all? These and other anguished questions shot through his frightened mind as he tried to prepare himself for the agony to come.

But, suddenly, Erpenbeck was interrupted by a loud knock at the door.

'What is it? I'm very busy here.'

'Sorry, sir', said a voice from outside. 'Phone call for you from your office, sir. They want you to ring back immediately.'

'Donnerwetter. Very well. So, Johann, our little chat has been delayed for the moment, but I'll be back soon, never fear. And, remember, part of the pleasure is the anticipation of what is to come. And, when I've done with you, I think I'll turn my attention next to your dear wife. She must be quite an attractive young woman under that cute nurse's uniform.'

Chapter Twenty-Six

Thomas said goodbye to his wife and left the house. He had decided not to ring Max, as he was convinced that Johann's arrest was not just a random occurrence but a calculated and cold-blooded act based on information which could have pointed the finger at Max or any one of the rest of them.

As he drove through the empty streets of the city, he pondered how it was possible for Johann to be targeted and arrested. He was sure that Max and Rudi were both fully aware of the potential dangers they were facing and tried to determine who, if anyone, could have found out about Johann's identity and his activities.

He was particularly concerned about the 'hospitalisation' of SS Leutnant Erpenbeck because he was now sure that, once that dreadful man had recovered from the shock and humiliation of what he had undergone, he would by now have regained his arrogant self-assurance and must have been moving heaven and earth to try and track down his tormentors. He turned into Max's quiet side street, parked the car and looked carefully up and down. He crossed over to the building where Max lived, pressed his bell and waited. The response was almost instant.

'Who is it?' Max's voice was distorted by the tinny speaker but he clearly sounded concerned.

'Me, Thomas.'

The lock buzzed and Thomas let himself in. He walked along the corridor as quietly as he could and, when he reached the apartment, Max was waiting for him. They shook hands and Max closed the door after looking nervously up and down the hallway. He gestured Thomas to a seat, but he remained standing.

'I was still up when you called. I rarely sleep until well into the night. What is wrong, Thomas?'

'We have a serious crisis on our hands and we've got to act quickly.'

He explained that Elise had rung him at home and told him about Johann's arrest.

'The poor woman sounded frantic and we simply must try and do something to help Johann.'

'Where do you think he is now?'

'Almost certainly at Gestapo Headquarters in one of their rather unpleasant interrogation rooms. What bothers me most is that I suspect Erpenbeck is behind the arrest, although how he has managed to pinpoint Johann defeats me. We have been most careful about keeping information about our group strictly confidential. Anyway, now he has got his hands on Johann, he'll be doing his utmost to extract from him the names of the rest of us who were present when he was in that hospital bed.'

Max scratched his head thoughtfully.

'But how do you propose getting into Gestapo Headquarters of all places? I assume we'll need the acting abilities of Rudi to assist us but we've got to gain entry to the building first and do so without attracting adverse attention.'

'That's where one of my lesser-known talents comes to the fore,' said Thomas with a conspiratorial smile. 'You may recall that the building which the Gestapo took over a couple of years ago was previously part of a municipal office complex. As it happens, I used to work there before I became Chief Engineer for Transport in the city.

'There were all kinds of problems with keys being lost, damaged or misplaced, as a result of which, people couldn't gain entry to their rooms and many lorries and other vehicles which had been parked overnight couldn't be sent off to do the day's work the following morning. So, I set up a bank of spare sets of keys and began to introduce a system of master keys. At the same time, I became fascinated by the abilities of the locksmiths I engaged.

'As a result, I became pretty skilled at literally opening doors and I also acquired my own set of master keys for the entire building. Which I happen'—he dipped his hand into his coat pocket and withdrew a metal ring holding several keys—'to have kept in a drawer at home in case there were any problems with the locks at a future date.'

'Brilliant,' said Max, 'I suppose that you can open street doors as well as internal doors?'

'Indeed I can. We are going to enter Gestapo Headquarters via a little-used rear entrance which can be accessed from one end of the underground car park, and that means we can gain access slightly more subtly than Johann and Rudi did with those goods wagons at the railway station.'

'You're absolutely right, they could have made use of your services then. Keys do tend to be a little quieter than bolt cutters, so they tell me. Shall we go now and call on Rudi?'

'Absolutely.'

Rudi's apartment was situated in a rundown quarter of the city, at the end of a cul-de-sac. Thomas parked the car and Max said, 'Let me go and wake him up. You can be turning the car round, ready to drive off quickly, just in case there's a problem.'

Max entered the apartment block, which had no main entrance door, and knocked gently on Rudi's ground-floor apartment door. Silence. He knocked again, this time a little more firmly. Still no response. Aware that he might waken the warden in charge of the apartments, he exited the building and walked swiftly round to the side, where he located what he hoped was one of Rudi's windows.

This time a couple of taps on the glass did the trick. Rudi's pale and fearful face appeared through the curtain. He smiled faintly and waved when he saw Max and gestured that he would open his door for him.

Max quickly explained about Johann and told him about their plan to search for him at Gestapo Headquarters. Outside, Thomas waited anxiously for the two of them.

Ten minutes later, Max emerged, followed by Rudi, who was carrying a large holdall. 'I've stuffed a couple of uniforms in this bag in case of need. And I'm pretty sure we'll be requiring them tonight.'

When the two piled into Thomas's car, Rudi said, 'I'm glad you didn't make too much racket just now. The block warden in the apartment next to mine is a red-blooded Nazi and would report me the second I appeared to step out of line.'

They stopped the car a couple of streets away from the back of the headquarters building. On the way there, Rudi had struggled into a Gestapo uniform and, when Thomas got out of the car, he donned the shiny dark grey overcoat and a broad-brimmed hat of a plainclothes Gestapo officer.

The plan they had concocted in the car involved Thomas and Rudi dragging Max, who would be acting the role of a prisoner, along the basement corridors in search of Johann, though how they were going to find him without shouting out his name and drawing attention to themselves had not been worked out in any detail.

'This way,' whispered Thomas, turning down a flight of steps to a metal doorway. He stopped abruptly. 'Damn.'

'What's wrong?' asked Rudi.

'This is a brand new door and I don't have a key for it.'

'So what are we going to do?'

'We are going'—he fished a set of skeleton keys out of his pocket—'to put my skills as a lock picker to the test. Stand back and prepare to be amazed.'

Thomas examined the lock carefully, then selected one of his tools and set about trying to unpick the lock. After several attempts, Thomas was close to admitting defeat.

'Can I try something?' said Max, tentatively.

'Surely.'

He reached forward, twisted the handle, and pushed. The door swung open, creaking a little on its hinges. Rudi and Max gave a nervous laugh.

'That was a bit too easy,' said Thomas contritely.

'Just wanted you to conserve your energies for the real tasks ahead,' smiled Max.

They peered into the gloom. A set of steps led downwards and disappeared round a corner to the left. Thomas edged past the open door and the others cautiously followed him. When they reached the turn in the steps, Thomas stuck his head around.

'There's another door,' he whispered. 'It is almost certainly locked, but this time it should open with one of my master keys.'

He reached into his pocket and drew out his keys again, selected one, and inserted it into the lock. Nothing. A second key gave a satisfying click and the door opened.

'We're in,' he whispered.

Slowly, he pushed at the door. It gave access to a dimly lit corridor with doors alternating on either side, but this part of the basement area did not appear to be in use. The three of them walked cautiously along the corridor to another door at the far end. Thomas unlocked it with the same key and pulled it slowly towards him.

Their senses were immediately assaulted by the stench of disinfectant and human excrement, overlaid by the tart odour of raw fear. Then came the sounds, muted groans, angry raised voices, a scream of agony and despairing sobs. Distant doors slammed, boots clattered along concrete floors. The subdued lighting cast dark, menacing shadows.

'Where shall we start?' whispered Rudi. 'We can't very well call his name out, can we? In any event, the poor man may not even be conscious. And, if we're really unlucky, he'll be a corpse already, if he's even here, that is.'

'I don't think he's dead,' said Thomas in an undertone, 'Erpenbeck will be anxious to make him give up our identities, then force him to suffer for as long as possible before finishing him off.'

He looked from left to right. 'Let's start with this door over here, Interrogation Room One.'

Thomas tried opening the door but it was locked. He selected a different master key and turned it gently in the lock. He swung the door open and stepped inside.

His nose was assaulted by the vile stench of human waste and burning flesh. Hunched in a corner lay a prisoner, a man, completely naked, with hideous burn marks across his back. He appeared to be unconscious and near to death. Thomas twisted his head sharply away from the grisly spectacle.

'I think this poor bastard is too far gone for us to be able to help him. He looks as if he wouldn't be able to make it to the corridor, let alone get out of the building.'

Reluctantly, he closed the door, locking it behind him. He listened keenly for a few seconds before moving on to Interrogation Room Two. From inside, he could hear an angry voice being raised. Thomas put his ear to the door. A second voice responded, a barely human wail of despair, pleading innocence.

'That's not Johann either. Let's move on.'

No sounds could be heard from inside the third interrogation room. Maybe, thought Thomas, it was empty and waiting for the next unfortunate individual to be dragged here to be tortured and murdered. Still, he tried the door, found it locked, but opened it with a practised twist of the master key.

Inside, the room was lit by a single low-intensity bulb and appeared to be empty. Then, as their eyes grew accustomed to the gloom, they could gradually make out a gruesome sight.

At the far side of the room, hanging from the ceiling by a rope suspended from a butcher's hook was a hooded figure, naked except for a pair of soiled briefs, feet barely touching the ground.

'No luck here either, it seems,' said Thomas as he turned to go, but Rudi stopped him.

'That fellow's about the size and physique of Johann,' he whispered.

'So are any number of people,' countered Thomas.

They were about to leave the room when Rudi held them back again. 'Just hang on a second… Look, I think I see something I recognise.'

He pointed at the man's lower leg. 'Take a peek at that deep scar with stitches on it. Didn't Johann cut his leg rather badly when we were making our escape with the Birnbaums from the goods yard?'

'You're damned right. That must be Johann. I'll lock the door. You get him down from that bloody hook.'

He was about to dash and secure the door but, before they could release Johann, a pair of military boots pounded along the corridor outside and came to a halt. Thomas, Max and Rudi flattened themselves against the wall by the door. The door swung open and Leutnant Erpenbeck strode into the room. He picked up the horsewhip lying on the table.

'Now, Dr Johann Voss, I think I have kept you waiting long enough. At last, the real entertainment is about to begin. And, I can assure you, you will talk. Sooner or later.'

Erpenbeck flung the horsewhip back as he prepared to deal Johann a vicious blow across his bare shoulders, but the door was slammed shut behind him. There was a brief scuffle and a loud thud as he collapsed on the floor, coughed and passed out.

Thomas stood over him, rubbing the knuckles of his right hand as he gave Erpenbeck a couple of thoughtful kicks.

'One of my best punches that, a right hook to the jaw. I'm glad I haven't lost my touch completely. I'll lock the door while you two release poor Johann.'

As they eased Johann to the floor, Thomas joined them, removed the hood, carefully untied the gag and pulled the dirty cloth out of his mouth. Johann blinked, bewildered, in considerable pain and very frightened. His lips formed the words, 'Thank you', then his head tilted forward and he lost consciousness for a second or two.

'Thank, God, Johann, we've managed to find you. Now, let's get you out of here as quickly as we can.'

Rudi came across from the table, the glass of schnapps in his hand. 'Johann, open your eyes and take a drink of this.'

Johann managed to choke down some of the fiery liquor, shook his head and whispered, 'How did you get in here?'

Rudi replied, 'Thomas had a set of master keys but he'll explain to you how he got them later. Now, we must go.'

Max intervened, 'We can't just leave Erpenbeck here. He'll raise merry hell and we'll all be pursued until they string the lot of us up like Johann was just now. He clearly knows all about us.'

'We are going to have to think of some way of preventing him from talking,' urged Max.

Thomas held up a hand. 'I have an idea. A little brutal, perhaps, but it should serve to stop him from betraying us and also teach him part two of the lesson he should already have learned the first time around. You must all bear in mind the fact that Erpenbeck came into this room determined to torture Johann to death.'

Thomas explained to them what had to be done, and they reluctantly agreed that this was the only way of keeping themselves from falling into the hands of the Gestapo.

They stripped off Erpenbeck's uniform and gently eased it onto Johann, who tried not to cry out with the pain of bruised muscles and torn flesh. The gag was stuffed into Erpenbeck's mouth and the hood placed over his head.

'I'm going to ache for months,' croaked Johann.

'You'll have plenty of time to enjoy your recovery but, right now, if you could manage to assist us a little by undoing the other end of that rope, it will help Rudi and me to prepare our dear Leutnant for his just chastisement.'

Johann gave a half smile and, when he feebly tried to loosen the rope, Thomas rushed over to help him.

As they continued with their work, the sound of boots once more echoed along the corridor. They paused outside, and there was a loud knock on the door.

Rudi put a finger to his lips to silence the others and then called out in a peremptory tone, 'What is it? I am very busy in here.'

Voices muttered outside, then, 'Sorry. We were told Interrogation Room Three was available. We'll just try a room further down.'

The boots clattered away down the corridor as they all gave a sigh of relief and went back to work. Together, they bound the still unconscious Erpenbeck, yanked the hood hard down over his head and hoisted him up by the meat hook suspended from the ceiling.

Thomas went across to the desk and picked up a sheet of paper. 'Looks like an arrest warrant. Let's modify it a little, shall we? It already has the unnamed prisoner down as a Communist activist.' He thought for a moment. 'Let's also brand him as a homosexual offender against the New Germany.' He scribbled a few words and looked up at their prisoner.

'We'll have to give him a tickle with the horsewhip to make him look a bit more authentic,' he said, and Rudi volunteered for the task.

One crack of the whip and an ugly bluish-red welt appeared across the middle of Erpenbeck's back. A second flick and the pain of the blow must have caused him to regain consciousness because he started to moan and twist and turn in a vain attempt to break free.

Johann gestured at the pile of clothing on the desk and said to Rudi, 'You may recognise that little lot from your escapade at the bank. Perhaps you could put a dress on him to add an authentic touch to the charge sheet.'

Rudi nodded eagerly and went across to pick up one of the items of female attire. He handed it over to Thomas, who smiled and went up to the hooded figure. He spoke in a quiet, venomous tone.

'SS Leutnant Wilhelm Erpenbeck, you did not learn your lesson from us the first time around, so perhaps you will do so on this occasion.

'We are going to leave you here to the tender mercies of your colleagues, who will doubtless go about their labours with their usual enthusiasm. Not least, of course, because we have changed a couple of details on the arrest form on your desk. We have left the space for a name blank, but underneath 'Communist political criminal' we have added 'rampant homosexual' and, to make that a bit more credible, we thought we would add an item of female clothing to your young and masculine body. One padded bra, which has already seen combat, so to speak. I trust it fits you snugly, Leutnant.'

Thomas lifted up the bra and attached it around Erpenbeck's chest. 'Now you really do look like one of the homosexuals you have been pursuing so ardently along with the Communists and Jews. If I had half-an-hour to spare, we would have performed a circumcision on you with a pair of blunt scissors, but time presses and we really must make good our escape.'

Johann struggled into Erpenbeck's greatcoat and, as he did so, he noticed a black briefcase on the floor by the desk.

'We should take this with us. It might contain useful information and, at the very least, it's a valuable prop.'

As they were leaving, Johann moved close to Erpenbeck and whispered in his ear, 'Whatever happens to you next, and it won't be very pleasant, do remember the names of Naomi and Ruth as you writhe in agony and beg your captors to kill you. Although, I doubt if they will hear much of what you have to say, given the fact that you are very efficiently gagged.'

The hooded figure wrestled violently to try and free itself but, when Thomas tied a knot, it stayed tied.

Chapter Twenty-Seven

As they moved swiftly down the corridor, two Gestapo officers appeared suddenly from one of the other interrogation rooms. They had clearly just completed dealing with a prisoner and were smiling and joking with each other as they locked the door. When they saw Thomas and the others, they stopped and looked questioningly at them.

Rudi quickly assessed the situation, stepped forward and snapped in his best Gestapo Kriminalinspektor tone, 'Have you finished your work in there?' He nodded towards the door they had just closed.

'Yes, sir. Our man has sadly just passed away from, er, natural causes.'

The other officer smirked. 'About as natural as they get down here.'

Rudi laughed in reply. 'Did the fool try and catch a bullet between his teeth?'

'Something like that, sir.'

'Right then. Could you do us a favour and give your attention to the gentleman in Number Three? He's a Communist and one of the local homosexual community as well, so we'd be obliged if you could ensure that he might be persuaded to end his days by means of one of your natural causes. The necessary paperwork is on the desk. Do take your time with him. We, unfortunately, have to go out on pressing business, as we have a couple more potential customers to be arrested.'

'I think we could manage that, sir.' The two officers laughed and moved past them on their way to Room Three. Erpenbeck, it seemed, was about to enjoy the benefits of a natural death, although none of the group relished the prospect of causing the demise of another human being, however vile.

It was approaching four in the morning as they removed their uniforms, bundled into Thomas's car and prepared to drive off. Johann, his voice still hoarse, suddenly cut in,

'Stop a moment before you drive off. First, many, many thanks for getting me out of that dreadful place. I'd be dead by now if it wasn't for you all. But we must pause for a moment and think. We are pretty sure that Erpenbeck will be finished off by those fine Gestapo men we met just now in the corridor. However, we really must tidy up after him, so to speak.'

'What do you mean?' asked Rudi. 'Our priority is to get away from this place and drive you back home so that lovely wife of yours can tend to your wounds.'

Johann eased his aching body around to address them. 'No, we must sort this business out properly before anything else. Erpenbeck must have come here by car and my guess is that what he was doing was not entirely officially sanctioned, but that he'd had the help of a couple of friends in the Gestapo who arrested me, allowed him access to the interrogation room and acted as his aides. His car must be somewhere around here, and'—he fished into the briefcase—'you're not the only one here who is a wizard with locks. Here are Erpenbeck's keys. I believe he drives a black Mercedes. We must dispose of it before we do anything else. It would be a little awkward if his car was found abandoned inside Gestapo Headquarters.'

Rudi spoke up. 'You're right, Johann. We have to cover our traces thoroughly, even though we're all desperate to get you back home to have your injuries treated.'

There was a short silence as they considered what they should do next.

'First,' said Rudi brightly, 'we must find the vehicle.'

'Not a problem,' said Thomas. 'He would park in one of the visitor spaces in the underground car park. And there shouldn't be too many black Mercedes around at this time of night.'

'But once we discover where the car is, we have to decide what to do with it,' Johann insisted.

Max had been quiet for some while. Suddenly, he spoke up. 'I have been giving the matter some thought. Erpenbeck will, we hope, be shortly deceased, and I suspect that there will be little reverence for the body. It will just be piled into the back of a lorry and ditched in a mass grave.

'However, if we can persuade people to accept an alternative scenario, we can ensure that everyone will conclude that Leutnant Erpenbeck died elsewhere, as the result of a tragic accident. I don't know if you are familiar with the side road leading out of the city towards the little town of Lauf an der Pegnitz, but there's a bridge over the river about halfway there immediately after a sharp left bend. I nearly came to grief there myself a little while ago and I was wondering if Leutnant Erpenbeck might be driving along that road a little too fast and failed to make the turning.

'The car would end up in the river, with his greatcoat and briefcase in it, but the driver's door could have come open in the force of the crash. The deceased's body will have drifted in the strong current and, after a cursory search, he'll simply be reported as an accidental death. How does that sound—for a death by natural causes?'

'That has all the makings of an excellent plan,' said Johann. 'Let's do it.'

Some twenty minutes later, they had left the outskirts of Nuremberg and were well on the road towards Lauf. Thomas drove Max and Johann, and Rudi was at the wheel of the SS car. Thomas's rear lights flashed several times to warn Rudi that they were close to the bridge, and they drew up together by the roadside.

Johann rummaged through Erpenbeck's briefcase and said, 'There are a couple of files here which might be of interest to us, but the rest is just the ordinary stuff people take with them, including a fairly elderly-looking sliced sausage sandwich wrapped in a cloth, and a half drunk bottle of schnapps.'

He removed the files and handed the briefcase to Max. Thomas stepped out of the car and went forward with Rudi to examine the lie of the land. The road before them made a sharp bend to the left immediately before the narrow bridge and, to the right, there was a flimsy paling fence stretching across a steep drop down a grassy slope to the waters below.

Rudi said, 'I'll drive at the fence and try and knock it over so the car will roll down the slope more easily.' He returned to the driver's seat and jerked the car forward. With a satisfying crunch, the fence collapsed and he braked hard to stop the car from sliding down into the river with him in it. He opened the door, jumped out and gave it a hefty kick.

'Come and help me bend the driver's door back,' he called. 'We need it to be forced open so the police will assume that Erpenbeck's body was thrown out by the impact and floated down the river. Johann, you stay in the car. You are in no fit state for physical exercise.'

Five minutes later, Erpenbeck's Mercedes, its passenger door wrenched open by their combined efforts, was crashing down the decline and landed in the Pegnitz with an impressive splash. Half a minute later, only the roof of the car was visible above the fast-flowing river. A second or two after, that too had disappeared.

As they stood watching, the sound of an approaching vehicle could be heard. 'Quick,' said Thomas urgently, 'open the bonnet. I'll look inside and pretend to be searching for a fault. There's a torch in the boot. Get it for me.'

A pair of bright headlights swept across the trio as they solemnly inspected the internal workings of the engine compartment. The other vehicle slowed down, then stopped. Out stepped a policeman, who sauntered officiously towards them.

'Thank goodness for small mercies,' said Max under his breath. 'It's the local police not the Gestapo.'

'Can I ask what you gentlemen are doing here at this hour?' The police officer's words were polite but his manner was wary and somewhat aggressive.

Thomas lifted his head up from inspecting the engine and said, ''Morning, officer. The trouble seems to be a loose plug lead, but it won't take long to fix it.'

The policeman nodded but persisted in his questioning. 'Running repairs I can understand, but it's a pretty odd time for anyone to be out and about on our roads so, I must ask you again, what are you doing here at this time in the morning?'

Rudi came to the rescue. 'We've just spent a very pleasant night at the Sommerkabarett, officer. It's my birthday and we have been celebrating. The evening's performances were pretty amazing and I can heartily recommend them. The comedians were especially funny.'

The policeman shuffled his feet uncertainly. This seemed to be a genuine enough situation, but he sensed that the trio were tense and ill at ease.

'And the fellow in the car?' He nodded towards the back seat.

'He's lost to the world. Too much schnapps, I'm afraid, and his wife will not be best pleased with him when we get him home.'

The officer hesitated for a second, then said, 'All right, gentlemen. You may continue on your journey.'

He got back into his vehicle and switched on his headlights. Thomas closed the bonnet and watched anxiously as the policeman prepared to drive off. But, suddenly, the officer seemed to change his mind, as he got out of the car again and strode back towards them. He pointed to one side of the bridge.

'Do you see that damaged fence over there?' he asked.

Thomas twisted his head around, trying to act as unconcerned as possible. 'Oh, that. I believe that was caused by an accident some time ago.'

'Really?' said the policeman. 'I haven't worked this area for a month and the damage looks fairly new to me.' He took a couple of paces towards the fence.

'Officer?' asked Thomas. 'May we continue now?'

The policeman paused, moved away from the fence and said, 'Yes, I suppose so... No. There is just one further matter.'

Thomas and the others strained to act normally, but their nerves were taught as piano wire. What could the damned man want now? Had he seen some kind of fault on the vehicle?

'And what is that?' Thomas asked nervously.

'Well...' said the policeman, 'you informed me that you had been attending the Sommerkabarett.'

'Yes. Indeed we were.' Thomas was making a valiant attempt at sounding nonchalant.

'Sir, I have a question to put to you. Did you see Little Marlene performing?'

'Pardon?'

'Little Marlene. Was she on stage this evening?'

Rudi cut in. 'Are you referring to the comedian doing the Little Marlene routine?'

'Yes, sir. I saw her a fortnight ago. She was brilliant.' 'You mean… ..' Rudi cheekily switched his voice over to that of Little Marlene, 'Oh, Mr Hitler, can I sit on your knee, please? And why would I want to do that? So I can see Austria from up here and check if we've taken it over yet… '

The policeman guffawed, then said, 'That's her all right. Not a particularly good imitation though. I give you four out of ten.'

Still chortling, he waved them off before making his way back towards his car.

'Let's get out of here!' said Thomas. He drove off slowly as if they did not have a care in the world. As the police car's lights disappeared round a bend, he twisted his head round to Rudi and said laughing, 'He didn't think much of your attempt at Little Marlene, did he? Four out of ten, that's hardly a ringing endorsement.'

'Let me tell you a story,' Rudi countered defensively. 'Once upon a time, the great opera singer Enrico Caruso came back from the dead and entered a Caruso look-alike singing competition. He came ninth. I rest my case.'

They all laughed uproariously, partly at Rudi's joke, but also with huge relief at having emerged unscathed from a potentially dangerous situation. Fortunately, the police officer was so preoccupied with the broken fence that he had not noticed that the carload of revellers was actually returning the way it came, back to Nuremberg, rather than onwards to Lauf.

Chapter Twenty-Eight

The next morning, Johann woke quite early to find Elise sitting in a chair by the consulting room table on which he was lying. She was observing him closely with a concerned expression on her face. His whole body hurt, which was not surprising, since his injuries were found to be more extensive than she had first thought, with two suspected cracked ribs and all manner of cuts and bruises, many of which required stitches, but his lacerations from the whip were painful rather than serious. His sleep had been restless and he had clearly been badly affected by what had happened to him.

When he arrived back from Gestapo Headquarters with Max, Thomas and Rudi, Johann had managed to tell Elise about his interrogation as she tended to his injuries. He was tentative when it came to explaining what had happened to Erpenbeck, but she responded instantly that he thoroughly deserved his fate. She had snapped curtly that a man who treats people like animals should expect no mercy at all from his fellow human beings.

After he had taken a couple of sips of coffee, Johann recalled the folder of files which he had found and asked Elise if it had been safely brought back.

'Yes, Liebling. They're here on the desk. Thomas told me to let you have them, but you must concentrate first on getting yourself on the road to recovery. You have had a truly dreadful experience, and it will take a long time for you to become fully well again.'

'Just leave them on the side table and I'll look at them when I've rested.'

Elise busied herself checking his bandages and replacing those which had become badly bloodstained. When she had finished, she gave him painkillers and told him to rest. She would check him again in a couple of hours and, in the meantime, she would busy herself cancelling appointments and doing administrative work for the practice. Thomas, Rudi and Max were in the sitting room talking over the night's events and waiting to speak to him. They would have to wait until he had had a proper rest, she insisted.

Johann slept for another couple of hours and, when he woke, it was near midday. He was reaching out to ring the bell to call Elise when his eye fell on the files he had taken from Erpenbeck's briefcase. I'll just look through these papers, he thought, and see if there's anything of interest in them.

The first of the two documents inside appeared to be a report by an agent who was trailing a local businessman. The latest entry described the man's visit to a house in the red light district, where he stayed for about twenty minutes and then re-emerged 'with a definite smile on his face', according to the agent.

Johann laughed painfully and turned to the second set of papers. This time the report was slightly different. It appeared that the agent had also been tasked with trying to find some reason to arrest and charge a top official in the local authority. The man had clearly failed in his endeavours and he ended by proposing that the suspect should be implicated with the businessman and his visit to the brothel in the previous file. He could then be indicted for immoral conduct and suitably dealt with. Odd, thought Johann, there's no reference to a name, just Case NU4566. He was just replacing the two sheets of paper, when he felt a piece of card inside the folder.

He retrieved it and found that it was a small photograph. On the back was the number NU4566. He turned it over and… Oh, no, he said to himself. It can't be. He rang the bell on the table urgently.

Elise rushed in to see that Johann was very distressed. 'What's the matter, Liebling? Are you in pain?'

'Is Thomas still here?'

'Yes, Thomas and Max are both in the sitting room hoping to talk to you, but Rudi had to go off to prepare for this evening's performances.'

'Could you ask Thomas to come and see me? Just Thomas.'

'May I ask… '

'Later. I'll explain everything to you when I have got this problem sorted out. Just tell him to drag himself away from whichever bottle of our wine he's checking out and come. Now. Something really bad has turned up but don't say a word to him.'

Mystified, she left the room. Johann quickly scanned through the documents again and took another anxious look at the photograph. The door opened and Thomas peered into the room.

'Well, Lazarus rises from the grave.' Thomas was in a cheerful mood, made all the merrier by the half full glass of red wine he was clutching in his right hand.

'Please, Thomas, take a seat. First, I must thank you again —all of you—for risking your lives and coming to rescue me from that vile place. Now, though, I have something very serious to discuss with you, and I'm at a loss to see how we can deal with it.'

Thomas leaned forward in his chair, looking extremely concerned. 'What are you talking about? What's going on?'

Johann reached over to the folder on his desk. 'You remember that I removed these documents from Erpenbeck's briefcase before consigning it to the waters of the Pegnitz? Well, I have just looked through them, and one of them makes pretty grim reading for you.'

'Me? Why on earth should I figure in Gestapo files?'

'It's not just that you make a star appearance in this document that worries me, Thomas, although that in itself is pretty bad. The worst part is that someone is trying to set you up as a criminal of some kind with the intention of having you transported to a concentration camp and almost certain death. What we must find out first is who is behind this and why on earth they are gunning for you.'

Thomas looked confused and horrified. 'I don't understand what you're talking about, Johann. Just tell me what's in the bloody document, please, never mind how bad it is.'

Johann showed him the agent's report and then the photograph of Thomas with the case number on the back and explained the contents of the two files.

For a full minute, Thomas sat there in total silence, staring at the sheets of paper which might well have condemned him to death but for their chance presence in Erpenbeck's briefcase. Then he rose to his feet and began pacing back and forth. 'I-I cannot begin to see why anyone would want to try and destroy me like this. I could understand an employee with a grievance seeking to attack me in some way, but not in this brutal fashion. And there's no hint in the agent's report about our group and what we have been getting up to, so our little adventures still appear to remain undetected by the Gestapo. That is, except for the late Leutnant Erpenbeck.'

Johann nodded in agreement. 'Trouble is, Thomas, that someone out there is bent on doing you serious harm, and we can only hope that this report is the only document about you in the files. Thank God, it has the appearance of a preliminary response to a request from someone in the Gestapo or SS. More likely SS, given Erpenbeck's position and rank.'

'Thomas, you should... ' His voice trailed away as he saw that his friend was deep in thought. He had stopped pacing and was staring blankly at the opposite wall, which was cheerfully decorated with a chart of the human skeleton.

'Thomas?'

He turned to look at Johann in a dazed, distraught manner. 'I just cannot comprehend what is behind all this. All I can suggest is that we go through the document closely again, and see if there is some kind of clue as to who or what is behind this wretched business.'

Johann said, 'Right. I'll read the report out loud and see if that helps to give us an insight into what exactly is going on.'

Thomas nodded and Johann began reading slowly, pausing at the end of each sentence. He was nearly halfway through the report when Thomas suddenly leapt to his feet and called out, 'Stop!'

Taken aback, Johann paused and looked inquiringly at his friend.

'S-sorry, I did not mean to shout like that. But we're looking in the wrong place for the answer, or at least the beginnings of an answer.'

'What do you mean, the wrong place?'

'Well,' said Thomas roughly, 'I am being remarkably stupid here, making you read through the document when the answer is literally staring me in the face.' He reached out and grabbed the photograph from the table. 'That's the explanation or at least the starting point for one, and the more I think about it, the more disgusted and saddened I become.'

'Thomas, please, take it easy. Sit yourself down. Now.' Thomas reluctantly obeyed. 'Count up to ten or whatever it is you do to calm yourself. Then, tell me, quietly and slowly, what it is you find so shocking about this document.'

Thomas held up the print. 'It's not the document at all, it's the photograph. That's where the explanation is to be found. Look at it. Closely.'

Johann took it and shrugged. 'It's a head and shoulders shot of yourself. The background isn't too clear, but it looks like some kind of building with a garden.'

'No,' said Thomas, 'don't look at my ugly face, look at the paper on which the print has been made.'

Johann examined it carefully, then said, 'That's odd. Three sides of the photo have a crinkly decorative edge, but the right-hand side is straight cut.' He stared closely, then added, 'No, it's not straight, not quite. It's almost as if it's half a photograph which has been sliced in two with a pair of scissors.'

'And, there, dear Johann, lies the explanation of what this is all about.' He twisted the photograph round and round in his hand. 'First, the crinkle cut edge. That's the standard way in which developed prints are processed by the Foto Porst, the leading photographic shop in the city centre just along the street from the Sommerkabarett.

'But, that's not all. I recognise the photograph itself now, although, at first, I was too shocked to do so. It was taken outside my parents' house in a little village to the north of the city. Nothing special about that, you might think. But the important point is the bit that's missing. The original photograph showed me in my parents' front garden, just as the roses were coming into bloom, as I remember, and next to me in the photo—was my dear wife, Gertrud. It was my father who took the picture.'

Johann gradually realised the significance of what Thomas was saying. 'You mean that this photograph was somehow removed from your house, cut in two and handed over to Erpenbeck with the intention of sullying your name and getting you arrested and worse?'

Thomas sighed, his face grim with anger. 'Not just "someone", Johann.' He looked earnestly at his friend, his face contorted with shock and dismay. 'I have been a fool, an utter fool, and not for the first time in my life.'

Thomas paused, struggling to control the emotions which were clearly raging within him, and Johann waited patiently for him to continue.

'There is something I have to tell you that I have been too ashamed to admit to anyone. My wife,' he uttered the words slowly and emphatically as if pronouncing sentence on her, 'is not just a theoretical admirer of all things National Socialist. She has recently been having a sordid affair with one of the leading Gestapo officials in the whole damned city. And it must be Gertrud herself who gave her lover this cut-out portrait of my charming features so that he could go to his friend and colleague, Erpenbeck, in order to try and find a way to blacken my name. That would allow her to get rid of me and then be swept up publicly into his loving arms. And the owner of those loving arms? They belong to none other than Fritz Mergel.'

Johann looked horrified. The name Mergel was notorious throughout Nuremberg as that of a thug and bully who had a serious criminal past and had fought his way into the position of Deputy Chief of Police through his dedication to the Party and his merciless crushing of anyone who dared to stand in his way. Rather like Bucher, he thought grimly.

'A couple of weeks ago, I was driving home early one afternoon and, as I turned into our quiet avenue, a black Mercedes coupé nearly sliced me in two as it swept out into the main road. The driver was none other than Fritz Mergel, his podgy face familiar from countless appearances in the local press, kissing babies at social events, presenting awards to police officers for some casual act of brutality, heiling Hitler at the Party Congress rallies, and generally being a top-drawer leading citizen of the New Germany.

'When I walked into the house, Gertrud was standing at the top of the stairs in a négligé. She claimed that she had been unwell and had only just risen from her bed. The latter part was true, but it was pretty clear to me from her flustered demeanour that she had, not to put too fine a point on it, been expressing her devotion to the Party and its local Deputy Chief of Police on her back in a very practical and sexual fashion. I demanded to know what

Mergel had been doing in our house and she just laughed in my face.

'Because of her blind devotion to the Party, our marriage had more or less fallen apart several months before, a fact which I had been trying to keep private for the sake of our children, but her blatant unfaithfulness shocked me to the core. I told her to pack her bags and leave, which she did without a murmur. Clearly, Herr Mergel had already been preparing a love nest for them both, and she was gone within the hour. I had to call my elderly mother in to help look after the children who were pretty devastated by the sudden departure of their dear mama.'

'I'm so sorry, Thomas,' said Johann.

'She had been seduced long before by the whole glitz and glamour of the high life in the Nazi Party. Like countless other women, she believed that Hitler walked on water and could lead us all into the Promised Land. Mergel just happened along when she was at her most vulnerable and swept her off her feet and into our marriage bed. The woman she had become was no great loss to me, but it was shameful how she had destroyed the life we had built together for ourselves and our children because of her slavish devotion to the Party and her blindness towards its violence and thuggery.'

He paused again, close to tears. He was so outraged by this betrayal, that it was only after several seconds thought, that he realised the full implications of her actions.

He continued, 'But, now, it appears, she and her paramour did not rest content with flaunting their supposed amorous entanglement but are determined to have me removed from circulation in the process. And, for once, I am at a total loss as to what I should do.'

Johann looked compassionately at Thomas.

'Would you mind if I asked Max to join us so that I can tell him what you have just told me? I have the beginnings of an idea which could turn this situation to your advantage. After all, you, Max and Rudi came to my rescue at a time when my own situation appeared to be beyond all help.'

Thomas nodded reluctantly and went to fetch Max. When the two of them came back, Johann explained what had happened and Max expressed his deep regret that Thomas had got himself entangled in a painful and potentially disastrous situation which was none of his making.

Johann said, 'The reason I asked you to join us, Max, is that I believe you can be of considerable assistance in trying to turn this awful situation around.'

'Anything to help, but how can I possibly be of use? Love affairs are not exactly my area of expertise, so I don't see how I could help you.'

'You have a young protégé called Kaspar, who, as we saw when we were bringing about Bucher's downfall, is a genius with a paintbrush. I wonder if he is equally gifted when it comes to forging documents and signatures?'

Max nodded thoughtfully as he began to realise how Kaspar's special talents might be put to use in assisting Thomas. 'You mean, Kaspar could take this report from the agent, tamper with it appropriately to make it seem that Mergel rather than Thomas is the person under suspicion and change the document to make it appear that evidence against him has been found in abundance. Then you could ensure that the document somehow finds its way into the hands of the SS, who are no friends of the local police force at the best of times.'

'Precisely. If Kaspar can forge a painting, I bet his abilities also stretch to imitating someone's handwriting.'

'But,' asked Thomas, puzzled, 'how do you propose to get the modified document to the SS?'

'I don't,' said Johann with a smile. 'You are going to do that. But we now need to find an official-looking photograph of Mergel, and I bet Rudi with his connections with the Double Eagle unit could organise that for us. I also think it's time to call another meeting of the group next week and, on this occasion, I think we can risk a visit to the Mautkeller and the Castle Room.'

It did not take long for Kaspar to produce a revised document, effortlessly copying out Johann's version of its contents which implicated Mergel in all manner of corrupt and immoral activities. It was sealed together with his photograph, which Rudi duly obtained for them, and passed it over to Thomas.

In his office that afternoon, Thomas reached for the telephone and asked his secretary to connect him with

Gestapo Headquarters. He wished to speak, he said, to a senior officer about a serious breach of security. Not long after, he was put through to a pompous-sounding Kriminalinspektor. Thomas took a deep breath and spoke,

'Thank you for taking my call. I am the Chief Engineer for Transport at the central workshops, and it has come to my attention that a folder of state documents marked "Secret" and bearing the address of your headquarters here in Nuremberg has been discovered lodged behind a seat in one of our trams.

'The cleaner who found the documents has been questioned at length and he has stated that it is most probable that the documents fell there by accident and that they have not been opened or tampered with. I can personally confirm this as I have the sealed folder in front of me on my desk. It occurred to me that it would be most tactful to contact you informally, as the loss of such material could be embarrassing to yourselves, and I would not wish for such a thing to become public. I suggest that you arrange for a courier to call round to collect the dossier at your convenience?'

The voice at the other end of the line had begun by being sharply officious, but it became very conciliatory when Thomas pointed out the potential scandal that such a discovery might cause.

Thomas was thanked for his tact and discretion in this matter and, yes, a courier would be calling round later that day to collect the documents.

Extract from the Nürnberger Zeitung,

A local police officer has been commended for his diligence in discovering a motor vehicle which had crashed through wooden barriers on the road to Lauf an der Pegnitz and became submerged in the river. Tragically, the vehicle had been issued to a young SS officer, Leutnant Wilhelm Erpenbeck, who had been marked out for a dazzling career in the service of the Reich. His greatcoat and briefcase were found in the vehicle. The driver's door had been wrenched open by the force of the impact, and it is believed that the Leutnant's body was swept away by the strong current. No remains have been found, despite an extensive search. Yesterday, a memorial ceremony was held at the Hitler Barracks and a commemorative plaque was unveiled to this very promising young officer.

Extract from the Nürnberger Zeitung,

Disgraced Deputy Mayor Fritz Mergel has been found guilty by a summary People's Court of crimes against the state and sentenced to death, including extorting money from local businesses, immorality and conduct generally unbecoming a public officer. His replacement will be appointed in due course.

Chapter Twenty-Nine

The meeting had been arranged for eight in the evening at the Castle Room in the Mautkeller and everyone except Thomas had arrived a quarter-of-an-hour or so earlier. There was a sense of mystery and tension in the air, as the meeting had been originally called to determine what direction the group should now follow, but they had also been told that Thomas had an announcement of some importance to make. They were all filled with curiosity as to what it might be. Thomas himself arrived shortly after the appointed hour.

'I am sorry to keep you all waiting,' he said, 'but there was a rehearsal for the grand parade to the Party Congress this afternoon, which meant that just about every tram route in the city was disrupted and I had to do my best to sort out the mess. Individual units were everywhere they shouldn't be, half of them without drivers because they were participating in the parade, and the situation is only just returning to normal. However, here I am, and I'm sure you are keen to know what I have to tell you. First things first, though.' He walked across to the side table, drew himself a beer, came back to the refectory table and sat down.

'What I have to disclose to you is, I believe, of considerable significance for all of us. So, I'm going to deliver a bit of a speech, which is not something I am especially good at. But here goes. Let me start by saying that I am truly grateful to Johann and to the rest of you for allowing me the privilege of taking part in your little escapades. That may sound more than a little pompous, but I really do believe in the importance of what we have achieved. It has been essential for us all to be able to undertake those operations which either assisted folk who were being persecuted or sought a measure of vengeance against the very worst kind of Nazis.

'I don't use the word "vengeance" lightly, I really believe that it is vital that these evil people should be confronted with the sheer inhumanity of what they are doing on a daily basis and brought to account for it. Even if it means, in the case of Leutnant Erpenbeck, that he would meet a sticky end. His vicious treatment of Ruth was truly repulsive, and he was determined to kill Johann and the rest of us. Remember, too, he had meted out similar vicious treatment to countless others who have challenged the political orthodoxy or have offended in other ways against the state.'

Around the table, heads nodded in serious agreement. 'Next, I am delighted, and I'm sure you are too, that we have achieved a couple of remarkable successes, so outstanding in the case of Leopold Bucher, in fact, that the thought must have occurred to each one of us: how are we going to surpass that?'

He paused for a drink, then continued in a more serious tone.

'Maybe we could achieve larger successes in the future, but there is one fact which is, unfortunately, staring us in the face, which is that Johann came perilously close to getting himself killed the other night because, somehow, Erpenbeck managed to discover his identity. And, as you will know, I myself came close to being arrested and carted off to a concentration camp as a result of the machinations of our beloved and late lamented Deputy Mayor Fritz Mergel. Many thanks to you, Johann, for coming up with a way of digging me out of that hole.' He paused, took a deep draught of beer, looked seriously at the others, then continued.

'When we stand up in the face of a vicious and determined régime, it is almost inevitable that, in due course, there will be victims on our side too, and if it involves someone dying for our cause, we have to agree that's going way too far. We are not soldiers. We are ordinary citizens. And the fact that Max's secretary, poor girl, was forced into giving away key information about us demonstrates just how ruthless and determined our enemies are. So, what are we to do?'

He looked at each of them in turn.

'Do you—you—or you want to call an end to our activities as a group?'

One by one, they shook their heads.

'All of which means,' continued Thomas, 'that we find ourselves in an almost impossible position. As Johann has said to us more than once, one good deed isn't enough, you have to keep on doing good deeds if they are to make any real impact. But, if that means shortening our life expectancy and making the last hours of that life singularly unpleasant, as very nearly happened to Johann, I do not believe it merits a sacrifice of that order. Not least, because if you are dead, that severely limits your ability to keep on doing deeds whether good or bad.'

A ripple of nervous laughter ran around the table. 'However, I am convinced that we have inadvertently found a way out of this paradox, in which we seem unable to go back and almost dare not go forward, and that lies in an unexpected side effect of what we have achieved collectively. Let me take the most striking example of us all, Rudi.'

Rudi blushed with embarrassment.

'Largely, because of his brilliant acting abilities, Rudi now finds himself in the remarkable position of being able to serve officially as a double to our dear Führer, and, as he's pointed out, to do some positive good in the process. That alone means that our small efforts have not been in vain. He at least has lit a very bright candle in the darkness which surrounds us. Through Rudi, we have made an impact on the wider world and, God willing, he will go on doing so for a long time to come.

'But what about the rest of us? Do we continue as the leftovers of our little group, withdrawing into our shells and living off the memories of past glory, or do we perhaps seek to recruit new members? If we follow that path, are we imperilling our own lives and futures? I think we may well do so. But I am convinced that what we have all attained is not just a little pinprick which will have no genuine impact, but that there is somehow or other a cumulative effect behind our joint thoughts, beliefs and above all, actions. I have already cited Rudi as a shining example.'

He paused for another drink. The others looked at him curiously, sensing that his real point was yet to come and that it might yet be something pretty remarkable.

'I believe that our work as a group has gone about as far as it can in achieving its objectives, but each of us can build on what we have already done and move on to more significant achievements, not just Little Marlene here.'

Rudi bowed and the rest of them laughed again. 'Seriously, though, let's consider what each of us has achieved. I'll first let Johann and Elise tell you how they hope to move on.'

Johann cleared his throat, smiled at Elise and said, 'The treatment I received at the hands of Leutnant Erpenbeck was pretty brutal and, for that reason alone, we have decided to close our practice here in Nuremberg and to go and live near Elise's sister, Ursula, her husband, Wolfgang, and her family. There, I will be able to recuperate and, together, we will work hard to extend and strengthen their efforts to support and assist those who have fallen foul of the régime.

'I know that my sister-in-law and her husband desperately need the services of a small medical team, since many of the people who pass through their hands have suffered considerable injuries at the hands of the SS and Gestapo, and it will be an honour to contribute to that good work.

'One very important aspect of our activities will be liaising with individuals and organisations outside Germany who are determined to assist the oppressed within our borders, and Eli Birnbaum will play a leading role in this endeavour. Our efforts in helping the Birnbaums alone have greatly strengthened our possibilities for assisting others in the future, for which Elise and I are very grateful.'

Applause greeted his words, and Elise spoke in support of what her husband had said and to thank the others for sharing their experiences over the past months. She added that Eli Birnbaum had generously offered to ensure that they had enough medical supplies and other resources to continue their work for the foreseeable future. Then, before he revealed his own plans, Thomas invited Max to explain how his activities were going to progress in the future.

'Well done, all of you,' Max began. 'I feel that, in my case, simply continuing and extending what I am already doing is the very best I can aspire to and that I am playing a modest but meaningful part in protecting as much as possible of the artistic heritage of our country. I'll continue to dedicate myself to the task of concealing and storing away as many significant works of art that I can from the predations of the Nazi Party, and my young friend, Kaspar, is delighted to help me with that very special skill he has with paintings.

'I too am honoured by the opportunity to have been a member of our little group and it has helped me to break out of my academic ivory tower into the real world and confront and challenge the unpleasant facts of life in contemporary Germany.

'We must move on but, at the same time, we must keep in touch. Of course, I shall miss you all, but can I say on a personal level that I have recently gained more than adequate compensation for the potential loss of your close companionship.'

Max paused, blushed, looked sheepishly around the room and continued hesitantly,

'For some time, the relationship between myself and my secretary, Eva, has been growing into an affectionate and, may I say, intimate affinity between us. Last Sunday, I met with Eva, once again and, in response to my tentative proposal, she did me the great honour of agreeing to become my wife. I hope you will all be able to attend the wedding ceremony.'

Cheers greeted his words and toasts had to be drunk before Thomas himself could continue.

'We all wish you all the very best of happiness,' he said and paused for a moment.

'But I haven't yet come to the main purpose of my little speech. I have a piece of very significant news of my own to pass on to you which I am sure will delight you, as it will enable me to take our accomplishments to a much higher plane, where they, like those of Rudi, Max, Johann and Elise will have an impact way beyond the personal level and on to the regional and even national levels.'

The four sat completely silent, knowing that Thomas had something very important to reveal to them, but what it might be eluded them entirely. He paused, took a deep breath and continued.

'Last Thursday, I was summoned to the office of the Oberbürgermeister of Nuremberg. As you might gather, such an invitation is not exactly an everyday event, even considering my fairly senior position in the city, and I climbed the marble staircase of city hall with some trepidation. That concern was not lessened by the fact that, when I was shown into the Mayor's office, he was alone, sitting at his vast desk piled high with folders of important-looking documents and gazing out of the window at an impressive view of the main market square, the Pegnitz bridge and the river below.

'I had expected to be called to something like a meeting of a management group to consider the disruption to traffic and the life of the city caused by the rash of parades and processions which accompany the annual Party Congress. Or to look on the black side, I might have been facing a summary disciplinary tribunal for some imagined offence against the Party and its hierarchy. Such occurrences are becoming all too frequent nowadays, as we discovered only recently in my own troubles with Fritz Mergel. But, as I said, there was no room full of people.

'Just the Herr Oberbürgermeister himself, smoking a large cigar, who actually gave me a warm smile and rose to shake my hand. Then he waved me to a comfortable armchair to one side of his desk and planted himself in the chair opposite. The little circular table between us held two cups of coffee and he invited me to take a drink. I nearly dropped my cup at his opening words.

'"Did you know Leopold Bucher?" enquired the Mayor in a neutral, but not unfriendly, tone.

'I just about managed to control my emotions and replied in an equally non-committal manner, "It is always unfortunate when a senior member of the Party meets an unpleasant end."

'The Mayor stared at me for a full minute then he burst into laughter. "That's one way of putting it, Herr Direktor. It was a very curious set of circumstances indeed which brought about his downfall, as I understand it."

'He stared at me long and hard. I struggled to remain calm, dreading what he would say next.

'"My understanding is that reports of the events which caused his much-advertised charitable soirée in his new residence to culminate in a catastrophe were heavily censored by the authorities, to the point at which the presence of the Führer himself was swiftly denied, even though his speech had been supposedly transmitted on the radio. An outside broadcast crew was indeed in attendance, but nothing was actually sent out on air. Everyone who was present that evening has also been cautioned to hold their tongues. And the more I enquired, the bigger the mystery became as to what exactly had happened and why.

'"Regrettably, I was unable to be there myself on that particular occasion, but I managed to persuade one of my close colleagues to provide an eye-witness account. The poor fellow can still be seen stalking the corridors of this building half doubled up with ill-concealed merriment. I exaggerate, of course, but you do, I am sure, have some idea of what I am talking about?"

'"Er, yes, Herr Oberbürgermeister, I do," I replied limply.

'At that point, I had no notion of where this conversation was going, although, by this time, I was beginning to fear the worst.

'"I did ring Max Feinlein, the Chief Curator of the Nuremberg Museum and Galleries, who informed me in confidence that he had been ordered to step aside from the arrangements for that evening by the authorities, and that he had done so most reluctantly. His explanation was not particularly convincing.

'"But," he added, looking me straight in the eye, "what fascinates me is this. Why, if the Party wanted to get rid of him, and it clearly did, was such a complex and well-thought-out plan conceived and executed to bring about his public humiliation, including the alleged involvement of our Führer and three rather saucy paintings which cruelly parodied the purity and nobility of National Socialist art? The simplest thing would have been to send a truckload of SS soldiers around in the middle of the night and quietly carry him off for execution. Don't you think that's rather odd?"

'The Mayor continued to fix his stare on me. "Well, whoever it was behind the scheme deserves a medal of some kind. All of which, of course, has nothing whatsoever to do with the reason for my asking you to come and see me on this fine morning.

"'Let me be very frank with you, Herr Direktor. The departure of Herr Bucher did not cause a single tear to be shed in this entire building. In fact, the man was the very worst kind of individual who had fought his way up to high office ,not on merit, but because of his Party connections and, to be brutally honest, the vicious and inhumane manner in which he exploited them.

"'As one of my colleagues put it, he was like a cockerel who clawed his way to the top of the midden by clambering over the still-twitching bodies of his friends and enemies. And the same can be said for the equally swift disappearance of Fritz Mergel from the scene. His disgrace and execution were rapid and well-deserved, but, again, that episode raises many unanswered questions.

"'It is my considered view that the Party can and should prosper and grow without men of that venal and grasping nature in positions of power, and my role here as Mayor is to ensure that moderate voices are heard and respected in the governance of our beautiful city."

'The Mayor paused for what seemed an eternity. I sought to remain impassive.

'"And that is why, Thomas, if I may use your first name, after taking numerous private soundings about your effectiveness in your current post, your character, and—if I may say so—your independence of mind and action, I am asking you to relinquish your very senior position in the department of transport and join my team as a Deputy Mayor of the splendid city of Nuremberg. And, in this role, you can—how shall I put it?—continue to act as a force for tolerance and human dignity in a very brutal and uncertain world."

'I was dumbstruck. The man had more or less said in as many words that he was pretty sure of my involvement in Bucher's fall from grace and he also gave a none-too-gentle hint at a link between myself and Mergel's elimination.

'Now, here he was offering me one of the top positions in the whole of the damned city. For a second or two, I just sat there gaping with astonishment, but, finally, I managed to blurt out that I would be deeply honoured and that I would seek to fill the post to the very best of my ability, aiming always to maintain the highest standards of such a distinguished office.'

Thomas paused for his friends to absorb what he had just said. They all applauded him, raised their glasses to him and wished him well. Johann spoke up for them all.

'Many congratulations, Thomas. And thoroughly well deserved. That goes to prove, doesn't it, that even in the higher echelons of the Party, there are still men of dignity and honesty who are prepared to stand up and fight their corner. It demonstrates conclusively that our little battles haven't been fought out in total isolation and obscurity but that our efforts can now reach out to those of others seeking to put the brakes on the more extreme and inhuman aspects of the new Germany. Well done, my friend, very well done indeed.'

That evening, several beers found their way down the throats of the five members of the group who had dared to hope that their actions might have some positive consequences in an age of cruel inhumanity and grave peril.

They were just preparing to leave when there came a sudden, imperious knocking at the door. The five fell silent. It felt as if the temperature in the room had plummeted by several degrees. The knocking persisted, then the door was suddenly kicked open and two Gestapo officers strode arrogantly into the room.

'We have reason to believe that an illegal political gathering is taking place in this location and we have come to arrest you for violation of the law and acts of criminality against the state,' one of them shouted with all the venom he could muster.

'Do not move. Stay as you are,' the other added superfluously.

'Names and addresses,' ordered the first, while the second man noted down their hesitant responses.

'Now, you will all accompany us to Gestapo Headquarters,' ordered the first man.

For a moment, no one moved. Each appeared so shocked and horrified by the sudden appearance of the Gestapo that they were at a loss as to how they should react. Did this mean that their actions had been betrayed? Were they going to be dragged off to a concentration camp on the next trainload of goods wagons? The mood of delight and congratulation of a few minutes ago had suddenly evaporated into one of fear and deep apprehension. Each looked at the other, desperate to find a way out of this perilous situation.

Then, Thomas walked straight up to the first officer and, inches from his face, spoke calmly, 'No. We will do nothing of the kind.'

The Gestapo men, clearly unused to being challenged, were shocked and taken aback by such a confident rebuttal. The first officer stepped back then, recovering a little of his composure, he drew his gun, pointed it at Thomas and snapped,

'And why do you dare to challenge the authority of the state in this presumptuous manner? We shall be singling you out for special treatment, my friend, that's for sure.'

Thomas continued to stare straight into the man's eyes. 'Oh, I very much doubt that,' he responded in level tones. 'And if you intend to use that weapon, I suggest you release the safety catch.' The other four members of the group were fascinated by what appeared to be a battle of wills, one which appeared to be reaching a dangerous stalemate.

The Gestapo officer looked sheepishly at the gun, which he gradually lowered to his side as he looked at his colleague for support.

'Why,' continued Thomas, 'have you gate-crashed our private celebration in this thuggish and brutish fashion?'

'Private celebration?' snorted the first Gestapo officer, regaining his composure and still determined to maintain control of the situation. 'Our information is that this is a gathering of spies and terrorists planning attacks on the state and that you must and will accompany us to headquarters to face those charges.'

'Your information is, to put it bluntly, complete nonsense,' sneered Thomas. 'And I can prove it here and now.'

'And how do you propose to do that?' came the icy response.

'Quite simply. It was I who caused you to be summoned here this evening.'

The look of incredulity on the face of both officers was fascinating to behold. Before they could think of a response, Thomas continued, 'I had received information that some evil-intentioned individual had reported us to the Gestapo, hoping to gain personal benefit from our arrest. So, I told the Mautkeller manager to contact your Headquarters this evening just to see if they would send out officers to threaten to detain us. Which they obligingly did, and here you are to prove it.

'Now, let me tell you in simple language you might just understand that we are just a group of friends who meet to arrange charitable events for the benefit of the community, but on this particular evening, we have come together for a very important celebration. A celebration, in fact, of my recent appointment as a Deputy Mayor of the city of Nuremberg.'

The two Gestapo officers stood open-mouthed at his revelation, and the pistol swiftly disappeared into its holster. Thomas let the words hang in the air for a few seconds before concluding,

'And if you gentlemen would be kind enough to return to your headquarters and explain to your superiors that they are seriously misinformed about us, I would be most grateful. Otherwise, I would not care to think what the consequences might be for you, particularly when I bring this unwarranted intrusion to the attention of the Mayor himself tomorrow morning.'

The deflation of the Gestapo officers bordered on the comical. After a hurried whispered consultation, the first officer spoke up,

'There seems to have been some mistake, sir, Herr Bürgermeister, I should say. There must have been some error in the address.'

'Not at all, you were directed right here to this very room because I wanted to make it abundantly clear that I will not tolerate the Gestapo behaving so insufferably towards the people of Nuremberg, and, in particular, to myself as one of its leading citizens. Go back and report the error, and stay well out of my way in future.'

The two men reddened and moved to go. 'Just one more thing.'

They paused wretchedly and looked appealingly at Thomas.

'That page of your notebook with the names and addresses you wrote in it? I will have that, if you don't mind.'

Chapter Thirty

'We really must think of a suitable wedding present for Max and Eva,' Elise said as they cast their eyes over the untidy pile of boxes, furniture and assorted items which cluttered the sitting room. It was the day of their move to a comfortable farmhouse on the grounds of brother-in-law, Wolfgang's castle in the country, as they called it, and they were waiting impatiently for the removal van to appear.

Ursula and her husband, Wolfgang, had been particularly warm in their welcome to their relatives as prospective new neighbours, not least because of their medical skills, but most of all since Johann and Elise had told them in some detail of the attempts they had made along with their small group of friends to take a stand against the arrogant power of the Nazi Party and also to assist some of those who had fallen foul of its evil social and racial doctrines.

Ursula and Wolfgang Schmidt were already aware of the Voss's efforts to aid the Birnbaum family, who had stayed in their country house for several days waiting for a plane to leave Germany, and they were particularly delighted that Johann and Elise had achieved so much more besides with Rudi, Thomas and Max. It had been an

349

exciting time soured by the dangers which had threatened Johann's life and imperilled Thomas's reputation, but the experience had been worth every moment, good and bad.

Now, they had an opportunity to take their work in a new direction by assisting in the courageous efforts of Ursula and Wolfgang to offer refuge and support to some of the many victims of Nazi oppression in Nuremberg and the surrounding countryside.

Ten years previously, Wolfgang's reclusive uncle had passed away and had left him a splendid nineteenth-century hunting lodge in the middle of a large farming estate, together with a substantial sum of money. The grandiose building had been constructed in the style of a fortified manor house, with crenellated walls and even a moat crossed by a stone bridge. Hence, it was known to everyone in the family as 'Wolfgang's Castle'. Husband and wife had decided to move there at once, and when it became clear that Germany was persecuting Jews, Communists and other groups of so-called social undesirables on an industrial scale, they resolved to dedicate their good fortune to assisting as many of them as they could, exploiting the remoteness and generous accommodation of the hunting lodge for that purpose.

They soon recognised that most of the people in their care desperately wanted to leave the country altogether and start a new life abroad, and they found themselves becoming involved in a network of underground movements which helped such victims of Nazi terror to make good their escape. Johann and Elise were now anxious to become involved in the work of Wolfgang and Ursula, and they were keen to exploit this great opportunity to continue their positive efforts against the worst excesses of Nazism.

It would also offer Johann a far less stressful existence, as he reluctantly recognised that many months of convalescence lay before him after his brutal treatment by Leutnant Erpenbeck and that it would have proved unlikely that he could undertake the strenuous work of general practice again, even had he wanted to.

It was a very positive move for them and a new beginning, not least because, the day before, Elise had told her husband that she was expecting their first child. Johann's initial reaction to her emotional announcement had been one of mixed feelings. Part of him was apprehensive about the prospect of bringing a child into the world at such an appalling time in Germany's history, but he was also convinced that he could pass on to their new baby some hope for the future and that the child, boy or girl, could be encouraged to promote justice and an open society in the years to come.

Now, both husband and wife felt much more hopeful and confident about themselves and their lives together, despite a deep sense of foreboding that the follies of Nazism would inevitably culminate in a cataclysmic disaster for their beloved country. They were more than delighted that they had taken a modest stand, and with their small group of friends, had lit a candle or two and dispelled some of the darkness which blighted the lives of so many of their fellow countrymen.

There had been another positive outcome too. Since their last meeting at the Mautkeller when they had all reluctantly agreed to go their separate ways but to remain in touch with one another, the nightmares which haunted Johann for so long had not recurred, and his general mood had lifted with the prospect of a change of scene and more achievements to celebrate in the months ahead. He had also taken more pleasure in writing his diary entries, not least because the journal as a whole could now be passed on to his new baby when he or she grew up.

It was some time before Johann broke their silence. 'A portrait,' he said suddenly and Elise looked at him with a puzzled expression on her face. 'A portrait? What are you talking about, Liebling?'

'A portrait of Max and Eva as a wedding present, of course,' he replied. 'It could come from all of us, Rudi and Thomas too, and I think I may know the very artist who could produce a most suitable painting of the new couple.'

Elise smiled and nodded. Then a sudden thought occurred to her. 'As long as it's not like the second version of the paintings Kaspar created for that special evening with Leopold Bucher in the presence of our dear Führer.'

They both burst into laughter. But, after a little while, Elise noticed that Johann was looking around the room with a pensive expression.

'Will you miss anything about this house?' she asked with a worried frown.

'Not particularly,' admitted Johann. 'We have had good times here, but you know that life as a doctor in the city was becoming more intolerable and that, one way or another, change for us was becoming inevitable. But I know what I will miss.'

'And what is that, Liebling?' she asked.

'Walks in the evening round by the castle walls, although my little outings have been increasingly blighted by all that Nazi bunting draped over the historic buildings of our beautiful city. And there is one thing about this house that I definitely won't miss at all.'

He paused and she waited a little nervously for his response.

'The sound of hammering on the door at two in the morning,' he said laughing. Elise joined in with him. Impulsively, she reached out and grasped his hand and the two of them stood there quietly, lost in their own thoughts and memories.

Suddenly, there came a loud imperious hammering at the front door, and the two of them exchanged apprehensive glances, but when Johann turned the handle to look outside, they found before them two burly figures dressed in work clothes and behind them at the roadside a large removal van.

'You seem a little startled to see us, Herr Doktor,' said one of the men.

'Not at all,' replied Johann, 'I am pleased and not a little relieved. Shall we start with the consulting room?'

Epilogue

Across the road, two lorries loaded with building materials swung into the driveway of number 49 and made their way slowly up to the entrance. Under the portico, a group of men in overalls stood waiting to unload the vehicles. A wintry sun slanted across the house front, lending the frosty scene a picturesque lustre such as might be found in a work of National Socialist-approved art. The lorries squealed to a halt and the workmen set about their task. Scaffolding, planks of wood, bags of cement and other equipment and tools vanished through the double doors of the main entrance.

In the small former gatehouse opposite, the net curtains twitched as bony fingers clawed at the fabric, drawing the yellowing drapery a little to one side for the occupant to gain a clearer view. In the shadows, the outline of a short, middle-aged woman could just be seen peering out at the busy scene across the road. Briefly, her view was interrupted as a tram clattered along the central reservation, heading down the gentle slope towards the centre of the city. Its bell clanged officiously as it drew to a halt, unloading a couple of passengers before continuing on its way.

The woman peered out again as two men lugged a charred wooden beam out of the house and hoisted it noisily onto the flatbed of one of the lorries. As she moved to one side, a shaft of sunlight caught her face to reveal the pinched, embittered features of Marie Bucher, once all too briefly the fêted occupant of number 49, now reduced to virtual penury and eking out her lonely days in the one piece of property belonging to her deceased husband which local officialdom had permitted her to retain, namely, the gatehouse. The rest of his goods and chattels had been forfeited to the state before his execution.

On that evening when the alleged Führer came to open the Buchers' inaugural exhibition, Marie had promptly paid heed to her inner voice in the din and panic of the fire and had rushed through the smoke and crackling flames up the grand staircase to the master bedroom, where her extensive collection of jewellery was located. To her horror, she discovered that nearly all of it had already been spirited away, leaving only a few cherished pieces which she had locked securely away in a secret compartment of her dressing table. Earlier that evening, as the ceremonial opening of the exhibition was about to begin, a shadowy figure had crept up a back staircase to her dressing room and retrieved a large number of items of value, which were, in due course, passed on to the Curator of the Nuremberg Galleries and Museum for safe keeping.

With a meagre annual pension from the state, Marie now had barely enough income to eke out a lonely existence, living the life of a social pariah directly opposite the very house in which she had once fleetingly reigned as a doyenne of local Nazi high society. And, worst of all, she now resided in those very same cramped four walls which brother, Leopold, had so generously purchased for his miserable widowed sister, and which she declared still smelled faintly of the woman's wretched dachshund.

On that fateful night when she had telephoned her brother to inform him she was convinced the Birnbaums were about to take flight from the country, it was Marie herself who had forcefully persuaded Leopold to have the family arrested, and the tragic train of events that ensued flowed directly from her own avarice.

But Johann and his friends had acted together to mitigate, in some measure at least, the terrible human cost of her lust for the trappings of wealth. The Birnbaums now lived in exile, rather than facing a wretched death in a concentration camp, and they had the consolation of a positive future to look forward to, although their new existence was still over-shadowed by the tragic and senseless death of their younger daughter.

Marie's present plight was fitting punishment indeed. She was now compelled to eke out her days in full view of the spot where little Naomi had been crushed to death and directly opposite number 49, the splendid family home where she had touched the heights of Nazi fame and fortune before being condemned to a life of solitude and penury.

Angry and bitter tears stained her cheeks as she turned wretchedly away and, very slowly, let the yellowing curtain fall.

THE END

About the Author

Rex Last was Professor of Modern Languages at the University of Dundee from 1981-1991 after nearly two decades in the German Department of Hull University. He has written books on topics from Hans Arp, German Dadaism, E. M. Remarque and Erich Kästner to artificial intelligence and computer-assisted instruction for the language teacher.

He also edited the pioneering computerised Arthurian Bibliography and has translated a number of books including Willy Brandt's wartime memoirs, a study of Max Ernst, a biography of the early peace campaigner Bertha von Suttner, and an account of President Gustav Heinemann of West Germany.

Now retired as Professor Emeritus, he writes computer programs, designs websites and has written countless articles for a number of computer magazines. For information on his other current study guides, fiction and humour, please see the following pages.

For up-to-date information, check out my website at www.locheesoft.com.